PRAISE FOR SEAN GRIGSBY

"Grigsby's pulse-pounding sequel to *Smoke Eaters* is a worthy successor that expands on the series' already strong foundation of vivid action and meticulous worldbuilding… vibrantly imagined characters who ring with authenticity, and firefighter Grigsby knows just how to pull readers into scenes full of smoke and flame. Readers will delight in this fresh take on action fantasy."

Publishers Weekly

"Starting with its title, *Ash Kickers*, tells you exactly what type of ride you're in for then delivers on that promise with a story that hits like a Skyrim meets Ghostbusters battle royale. In it, you can almost feel Grigsby's glee as he mixes together supersized heroics, mythic creatures, snappy dialogue, and furious fight scenes to form a narrative that reads like a passionate homage to the action blockbusters we all grew up watching."

Evan Winter, author of The Rage of Dragons

"*Smoke Eaters* is a thrilling, exciting, funny and strangely heart-warming book, and Grigsby's experience as a firefighter shines through on every page, lending grit and realism to this rollicking ride of a tale in which firefighters become dragon-slayers. It's exactly as bonkers – and as brilliant – as you'd expect and I look forward to more from this author."

Anna Stephens, author of Godblind

BY THE SAME AUTHOR

Smoke Eaters
Ash Kickers

Daughters of Forgotten Light

Sean Grigsby

FLAME RIDERS

**ANGRY
ROBOT**

ANGRY ROBOT
An imprint of Watkins Media Ltd
Unit 11, Shepperton House
89-93 Shepperton Road
London N1 3DF
UK

angryrobotbooks.com
twitter.com/angryrobotbooks
Ride that flame

An Angry Robot paperback original, 2021

ISBN 978 0 85766 901 8
Ebook ISBN 978 0 85766 911 7

Printed and bound in the United Kingdom by TJ Books Ltd.
9 8 7 6 5 4 3 2 1

For Tammy

CHAPTER 1

There were about a dozen of them huddled in front of me, writhing together like snakes in a pit. By the light of my plasma lantern, their collective breaths rose like smoke against the cold. They all watched me quietly, waiting to see if I would take the bait. Of course I would bite. I'd run out of things to talk about.

"Tell us a story, Gilly."

The platoon always put me on what they called "brat duty." I didn't like the term or the job, but I was good with kids, so it was my duty to babysit while Colonel Calhoun and the others met with the town's adults to discuss business.

Calhoun called it business. I called it a shakedown, but only to myself. Dragon work accounted for maybe ten percent of what we did every day. Mostly we just roamed from settlement to settlement collecting our dues.

The kids in this town ranged in ages from as young as four all the way up to ten or twelve. They all looked like they could use a bath, but none of them wore rags or went barefoot. It may have been the apocalypse, but these were still American kids. No matter the hardships they endured on a day-to-day basis, their parents would have rather had their eyes gouged out by wraiths than to have their kids go without a t-shirt and sneakers.

The kid closest to me, a little girl who'd told me her name was Shequoia – the one who'd asked for a story – was wearing a pair of green Jesson Dragon Stompers. The shoes had to be older than she was. I knew because I used to have a pair myself when they first came out in stores. They were manufactured for only a year in 2119, and were quickly pulled from stock after a public outcry claimed an insensitivity to the dragon problem.

Everything was second- or third-hand nowadays. Shequoia's parents either found the Jessons in a dump or had saved their own original pair, thinking of the child they would have one day and what they'd wear when society tanked.

Shequoia's pair were raggedy as hell. As she sat on the ground, tapping them together, I noticed a big hole worn into the sole of the right sneaker and a loose heel on the left. Unless her parents had another set of shoes ready for her, they'd have to go scavenge or trade for some in another month or so. Kids grow like weeds at that age.

"A story?" I asked.

"Yeah!" all the kids said, keeping their voices down like I'd asked them to. "Come on, Gilly. Please?"

My name is Guillermo Contreras, but since that's usually a mouthful for children, I'd told them to call me Gilly. Only my family called me that, and no one in the New US Army addressed me as such. To my fellow soldiers, I was simply Contreras, the lowest guy on the totem pole, taker of all shit and unwanted duties.

I grabbed a stool that had been leaning against a shelf of dried goods and laid my rifle in its place. My sergeant had told me to take the kids into the storeroom while the adults talked, and you can bet I caught the implication of his statement. I was just a kid to everyone in the platoon, even though I was twenty years old and grown enough to die like any of them. My sergeant wasn't an adult. He wasn't even human.

Squatting onto the stool, I patted my knees and tried to think of some interesting tale to keep the kids busy. "A story. Hm. Well, I can tell you about the dragon we were tracking last week. It was a Wyvern that spits acid."

"No," all the kids groaned.

"We don't like the Army," one freckle-faced boy was brave enough to say.

Me neither, I thought.

"Okay, then." I looked around the darkened room as I tried to remember any fairy tales or fables I knew well enough to stumble through.

Towns like this – Wraith's End, they called it – didn't have much infrastructure or electricity. They were all powered by generators. There was no more Feed for news and television, no screened entertainment. No cities or any semblance of modern civilization. People were lucky if they had paper books and they eventually used them for toilet paper.

The few comforts society had held onto after the dragons emerged were quickly burned away after the New US Army took over dragon-slaying. NUSA wasn't connected in any way to the old American military aside from using the same lingo and looking the part. No one used the word "mercenaries" but I wasn't so naive I didn't see the truth. But even I, as a modern barbarian, was as much at their mercy as civilians.

I looked back to the door to make sure my sergeant or, worse, Colonel Calhoun, wouldn't stomp into the storeroom to hear what I was about to say next. Back to the kids, I hunched forward a bit. "Have you guys ever heard about the smoke eaters?"

A whispered *ooh* flitted through my tiny, captive audience.

I smiled. It was my favorite subject, but the only one I couldn't openly discuss. "The smoke eaters were a special group of people who could breathe dragon smoke and handle heat that would melt most people's faces off."

Shequoia twisted her face in disgust.

"They were heroes," I said. "They wore armored power suits that closed around their bodies and protected them from dragon teeth and claws. The smoke eaters could jump fifty feet into the air, shoot lasers out of one arm and fire-snuffing foam out of the other. And some of them even had laser swords they used to kill dragons as fast as you can blink."

Some of the kids blinked rapidly to see exactly how fast that was.

"Just like firefighters back in the day, they would ride out in big trucks with flashing lights and sirens, always ready to help those in need if a dragon attacked."

A little girl wearing a too-big Minnesota Maulers jersey raised her hand. "Did they fight wraiths, too?"

"You bet they did," I said. "They cleared dragon nests and caught wraiths with a special remote so no more dragons would show up in an area. They did it all. And the best smoke eater to have ever lived was a captain out of Ohio named Naveena Jendal. Do you want to see something?"

"Yeah!"

I knew they would.

Now, I could have been in huge trouble just talking to these kids about my holoreader. The New US Army confiscated all electronic devices from civilians and it was considered bad form to flaunt such things in front of them. Only soldiers were allowed to have holoreaders for official duties, but "official duties" usually meant watching old movies and recording videos of them hazing the platoon's FNG. That stood for "fucking new guy," and that had been me for the better part of a year.

I could at least say, with a clear conscience, that I'd had this particular holoreader since Christmas two years before, and I received it from my parents. I didn't rip it out of some twelve year-old's hands like the other soldiers.

"You have to keep this a secret," I said. "You promise?"

They nodded their heads, waiting to see what I was going to show them.

I flicked a finger across the reader's screen. A hologram rose into the air above the kids' heads: a blue-tinged, still image of a woman wearing one of the power suits I'd described. She was roaring and charging. On her head was a helmet that looked much like the ones firefighters used to wear, with added cheek guards. This wasn't your everyday hard hat. This was a smoke eater helmet. A bronze dragon sat at the top, its jaws holding a shield that read "Parthenon City."

Flames, caught in frozen motion, raged around the woman as she held her laser sword above her head. The laser sword protruded from her suit's right arm. It was the brightest part of the photo. In the bottom corner, a dragon spread its jaws wide, a ball of fire cresting out of its mouth. Its scaly skin was purple and it had at least fifteen horns curling from the top of its head in a nest of sharp points.

A few of the younger kids started crying.

"Hey," I said, "it's okay. Don't be scared. This is an old image of Captain Jendal. It's not happening right now. It's just a picture, a hologram. That dragon isn't really here."

"She looks scary too," Shequoia said.

"I know," I couldn't help smiling. Naveena Jendal was my personal hero. "But you have to be scarier than the dragons if you're going to fight them. That's what I want all of you to learn today if you don't learn anything else. You can't let the dragons and wraiths scare you. You have to be meaner than they are."

"But we don't breathe dragon smoke," a little blonde girl said.

"Maybe not," I said, "but that doesn't mean you can't do anything. You can listen to your parents. Do what you can to help everyone around you, not just yourself. Don't let the monsters make you scared."

"And what about monsters who are people?" Shequoia asked.

That melted away my smile. "That's a little tougher."

"What happened to the smoke eaters?" a little boy asked.

I leaned back on the stool and sighed, mourning something I never had a chance to know. "They were disbanded. Cities all across the country put a stop to their organization and turned dragon-fighting over to the New US Army."

"So there aren't any more smoke eaters?" Shequoia asked. Her eyes sparkled in the light of the hologram.

"There might be," I said. "But they stay hidden. The Army's longest-running job was arresting smokies who were still slaying in small towns. Now, if they find anybody who shows signs of being a smoke eater, they send them away to a prison in Ohio. Some people out there right now are smoke eaters and they don't even know it."

The door to the storeroom burst open. A bulky droid carrying a rifle marched in and scanned its red eyes over the kids before turning to me. He'd been constructed to look like a metallic bodybuilder, but apparently his manufacturer had also wanted to carve his face into something less intimidating. The result was something altogether more horrendous, and his voice was always cranked to maximum volume. "Private Contreras, get your saggy, brown ass outside and bring those squirming ankle biters with you."

"Yes, sergeant," I said.

Sergeant 5-90 looked one more time at the children huddled on the dirty ground before twisting his torso and marching outside on his clanky, tree trunk legs.

What was I doing with my life? This wasn't what I signed up for. *Join the NUSA, see the world!* Yeah, and the world was an ashen wasteland where I was relegated to wrangling a group of scared babies at gunpoint.

I guess it was a lack of alternatives and a desire to get out of my hometown that made me sign up. Sometimes I wished I would wake up one morning and realize it had all been a dream and I was back in Peoria, Illinois, and not freezing my ass off in Wisconsin. Granted, I'd still be cold in the Prairie State, but there's a warmth that family and a familiar place provide that you can't find anywhere else. Maybe I'd been worried that warmth would smother me to death some day.

The kids crawled into the corner farthest from the door. They looked at me as if I would tell them they could stay in the storeroom. Unfortunately, the droid was my superior and I had to do what he ordered if I didn't want to face punishment. And that could have been anything between being dragged by cables behind a spider tank or a swift placement in front of a firing squad.

I rose from the stool and grabbed my rifle. "It's okay, guys. Let's go outside. I'm sure me and the rest of the soldiers will be gone soon."

They moved to stand behind me, gathering in a clump.

We walked out into the cold afternoon, where the light was too bright and gray for my liking. Spring was a long way off. All the adults of Wraith's End stood facing us. Their faces were a mix of anger and fear. Some of their looks were directed at me, and that sat with me as well as a gallon of bleach in my stomach. I could only surmise the business meeting hadn't gone too well.

Behind them, our platoon's two spider tanks hummed and sent waves of heat into the air from their exhaust grates. The tanks only had four stiff legs they used to skitter over every type of terrain like waterbugs. But they still looked like spiders, so the name stuck.

Wraith's End was designated a town only because it was what you called a group of people struggling together to survive out in the ashes. It used to be a normal suburban street. Some of the houses still stood, barely. The asphalt had given way to dirt, but you could still see a few chunks of it here and there, lines and patterns of what used to be. The people of Wraith's End had built shelters out of metal sheets and boards, placing them alongside the still-standing houses, creating a sort of town square around the place we were gathered.

"Okie dokie," Colonel Calhoun bellowed. He paced in

front of the town's adults with hands at his hips and his large ion pistol holstered close. "Now we've got everyone here."

The rest of my platoon surrounded the grown-ups in a semi-circle, rifles drawn.

"You can't bleed a turnip," a townswoman said, shaking her head, breathing heavy through her nose.

"I can," Calhoun said. "And if I can't, I'll find something else to bleed. Line up those kids, Contreras."

It was rare for the Colonel to address me directly. It took me a second to realize what was happening and I didn't move until all the soldiers' and townspeople's eyes fell on me. The muscles in Calhoun's temples tensed under his beret, making it seem like rodents were moving under the buzzed, gray hair at the sides of his head.

"Yes... sir," I said. I turned to the kids. Shequoia was clinging to the back of my coat. "I need you all side by side, facing your parents."

The kids did as I asked, though several of them were sobbing and the one I had to carry to the end of the line refused to unlatch himself from my arms. I had to pry him away, though I ran a hand over his head to show there were no hard feelings. I didn't blame the kids for being nervous. Something in the air didn't feel right. This wasn't normal procedure.

"Kids," Calhoun said, "your parents are telling me they have no rations or any other resources they can contribute to the cause. I say that's a filthy lie."

A man in a brown bomber jacket mumbled something, but a soldier prodded him with the end of a rifle and shut him up.

"Now," Calhoun continued, "a lesser man would just

take everything in your storeroom and leave you to face the rest of the winter without food or a means to fend off the dragons. But I am above such larcenous activities. We have a symbiotic relationship. Towns like you provide us with resources, and we provide you with protection. It's a balance."

The colonel had to be crazy if he thought the kids would understand half the words he'd just said, but I knew it was all theatrics. He was really talking to the adults, and using the kids as a springboard for his message, really digging his hooks into the parents' skin. The adults behind Calhoun tensed and some of them struggled to hold back tears in their eyes. I felt for them, but it wasn't helping their kids any.

Buck up, I thought.

Calhoun took a big whiff of winter air, puffing up his chest and stretching the front of his fatigues. "I won't do anything to interrupt that balance we have, but I will do everything in my power to maintain it. By my estimation, little babies, your parents are hiding things from us and if they can't be honest about the supplies they have, they won't be honest with us about anything else, so it got me thinking."

I held my rifle a little closer to my chest, raising the barrel as far away from the kids as possible without drawing attention. It was never a good thing when Colonel Calhoun put his thinking cap on. And that was saying something, considering his ridiculous burgundy beret.

"Hiding things," Calhoun said. "They are hiding something. And what would they want to hide?"

No one answered. I couldn't think of anything myself. I thought this was just a showy way to shove these poor people around as an example. I didn't even think Calhoun had an answer, but he suddenly came to attention and barked, "Sergeant Five-Ninety!"

My droid sergeant, carrying his rifle in a count four position, leapt from where he stood and landed in the muddy snow in front of Calhoun. "Yes, Colonel."

"Relinquish your rifle."

"Sir, yes, sir." Sergeant 5-90 performed a few sweeping moves of the rifle before handing Calhoun the weapon.

As tense as the situation was, I couldn't help thinking, *What a show-off.*

"Sergeant," Calhoun said. "Please engage your flamethrower at the minimum setting and approach the first child in line at the far left."

All of the adults behind Calhoun shouted, but two of them were more upset than the others. They had to be Shequoia's parents, because she was the one Sergeant 5-90 walked toward. Shequoia screamed and backed away from the droid, who ejected a small stream of fire from its left forearm. Flames had to be about half a foot long.

"Private Contreras," Calhoun said. "Restrain that girl and hold her hand out, palm down."

My gut wanted to stay right where it was but the rest of my body moved forward, my hands slinging my rifle onto my back. I wasn't sure if other soldiers ever experienced the same thing, but I always got a sick feeling when it came to following orders, and it came over me stronger than usual right then.

Join the NUSA, terrorize children!

I placed myself behind Shequoia, put my hands on her shoulders. I wanted to tell her everything was going to be fine. But I couldn't. Because they weren't. I grabbed her arm and held out her hand. She fought me, wriggled and tried to pull away, but I was too strong.

"Let me go, Gilly!" she shouted.

"The only thing anyone would want to hide from us," Calhoun said, "the only thing I can think of, is a smoke eater. Well, we have ways of finding out who that might be. We'll start with each of your children first, then we'll make our way through the rest of you."

Sergeant 5-90 stood there, waiting in front of Shequoia. He hadn't been given the directive and would wait until kingdom come until Calhoun told him to do anything else. I felt just as much a robot, standing there with a scared little girl kicking at my shins.

"Sergeant," Calhoun said, "place your flame under that child's hand."

The adults were restless, pressing against the invisible line the armed soldiers had placed around them. The two drivers deep inside the spider tanks ejected their topside guns, turrets that looked like the tanks had grown lethal antennae. That got the crowd to settle, though their angry voices grew louder.

The droid sergeant stepped forward, close enough to where I could feel the heat from the flames flickering out of his arm. Shequoia was crying, screaming. I felt like she would melt in my arms as soon as the fire touched her palm. Even fire smaller than that could have set the world alight. Instead, they lit something inside me.

Sergeant 5-90 took another step.

"No!" I turned Shequoia away and grabbed my sergeant's arm, shoving the flames back with my bare hand. The heat cut my palm like a jagged dagger. I closed my eyes, convinced my winter fatigues would catch fire and that would be the end of my tour. I really hadn't planned it out too well.

Sergeant 5-90 ripped his arm away from me, killed the flames, swung his other arm around, and grabbed me by the throat. He lifted me off the ground, where my boots were dangling just above the snow. It was like being at the mercy of one of those claw games at an arcade. Breathing was a struggle, and if my sergeant squeezed any tighter, I'd have been decapitated.

Shequoia ran toward the group of adults and fell into her parents' arms. They all cried, dropping to their knees. She'd passed Calhoun on the way. The colonel gave her a brief, annoyed side eye but let her go. He was more interested in me at that point, marching over with his hands crossed behind his back.

Sergeant 5-90 twisted my head so that I had no choice but to face the colonel.

"Private Contreras." Even Calhoun's whisper sounded like a yell. "What is your fucking problem?"

I couldn't talk. 5-90's metal grip was too tight. I don't think Calhoun wanted an answer anyway.

"You should be flayed for this," Calhoun said.

"Colonel!" It was Shequoia's father. He gripped his family tight, lifted his head as tears ran down his cheeks. It may have been a trick of the winter light but it almost looked like blood flowed from his eyes. Some men have the ability to rip your heart out when you see them cry.

Calhoun looked back.

"Take whatever you want," Shequoia's father said. "Just leave."

Working his tongue at something stuck in his teeth, Calhoun turned to me. His eyes were gray blue, and I'd

never known that until then because I'd avoided eye
contact with him. He scared me. "All right, platoon. Go
through every inch of this town. Take whatever you need."

The other soldiers smiled, chewed on their gum, or patted
each other on the back as if they'd earned something. They
dispersed and began entering the shacks the people of
Wraith's End called homes.

"But not you," Calhoun said, and this time he was
talking to me. "Sergeant, drop him."

When the metal hand let go I fell to the snow, coughed,
and gagged. Rubbing your neck after such experiences
never does anything, but your body has this natural
response you just can't help.

"Contreras." Calhoun loomed over me and I wanted to kick
him in his square jaw. "You're going to strip. All the way down
to your boxers or briefs. And I sure hope you didn't take the
term too literally and go commando today, because you will
be relinquishing those fatigues and that jacket. You've lost the
right to wear them."

I blinked, already beginning to feel frozen on the snowy
ground. He couldn't have been serious.

"I'm serious," Calhoun said. "Hustle and get those greens
off your scrawny brown ass."

I moved to push myself onto my feet, guarding the
hand that had come in contact with Sergeant 5-90's
flamethrower, but there was no pain when there should
have been, not even a slight radiating of scalded skin.

"And don't even think of seeing Reynolds for that hand,"
Calhoun said as he turned and walked away. "You acted
like a dumbass, you can live with the burns."

But that was just it. When I stood and looked down at
my palm, there was no scalded flesh or charring. My skin

was just as clean and unblemished as it was before, besides the freckle that had sat in the middle of my lifeline since I knew what one of those was. At first I thought I must have knocked Sergeant 5-90's arm away at the perfect angle. That wasn't it. Even if I'd only touched his arm, the metal would have scorched me as much as the fire.

I'd touched both. Neither had hurt me.

The droid sergeant had been watching. His electric eyes could have bored holes into me the way he stared, and I wouldn't have been surprised if he had some hidden feature where he could actually eject drills from his eye sockets. I quickly folded my arm behind my back and stood at ease.

5-90 didn't waver his gaze. "Strip, you maggot. Let's see how Spanish balls fare in the cold."

My family was originally from El Salvador, so that irked me.

"Do it now, Contreras. Or do I have to treat you like a simpleton whore and do it for you?"

It was easy for him to say. He didn't feel how cold it was.

CHAPTER 2

Someone once told me that freezing to death was blissful. I'd forgotten who'd said it, but they were clearly an absolute moron. Freezing was like being stabbed with a million tiny knives over every part of your body while having specific parts of your anatomy burned inch by inch, both done very slowly and carelessly. Then things go numb and you worry you'll never be able to move them again, even if by some miracle were you to survive. It got really scary when your body started shaking on its own. That's when you knew you weren't in control anymore.

We were ten klicks outside of Wraith's End. We were heading toward what had once been Illinois, and I just hoped I wouldn't have to hobble over the state line in nothing but my boxers and boots.

I had my rifle with me, but I'd been ordered to hold it in both hands above my head, arms straight, until told to do otherwise. The rest of the platoon had been ordered to turn and shoot me in the head if they caught my arms dropping.

I'd been put at the rear with one of our spider tanks, and every other soldier, whether they rode in a tank or marched on foot, kept their eyes forward as we made our way down the road. When I felt it was safe enough, I'd drop my shoulders a bit to release the tension. Sometimes I'd drop one arm altogether and quickly return it to the rifle once the pain had subsided. It quickly returned, though. The soldiers in the spider tank never caught me, but a few of the ones marching ahead would look back often enough that it was risky.

Sometimes I wondered if most of them had joined NUSA for a chance to kill people, or to at least have so much control over their victims they'd wish they were dead. I used to think every person had an underlying, buried bit of humanity, no matter who they were or how badly they behaved. I used to believe the old stories of redemption, where one flick of a magic wand or a song belted out by a mass of innocents would make their hearts grow three sizes and pump empathetic blood. Most people like to think that, but after living and fighting beside these jagoffs, I can tell you redemptive humans are the minority.

But that didn't stop me from looking for them.

I began coughing so hard it made my lungs ache. Throat full of cotton. It was hard to think of anything besides how cold I was and how difficult breathing had become, but along the road I tried to keep my attention on the few points of interest we passed. The last one was a road sign saying we'd entered Sylvania. Part of the sign had been burned, but not so much I couldn't read it. Dragons are silly creatures with the things they choose to burn and those they leave alone. In one small town I saw a torched hospital, but the funeral home next door hadn't been touched by so much as a puff of smoke.

Maybe the scalies had a sick sense of humor.

One of the soldiers ahead of me slowed to allow the

rest of the platoon to pass. She paced her steps so she was marching just ahead of me, close enough for a conversation. Her name was Reynolds, and she was about the closest thing I had to a friend.

"How's your hand?" she said.

"Wha... what?" I said. My damned teeth were chattering and my nipples looked like purple torpedoes.

"I saw you shove 5-90's flames away from that kid. You need some antibacterial and a bandage wrap."

"It's not bad," I said. "I'm fine, Reynolds. Rather... have my uniform back."

She glanced at me over her shoulder. Her hair was hidden under her helmet, but her half-lidded, green eyes and thin, crooked lips were out in the open. Her eyebrows were golden brown, like perfectly-baked cookies. I'm sure that's a strange way to describe thin lines of facial hair, but it's the first thing I thought of when I first saw them and I loved cookies more than most people love breathing air.

"I told you to call me Sarah," she said.

There was no way in hell I was going to call her that in front of the other guys. It would have slapped a target on her back. Maybe in the quiet times we shared, talking about our families and where we grew up. Maybe then I'd let a "Sarah" slip once or twice. I liked how it sounded.

She should have known better than to be my friend.

"Sorry," I said. "Forgot. I've just been a little busy freezing my ass off."

"Yeah, and that's your own fault. You should have just done what Calhoun told you. He wasn't really going to hurt any of those kids. It was just a scare tactic. You weren't at the meeting with their parents. Those people were holding out on us."

I gritted my teeth. My whole face tensed. I looked down at my boots crunching against the ash and snow. "He was going to have 5-90 burn her. Droids don't understand bluffing, they just do what they're told."

"Colonel would have stopped him in time."

"I guess it's going to take something bad happening to convince you," I said.

"With an attitude like that, you'll never get to see the Big Base."

I blinked and shivered, thinking about it. The Big Base was supposed to be the hub of all NUSA operations. To hear the other guys talk about it, the place had all kinds of food long-thought to be extinct, like cheeseburgers, hot wings, and those little packets of ketchup. It also had warm beds and even a ping-pong table. But despite all their talk, none of them had been there. No one besides Calhoun and 5-90. I'd been on the road with the colonel and the First Platoon since they'd picked me up in Illinois. It had been a year of boots against the ground, uncomfortable cots if you were lucky, and roving to a new settlement to keep our bad reputation alive and well. I'd labeled it a pipe dream early on. If the Big Base was real, Calhoun would have been there instead of out here with the grunts. If it *was* real, I'd never see it.

"I guess not," I told Reynolds. "Now leave me alone before one of us gets shot."

She should have marched ahead, but she slowed her steps and walked beside me. "When we stop, I'll look at your hand. I don't care what Calhoun said about it. He was just mad at you. You're no good to the platoon if you've got gangrene and can't hold a rifle."

"Apparently, I'm no good to the platoon one way or

another." I kept my eyes away from her and bit back a groan when a sudden wind gust sliced at my skin.

"I won't leave you alone until you say yes," Reynolds said.

She was taller than me, but her presence wasn't threatening like some of the other soldiers, and it wasn't just because she was the platoon medic. Reynolds had a confidence and a demeanor that warded off assholes where I seemed to attract them. She'd been nothing but pleasant with me, but she also never seemed to give a shit when I got hazed by the other guys. A pure neutral, she acted like my friend when we were alone and like the rest of them when it was time to put on the platoon persona. I blamed her for such obvious bullshit, but I understood it enough not to call her out on it. Obviously, we didn't have any romantic thing going on, but it walked on the same legs as some private affair. I felt cheated and used.

"My hand's fine," I said. "I barely touched the fire."

"Bullshit. I saw it all. Your hand went through that fire stream and connected with Sergeant's arm. I'm surprised you didn't scream and crumple into a fetal position there in the snow."

"But I didn't, and I'm still able to hold my rifle just... just fine." My arms shook, elbows bending a bit. She was more concerned about my dumb hand than she was about potential hypothermia.

"Okay," Reynolds said, sawing a gloved finger across the underside of her nose. "But when you come crying to me later about it. I'll tell you I told you so."

"Fair," I said.

"And I won't be gentle with you either."

"For f... fuck's... s..." I couldn't finish my sentence – at first because I was shivering so much, but the rest of the words fell from me when a roar boomed through the clouds above us.

"Platoon!" came a shout from the front of the line. "Halt!"

The sky was overcast, gray stretching to every point of the horizon. We hadn't seen the sun in a few days, but right then, just on the other side of the clouds, I could make out the shadow of a dragon flying over our heads. Its wings were spread, straight and unmoving. It glided without a sound and if it hadn't announced its presence, we would have never known it was there until it was too late.

It was already too late.

"Get in defensive formation," Sergeant 5-90 was giving the orders, shouting in a voice that sounded like microphone feedback.

I rushed forward, as fast as my stiff legs would move me. But I kept my rifle above my head. I hadn't been told to drop it yet.

Our two spider tanks reversed and began circling all of us who were on foot. The tanks' energy cells went into overdrive as they shifted into attack mode and lifted their turrets to the sky. It sounded like the machines were screaming and the screams got louder with every second. The tank legs rolled around us clockwise while their turrets spun in the opposite direction, searching for the dragon. This position was supposed to protect us, but I felt more like one of several sardines chunked into a bowl for the dragon to fly down and devour. There was safety in numbers but clumped numbers like this also made an easy target.

"Private," Sergeant 5-90 broke through the platoon and stopped in front of me. "Drop your arms and carry that rifle like a real soldier."

"Thank you, sir," I said, lowering my arms and cradling my weapon against my bare chest. "Sergeant?"

"What the hell do you want, Private?" His metal frame clanked as he stomped closer. The nearest soldiers looked on. "Don't you see we have a scaly about to drop on us?"

"I know this m... might be a bad time." My lips felt like iced rubber. "But do you... think I can get my fatigues back?"

5-90 leaned back on the hinges at his waist. His eyes turned a frustrated glow of yellow. He sliced his right arm into the air and pointed all of his fingers behind me. "Your clothes are in Tank Gx-900I. If you want them, you better get them now."

I turned and slipped my rifle strap over my shoulder. The rest of us never called the tanks by their serial numbers. We just called them Tank 1 and Tank 2, and they were still hard to tell apart, though Tank 2 had a slightly newer paint job thanks to a town in northern Wisconsin we passed through a couple weeks before. Tank 2 was the one that held my clothes. Calhoun always rode in Tank 1, so I hoped it was a sign my luck had changed for the better.

"Watch it, Contreras!" one of the soldiers said as I made my way through the huddle.

"Get your naked ass off of me," said another, before shoving rough, gloved hands against my back.

I stumbled toward the rolling tank. The dirt beneath the machine sank and warbled with heat waves. It had already made a circle of melted snow around the platoon, marking its path. A crushing death followed by instant cremation would be the price for falling under its legs.

The good thing about most military vehicles was the overabundance of handles welded into every part of every vehicle. It wasn't a miracle that my hand found one of the metal bars.

"Open up," I shouted, running alongside the tank as it dragged me along.

My fingers were so damned stiff, it took me a second to ball them into a fist. I reached back to knock on the side hatch. They'd have to open if I banged hard enough on the door. What did they have to lose? They were swaddled in a cocoon of heavy metal and I didn't have more than a few stitches covering my ass.

A huge, dark blur dropped out of the clouds. It came with a guttural howl and wings that clapped like thunder. The dragon's claws dug into Tank 2 as if it was made out of thin aluminum, and dragged it into the sky, ripping the handle from my hand.

I stumbled backward into the nearest guy. Looking up into his startled face, I said, "My clothes were in there."

"Open fire!" Sergeant 5-90 shouted.

All of us, clothed or not, raised our rifles and began firing lasers into the sky. Some soldiers didn't seem to give a fuck where they shot. The air above us turned into a chaotic burst of light, like when my Uncle Pedro used to get drunk and take over the Fourth of July fireworks.

We couldn't see the scaly, but we all could sense it. I heard its wings beating against the air. Its growl. I felt its danger hovering close, like a cone of heat traveling over my body. An unwanted spotlight. It was as easy as feeling someone creeping up behind you – that tingle running over your shoulders and up your neck.

My rifle gave off some heat as it fired and, being the only comfort I could find, I held it tight and discharged my shots toward the east. Most everyone else was shooting toward the north or west. I lowered my rifle for a second and looked to the clouds, just to see if I could catch any hint of the dragon. Just to see if I was right or losing my mind to the winter air.

A metallic groan sailed closer and Tank 2 dropped out of the sky. It hit the ground just ahead of me and began tumbling fast, kicking up huge chunks of dirt and rock. I dove out of the way, but the soldiers behind me weren't so lucky. The tank plowed over most of them and left red smears across the snowy ground. One guy got a spider leg through his middle before being dragged along into the flurry of the toppling machine.

Flames erupted from the tank as it came to a rest, and the nearest soldiers backed away from it, even though I knew they heard what I heard. The soldiers inside Tank 2 were still alive and crying for help. The platoon looked to 5-90, as if the droid would do anything outside of its programming.

"Defensive positions," Sergeant 5-90 blurted from his speaker, repeating the same line he'd used before. Back to basics, standard procedure. And that meant leaving the guys inside the burning tank to fry slowly while everyone else watched.

I admit no selfless bravery. Mostly, I thought doing something courageous and stupid would earn me some respect among my fellow soldiers and maybe a reprieve from what I'd done in Wraith's End.

It was just a bonus that I couldn't stand to see people in need left to burn.

Brushing off the dirt and snow from my body, I stiff-legged it toward the burning wreckage. If I was lucky, I'd not only rescue the soldiers inside the tank but also retrieve my clothes.

My breath burned in my lungs. All of the other soldiers at my back shouted for me to return to formation. "Don't be a dumbass, Contreras!"

"He must be cold as shit," one of them said. "Look! He's going to the flames just to warm himself."

Pounding came from inside the tank as I neared, the sounds of boots and fists beating against unyielding metal. If they couldn't get out, how was I supposed to get in?

The dragon beat me to the tank.

It landed on the underside of the spider and roared from head side to side, almost like it was expecting other dragons to show up and encroach on its kill. The scaly was oily black with splashes of purple curling along its sides, running all the way to the end of its spiked tail. Its wings had sharp points at each angle that looked like they could sever a man's head. The jaws and teeth looked like they were made out of volcanic stone, and its body had enough thick, stringy muscles that it could easily crack open Tank 2 like a boiled crab.

All of that made me want to crap my boxers and run away crying, but it was nothing compared to its eyes. The dragon's eyes glowed with nuclear green flames that flowed from its sockets, but they didn't move like any fire I'd ever seen, dancing slowly upward around its two shiny black horns.

The world turned muffled and numb. Sergeant 5-90 shouted something and then a storm of red lasers began striking the dragon. It didn't seem to be doing any good. The lasers would hit the dragon's scaly hide, send up a small puff of black smoke, and that would be it. No blood, no scaly flesh slicing into ribbons. The dragon didn't move from the tank. It began to heave. And then, raising up on its hind legs, it showed me its underside. A tiny spark of green throbbed from within its black scales. The light quickly grew bigger and brighter.

"Oh," I said. It came out like an involuntary gag reflex.

I'd told the kids in Wraith's End about a dragon we'd been tracking. What I hadn't told them was that we'd never found it. Instead, it had found us.

A rushing sound came from the scaly's throat as it bent over and spewed steaming neon green acid onto the spider tank under its feet. The tank's metal melted away like cotton candy in the rain. I didn't hear any of the trapped soldiers any more. They were no longer there. The tank had become a puddle of green and silver sludge.

I ran toward the rest of the platoon. Our remaining tank skidded in front of me, kicking up snow and dirt. Its turret blasted a quick cone of energy that flew over my head.

The dragon leapt into the air with a high-pitch yelp and landed on the other side of the platoon. It spread its wings, challenging Tank 1 with a hiss. A couple soldiers thought they could get the jump on the dragon from the back, but with a tail flick they were tossed away with a three-foot spike wound through their chests.

Showing their commitment to insanity, the platoon kept shooting their lasers at the dragon with the same result. The big scaly turned its head and heaved again. Its acid spit had a lot more pressure behind it this time, rocketing out of its throat like a fireball. Most of the soldiers in the line of fire got out of the way but some of the acid splashed up from the ground and coated a guy's arm. He screamed as his flesh and bones corroded and oozed onto the ground.

Sergeant 5-90 charged the dragon. Like everything else he did, his movements were calculated and precise. Each footfall was perfectly timed, and only he would have been able to fire his rifle while in a full run. Sensing the droid approaching, the dragon turned and swiped a claw. 5-90 sprang off the scaly's arm and landed on its head. The dragon thrashed but 5-90 held tight to one of its horns, riding it like a bull.

But this dragon was smart. It flexed its shoulders and used one of the sharp points at the top of its wings to clip the sergeant and send him tumbling to the ground. The dragon clamped its jaws onto 5-90's leg and lifted him. The sergeant dangled, shooting his rifle wildly. The soldiers on the ground dropped onto their stomachs to avoid getting hit. I guess the dragon didn't like the taste of metal. With a jerk of its head, it threw 5-90 away. The metal man soared for twenty feet and landed in a crumpled ball. He didn't get back up.

I'd never been in a dragon fight before. Most of the ones we'd killed were smaller types that weren't so hard to beat: Lindwyrms and a small nest of adolescent Poppers. I'd never gotten the chance to shoot any of them. My training had been a half-assed, on-the-job instruction of what certain hand signals meant and to do whatever my superior told me. Turn this way. Shoot that way. Target practice was usually done on clumps of ash and empty bottles after a night of getting fucked up on grape juice.

The Army knew next to nothing about dragons, but I hadn't known that until I'd signed on. Up until then, I spent my nights reading all of the smoke eater training courses I could find archived on the Feed. I thought my dragon knowledge, limited as it was, would be an asset to the New US Army. That had been my first mistake. When the platoon found a dead scaly that'd broken its neck in a dried-up river bed and couldn't figure out what kind it was, I tried to show off, tell them the difference between a Drake and a Wyvern. They didn't like that very much, and I'd been a pariah ever since. But you can't fight what you don't understand, and NUSA's abhorrence for science was about to get us all killed.

Tank 1's turret spun toward the dragon, *tick, tick, tick.* If the tank could land one good shot, the dragon would be toast.

My legs were burning and I was sure I'd gotten frostbite on my nether regions, but I shuffled around Tank 1 for a better shot. The dragon puffed up again, its chest swelling bright green, like a bullfrog's throat about to burst. The rest of its skin shifted away from the chest, looking like armored platelets. No wonder the lasers weren't getting through. The chest, though, was a soft, stretched-out balloon of glowing acid.

Tank 1's turret began whining, revving up. It wouldn't build up energy in time. The dragon would fire first. I raised my rifle, looked down the sights, and pushed air through tightened lips as I squeezed the trigger. Just like I'd been taught.

Three rounds rocketed from my rifle and struck the dragon in its swollen chest. The glowing bulge burst open with a *pop*. Green acid splattered the ground, oozed from the wound and dripped from the dragon's jaws. It stood there motionless for a moment, then tilted forward, crashing to the ground. Dead.

I lowered the rifle and blinked at the dragon and the volatile acid flooding the ground around its corpse. A steamy foam formed as the acid ate away at ash and snow.

I... killed the dragon?

It was quiet except for the whine of Tank 1's turret and even that faded away after a while. The other soldiers stepped cautiously toward the acid dragon and then looked toward me. A few of them did a double-take and one guy blurted, "Contreras killed it? *Contreras?*"

I was just as surprised as he was.

They were all staring at me.

Reynolds appeared from the other side of the dragon and began clapping. Then she hooted a few times. I was about to tell her to stop before her one-woman show sentenced me to a midnight blanket party where all the guys would hold me down and take turns pelting me with boots and socks filled with roadside stones. But someone shouted, "Medic!" and set her to running across the snow to the guy with the melted arm.

The other guys started clapping.

Rifles were lifted above heads. Smiles were shown. Fingers pointed toward me while appreciative thumbs were raised. I didn't trust any of it. Not at first. But my skepticism melted away after their praise went on long enough. If you eat nothing but shit for a year, you're grateful for the stale cracker someone tosses you.

I grinned. But it lasted half a second.

An eerie white glow approached from behind the other soldiers. It had shown up like a fog. First nothing, then a floating torso and gnashing teeth. Then the shrieking and moaning came. Any sense of camaraderie in me left without a note. I turned and started running in the opposite direction. The platoon be damned. My clothes be damned. I'd rather freeze to death than deal with a wraith.

The sound of loose electricity caused me to look up. Another glow sped toward me. White hot sparks flashed from its center. Then it started making noises. Moans of someone in terrible pain. All this from a floating orb – but it took less than a blink for it to form into the shape of a ghostly woman who looked like she'd been burned, drowned, and ripped in half. The wraith had a strong likeness to one of the soldiers in our platoon. One who'd just gotten killed.

These were the result of dragon-caused human fatalities. Vengeful spirits that defended dragon nests and drew other scalies to an area for extra protection and mating.

Wraiths.

I'd say a chill ran up my spine, but I was too cold to know. I skidded to a stop and chugged my legs backward, changing my direction. It didn't make a difference. Wraiths were appearing all around us. One ghost slashed its sharp fingers at Reynolds while she uselessly fired lasers through its body. Three other wraiths appeared to close the circle. They all began shrieking through their jagged, electric teeth. We were locked in, surrounded. The nearest ghost focused its burning eyes on me. It roared and flew over the snow like a bullet.

Tank 1 swooped in, rolling over the wraith that was chasing me. At the tank's sides, coiled rods ejected and gave off invisible waves of energy that warbled the air. I'd never seen anything like that on Tank 1. Tank 2 either, for that matter. And I would have known. The platoon had me clean the tanks every time we stopped in a town. Those rods were not standard NUSA weaponry.

The wraith popped out from under the tank, eager to rip my throat out, but it was sucked up into one of the rods poking out of Tank 1. A final flash of electricity spiraled around the coil before blinking out.

Gliding across the snow, the spider tank did the same

thing to the other wraiths. The platoon had scattered, every soldier for themselves, giving the wraiths plenty of targets to attack, but none of them got their kill. Tank 1 got there first, sucking up the ghosts like a heavy artillery vacuum cleaner.

When I finally got a chance to look around and tuck my hands under my armpits, every wraith had been taken out.

The platoon really cheered now. Hell, I would have clapped too if I could have felt my hands. But I was also wondering about the rods Tank 1 had used to capture the wraiths. I'd read about people using something similar. That was smoke eater technology. Stuff like that had been banned for ten years. NUSA wasn't supposed to have it. No one was.

The spider tank slid to a stop and the top hatch popped open. Colonel Calhoun appeared, taking off his beret to wipe the sweat from his head. He scanned the area around the tank, breathing like he'd just run a marathon. I thought he was checking to make sure there were no more wraiths, or maybe even to see how his platoon had fared in the fight. But when his eyes found me they didn't waiver. Calhoun tightened his jaw, tensed his eyes.

He'd been searching for me. And he had something planned.

CHAPTER 3

I paddled my feet in the bucket of hot water and reached over to scoop more canned peaches into my mouth with a plastic spork. At the center of the room a fire crackled inside a metal burner, lighting the walls with comforting splashes of orange. My new set of fatigues and a fur-lined bomber jacket lay on an air mattress in the corner. It had been turned down with fresh sheets and a very thick comforter. The pattern of dancing purple poodles didn't even bother me. I was wrapped in a white, terry cloth robe I thought was only reserved for fancy hotels, and I'd even put a towel around my head.

In short, I could have gotten used to that.

We'd stopped for the night in an abandoned town called Waukesha, just outside of Milwaukee. I say it was abandoned but the truth was NUSA had kicked out the residents for nonpayment and set it up as an Army detachment. It had all kinds of extra supplies for platoons out on the road.

When things went south and the cities were abandoned, metro areas became hotbeds of dragon activity. The scalies took full advantage of the clustered buildings, the burrowing subways, and the webbed layout of freeways. 5-90 had told me from the beginning we were to avoid areas like Milwaukee. Droids don't embellish. Our little detachment in Waukesha was closer to the big city than I cared for. And that went double for Lake Michigan. All sorts of abominations can multiply and crawl out of large, unregulated bodies of water.

On the way to Waukesha, Calhoun let me ride inside Tank 1. I was thankful for the warmth and the break from marching, but even more thankful he'd given me some spare clothes and refrained from speaking to me. There was no length of conversation I wanted to have with the colonel. Some of the other soldiers had good rapport with him, even shared dirty jokes, but I've never liked being on the radar. It makes me uncomfortable. I used to have a manager at the mall who would ask me all these personal questions like how my parents were and what I did on my day off. It wasn't what he said, but how he said it. His eyes would seem to bulge from their sockets, and he had this strange twist to his lips as if he was trying to catch me at something he could write a report over. I was convinced all failed interrogators ended up managing retail.

But something had changed after I killed that acid dragon.

I spent my time in Tank 1 watching the driver use the controls. There were a lot to choose from, but only a certain group of floating buttons were pressed during the trip. It looked pretty standard. Forward, left, right, reverse. And though I tried, I never found anything that would have told me how those wraith rods worked. Not only were there too many controls, none of them had labels. I couldn't wrap my head around it. If the platoon had this kind of technology the whole time, why didn't we know about it? Well... *I* hadn't known about it.

In Waukesha, Calhoun had other privates make up my room – it was really more of a one-person steel cabin. He had them boil water, find a clean uniform that fit, and get me whatever rations I had a hankering for. There wasn't much to choose from, but there were the canned peaches which always seemed to run out at chow time before I could get any. The other guys would snag every can while I was finishing up some dumb duty 5-90 had me doing. They'd mock me, too, when I would finally walk in, making sure I saw them slurping the last drops of fruity syrup right out of the can. They would exaggerate how delicious it was. Some moaned and gripped the cans to their chests. One guy named Smithers would always drop onto his back and begin humping the air as if the processed fruit had taken him to the heights of nirvana.

Not even Reynolds would save me a bite.

So yeah, I was enjoying myself in my comfy robe there in Waukesha. I dropped my spork into my third emptied can, humming an old song about moving to the country and eating a million peaches.

I noticed my right hand in the firelight.

There wasn't even a touch of redness to the skin. I tilted my hand to each side, closed and opened a fist. No pain. It was easy to believe I hadn't touched 5-90's flame or heated arm. But I had. I knew I had.

"Knock, knock." Reynolds pushed through the door, allowing a puff of frigid air to enter.

I dropped my hand, hid it in the pocket of my robe. "I always wondered why people say that instead of just, you know, knocking."

Reynolds closed the door and set her rifle against the wall. She laughed when she saw the towel wrapped around my head.

"I practically had icicles in my hair," I said.

She looked around the room and whistled. "Nice digs

you got, Contreras. You're going to make the rest of us scramble to kill the next dragon if this is the kind of reward you get. Sure beats burying the guys who didn't make it."

"I'm real sorry about that but–"

Reynolds's auburn hair fell onto her shoulders as she removed her helmet and tossed it onto the bed. The pack she'd been carrying on her back followed next. The air mattress bobbed a couple times before settling. I wish I could say the same for whatever was going on in my stomach. I don't think it was the peaches.

"But what?" Reynolds held her palms to the fire.

"It's about time I got some respect." I leaned back in my chair, a beat up leather recliner, but I overestimated and ended up springing backwards, kicking water from the bucket and nearly putting the fire out. The burner sizzled steam as Reynolds laughed.

"Careful with that big head you suddenly contracted," she said. "I don't have much gauze left to keep down the swelling. Anyway, I'm here about that hand."

"I'm fine." I shoved the hand in question a little deeper into my pocket.

"You don't have to act all tough with me." She stepped closer. There was nothing out of the ordinary in the way she walked, but it still made me feel weird.

"You know," I said. "Calhoun said I could have pretty much anything I wanted, within reason."

"Yeah?" She stopped, thinned her eyes. "So?"

"One of the first things, the main thing, I asked for was privacy. I just want to keep warm and relax for the first time in a year. Not trying to be an asshole, but if you don't mind..." I waved my left hand toward the door.

"Oh, shut up." She picked up her med pack and stomped

over to me. She grabbed my right arm and tugged, trying to remove it from the robe pocket.

"What the hell!" I pulled back but that only made her dig her fingers into my forearm. Hard. I yelped.

Instinct caused my other hand to leap up, to push her away. Everything stopped. She stopped. I did, too. Both of our eyes settled on where my hand had landed: her left breast.

My mouth fell open as my hand fell from her chest. Rage burned onto her face. She actually showed teeth. Dragons and wraiths didn't have shit on Sarah Reynolds.

I stammered to apologize. "I didn't mean to. It was an accid–"

Her hand sliced through the air and landed palm-first across my face.

I was at her mercy after that. She had my hand in hers and a flashlight in her teeth before I realized what was happening. With a weaker attempt, I tried to pull away, but she held my hand open, studying it under the white beam of her light. Her eyebrows came together and the flashlight soon fell from her lips.

Slowly, softly, she placed my hand in my lap. She patted it once. "Don't tell anybody."

"What's to tell?" I asked, rubbing my sore cheek.

She went to the bed and grabbed her med bag. Her hands seemed to shake as she dug into it. "I'm going to wrap it up. As far as everyone else knows, you got burned and I treated you. We're not going to make them think any different."

"I'm not hurt. I got lucky. That's all." I sprang from my chair. My wet feet caused me to slip on the metal floor.

Reynolds caught me by the shoulders. Then she grabbed

me by the cheeks. "You and I both know that's bullshit. You wouldn't have tried to hide it from me."

"I…"

Her eyes looked wet and I don't know if she was tearing up or if the firelight was doing something to them. "You're a smoke eater."

I backed away from her, minding my steps. "No. That doesn't make any sense. I'm just some private who was dumb enough to join up with the Army. Just a regular guy. There aren't any smoke eaters left."

"The fire test Calhoun was pretending to give to the kids today? They used to do the real thing all the time. That's how they found smokies. It's a genetic thing. You know what smoke eaters can do?"

"Yeah," I said. "Trust me. I'm very aware. But that's not me. I think you saw me kill a dragon today and this is some crazy way for you to process how someone like me could have done that."

"Someone like you?"

I pulled the towel from my head and let it fall to the floor. "Every one of you in this platoon has something against me. I was singled out the minute I joined up. I don't know what the hell I did, maybe it's just bad luck. Maybe there always has to be the one guy everyone else gangs up on and it's permitted because it builds some fucked up form of camaraderie. Who cares about the odd man out when the majority is doing just fine? I'll tell you this, though. I proved myself today and everyone who thinks they can run over me has another thing coming. I'm not a smoke eater, Reynolds, but I'm glad that dragon found us. I'm glad there are fewer assholes in this platoon for me to suffer."

She flinched as if I'd thrown a rock at her face. "How could you say that?"

"March a mile in my shoes," I said. "You'd say the same thing."

She shook her head, retrieving her helmet and pack. She left a roll of bandages on the bed.

"What?" I said.

She pushed past me.

"Did I say something bad about your friends?" It sounded so sappy, so petulant falling out of my mouth. But when a righteous pride takes over, you tend to let it burn.

Reynolds stopped at the door and turned to me. Her movements were sharp. Her jaw was tight. "Did you forget about that day at the lake? Our little swim?"

I shuddered every time, but I thought about it at least once a day. "No, you just act like you don't give a shit about me in front of everyone else. That makes you just as bad. Seriously, thanks for all the help you've been."

She groaned. No, it was more of a contained scream. "What do you think I've been trying to do? Just... wrap your hand and don't mention it to anyone. Everyone will forget. If you keep your hand down and your mouth shut. Past that, I can't help you."

She put her hand to the door.

"Wait." I stepped toward her, but stopped when she turned back and actually waited. A million things crossed my mind, a million things I should have said. The only thing to pop out was a question I'd been chewing on as much as the peaches. "How did the tank capture those wraiths today?"

She left me with a disgusted sigh. Her voice trailed through the doorway before it closed. "Ask Calhoun. I'm just the fucking medic."

Damned if I did, damned if I didn't.

The briefness of the open door left a chill in me. Of course, it could have been Reynolds's words. Either way, I got close to the fire and watched the flames dance. It felt good and I tried not to think about how much Reynolds must have hated me. I started thinking about how kids develop a fear and understanding of heat and the pain that comes with it. Do all kids have to experience a burn before they know not to play with fire? Or is it a societal rule that trickles down to each generation? Everyone *knows* not to jump off a cliff. Everyone *knows* not to touch fire.

What if I could?

I held my hand a little closer to the flames. Just a few more inches and I could have my fingers passing through them. One way or another, I'd know.

I pulled my hand away. I took a deep breath and looked around at my cozy room. As I climbed into my dry and lush bed, I was determined not to let Reynolds bring me down. I'd earned my good night.

My whole life I'd looked up to the smoke eaters and where had it gotten me? I could make something of myself in the New US Army. Maybe now we could start putting the hurt on scalies and not the people we were supposed to protect. I drifted off, thinking of ways I could improve things when I rose in the ranks.

It was less terrifying than thinking Reynolds was right.

CHAPTER 4

I woke up and couldn't move.

The fire had died and the room was dark, but I could sense someone standing in the corner. I could almost see their silhouette. They didn't move, but I knew they meant to hurt me in some way. I tried to speak, to ask who was there, but my voice didn't come. I was transported back to being a little kid, eyes darting around the bedroom, searching the shadows for monsters. I didn't even consider grabbing my rifle. I just wanted to run. But my legs wouldn't move.

The thing in the corner remained, watching me.

This wasn't the first time I'd experienced sleep paralysis. It wouldn't be the last. It always happened the same way. I'd wake suddenly and feel a malevolent presence and wouldn't be able to move. Reading about it later, I found out a lot of other people had experienced the same thing. My situation was not unique. It went all the way back before recorded history, eventually being explained scientifically. Everything was, given enough time and focus.

My family is Catholic and as a kid I swallowed religion like soda. The first time this happened I thought a wraith or demon had come to possess me, scratch me, or do whatever demons do. I remember lying in bed, paralyzed with fear, and claiming the blood of Christ over me. It seemed gross to ask for a deity's blood to coat you like barbecue sauce on a chicken wing.

Even a demon wouldn't threaten something so depraved. But that's what my abuela would always say: "I claim the blood of Christ!" So that's what I said in my mind over and over. I didn't know what else to do.

To make it less yucky, I imagined Christ's blood to be a golden light enveloping me like rays of sunshine. Not the crimson splatter of real blood. For some reason, it would always work. I'd begin to move and the shadowy presence in the room would disappear.

I got older and less superstitious, but the fear never changed. Each time it happened, I would forget every notion of scientific fact, any form of reason and logic. I'd be alone in whatever room I'd fallen asleep and would wake with the fear and the presence. I might not have been close with Jesus, but I'd take any help I could get. I would claim Christ's blood over me, though I hadn't prayed or gone to confession in years.

I did it there in my room in Waukesha.

But it didn't work.

After a few seconds of realizing I was awake, I still couldn't move or speak and the presence in the corner began to move toward me.

Oh shit! I thought. *My abuela was right and the demon finally broke through the veil.*

The shadow in the corner didn't float. It walked like a man. But it wasn't. And soon I saw the glowing blue of its eyes as it stepped closer. It placed one of its metal hands against my mouth and I fought to breathe through my nostrils.

"I'm here to test you Private Contreras." Sergeant 5-90 had turned his voice to its lowest setting. "Order sixty-seven. All suspected smoke eaters will be tested with fire or smoke and be detained if deemed valid."

I'd meant to say," You crazy metal fucker! Let me go!" But it only came out as mumbles against his metal palm.

I'd thought the acid dragon had damaged my sergeant in the fight, put him out of commission, but he was obviously well enough to walk and attack me. The fall must have shaken his circuits loose. He'd gone crazy. Haywire. He was taking it out on me. I tried to scream for help but he had his hand clamped so hard against my mouth there was no way I'd be able to alert anyone.

"I've been watching you, maggot," 5-90 said. "I suspect you of being a smoke eater. I must implement the proper testing."

"I'm not a smoke eater!" I tried to say. More muffled nothings.

5-90 lifted me off the bed and dragged me toward the door. "I've shocked your body with low-level diodes. You've been temporarily paralyzed from the neck down. A smoke test would be preferable, but I will implement a fire test for expediency."

The sonofabitch was going to burn me to death via procedures and logistics. I doubt Calhoun or anybody else knew I was about to be incinerated. In the morning they'd find a pile of ashes that used to be me. This was like what the Puritans did at the Salem witch trials. If I survived, 5-90 would kill me. If I didn't... better safe than smoky.

The sergeant's metal feet moved quietly. He was in no hurry. We were moving at a foot a second. My rifle lay against the wall by the door. If the droid didn't think of grabbing it

I was going to do my damnedest to get my muscles working and blow this bastard's head off before he could fry me like a campfire weenie.

I was dragged past my rifle. I could barely move my eyelids, but I was able to watch my weapon disappear from view.

Just because I couldn't move didn't mean I couldn't feel. When 5-90 had dragged me outside I felt the snow against my back, the roughness of the ground. Where was he taking me?

"I aim to make this quick, Private," the droid said. "I hope you understand, I'm just doing my duty."

Stars filled the sky. They were all I could see. I remembered a time when light pollution was so bad the only thing you saw at night was an empty void. Back when I was growing up, it seemed like the human race had killed the rest of the universe for our own benefit. No one gave a damn about astronomy or exploring other worlds. We had too many problems happening on our own planet. And soon society broke down and allowed the stars to return. Now they were my only witnesses.

I wasn't supposed to die like this. To be fair, I'd never considered when or where I'd kick the bucket, but I didn't think it would be this soon, nor at the metal hands of my own sergeant. Not because of a false assumption of superpowers I didn't have.

5-90 threw me into something hard. All the air in my lungs rushed out. Lying on the ground, I looked up and saw that he'd shoved me against Tank 1. It was a smart choice. The metal was flame resistant and the tank was wide enough to prevent me from escaping.

He lit his flamethrower, and moved closer with short, clanking steps. "Thank you for your service."

I didn't give a damn if I was a smoke eater or not, I'd do anything, say anything, whatever this metal asshole wanted. Just leave me alone! Turn the fire off! I could feel the heat, the biting, radiant tingles. Didn't that mean I would be in worse pain when the flames actually touched me? Didn't that mean I wasn't a smoke eater?

I had to beg, plead. Something to change the machine's mind. In thinking this, my body somehow reacted and I found myself kneeling on the ground with my hands pressed together as if in prayer. The shock from the diodes must have worn off.

The droid stopped and looked down at me, confused. I was in shock about it myself. It had been a long day.

"Sergeant," I said, but he didn't seem to care what I had to say.

He marched faster forward.

"Wait!" I spun around. I couldn't run because the tank was in my path. I grabbed one of the many handles welded into the frame and began to climb.

"Running implies guilt," 5-90 called behind me. "Don't be chicken shit, Contreras. Face the fire like a soldier."

"I'm not a smoke eater, you crazy machine!" I stood on top of the tank. My lungs burned and I couldn't stop gulping air. Box-like cabins surrounded us, dozens of them stretching out as far as I could see. They were all dark inside. All of the platoon had been trained to have lights out by twenty-one hundred hours and everyone kept to it. No one was awake. No one would know what 5-90 was trying to do to me. "Help!"

5-90 shot his flamethrower just over my head. I smelled singed hair as I flattened against the top of the tank. The droid lowered his arm to follow me with his firestream. I rolled away and grabbed onto the handle of the tank's hatch. I was vaguely aware that lights were appearing inside the nearest barrack cabins. Someone had heard me screaming. I just had to survive long enough for them to come stop the droid.

I opened the tank's hatch and fell inside. My knees hit something that left them stinging. Bare metal caught my back and heels, and I felt just how wet the snow had made my robe. But I was inside. I was away from the fire.

Metal clanked against the side of the tank. *Tink. Tink. Tink.* I felt a slight shift of weight. 5-90 was climbing after me. I stood and reached for the hatch. Flames flickered over the opening, inches from my face as I closed and sealed the hatch.

The droid banged his metal fist against the top of the tank. "Open up, Private."

"You'll have to get in here and drag me out," I shouted back. I instantly regretted saying it. He could have very well pried the tank open like a can of peaches.

"Sergeant!" Another voice came from outside. I couldn't hear it well through all that metal. "Disengage that flamethrower. What are you doing on top of that tank?"

Metal scraped against the hatch, followed by two thuds. I imagined 5-90 had gotten up and stood at attention. "Colonel, sir. Private Contreras has sealed himself inside Tank 1, disobeying my direct order."

There was a second of silence.

"You've been put on temporary leave, Sergeant 5-90. Why are you not charging your battery? Why is Private Contreras not in bed? What orders are you giving him at oh two hundred hours?"

"The order to burn, sir." He said it so plainly, so matter-of-fact. But what else would you expect from a droid?

I looked over the controls inside the tank. I had to figure out how to turn it on, use the PA system to tell Calhoun just how messed up 5-90's operating system had become. The view screen in front of me was dark. The smooth panels below it were just as blank. I began poking fingers all over the panels, hoping to bring the tank to life. As I was punching frantically, my eye caught a red switch to my left.

I shook my head – *fuck it* – and flicked the switch.

The tank jolted once and began to hum. Blue, sparkling lights sprang up from the panels with a hundred different operating commands. The view screen flashed on. I could see snowy ground and a few cabins where soldiers stood watching. They had their rifles against their shoulders and had obviously thrown on their fatigues in a rush. One guy only wore his coat and boxers.

"Private Contreras," Calhoun called. "Can you hear me?"

Turning the viewer around was easy enough. There was a camera icon and a left arrow. The tank hummed a little louder as it moved. I stopped it when Calhoun was in sight. The rest of the platoon was with him, including Reynolds. I found the button for the communication speaker, but missed it by a hair and accidentally hit the control to reverse the tank. It surged once.

5-90 dropped from the top of the tank, past the screen, and landed in the snow.

Served him right.

I hit the correct button the second time. "Colonel, Sergeant 5-90 isn't in his right mind. Er, whatever droids have. He attacked me in my sleep and dragged me from my quarters. He was attempting to burn me alive when I managed to escape in here."

Calhoun sighed in the only way a man of his position could, through his nose while he tightened his jaw. He looked down at the droid picking himself up out of the snow. "Sergeant, what the hell were you doing? Do I need to power you off until we get back to HQ-1?"

HQ-1 was Big Base. Pangs of excitement and disappointment sprang up in me at the same time. Things had turned around and now I found out we were heading to the promised land. The droid had messed everything up.

The soldiers behind Calhoun raised their rifles a bit toward 5-90. They didn't want to be the next victims of a haywire robot.

5-90 turned toward the tank. His eyes burned with digital hate. I knew he didn't have it in him; emotions weren't in a droid's operating system. But if he could despise a human, I'm sure I'd be the first on his list.

He turned back to Calhoun. "I was operating under Order Sixty-Seven. I suspect Private Contreras of being a smoke eater. The only option was to test my theory by putting a flame to his flesh and seeing if he burned."

"If you suspected that," Calhoun said, "why didn't you inform me immediately?"

"All privates are under my direct command." 5-90 twisted his head to pop out a cinch in his neck. It sounded like a gunshot. "You also ordered me not to disturb you unless it was absolutely necessary. I believed I was in my rights as a superior, dealing with the situation as I deemed appropriate."

The soldiers behind Calhoun lowered their rifles. The colonel looked back to them, then to the guys on the other side of the camp. Everyone had lowered their guard. The droid was making sense and that didn't bode well for me. I realized this was a trial, only no one was saying so.

"Colonel," I shouted into the speaker. "I'm not a smoke eater. He has no reason to do this to me. This is harassment. I'm a soldier in the New United States Army. I took an oath to serve and I don't see the reason for any of this. I'd just like to go back to sleep and back to my duties in the morning."

Calhoun looked toward me in the tank and then back to 5-90. "What gave you suspicions that Private Contreras was a smoke eater?"

Reynolds took a step back, farther away from Calhoun. She couldn't save me. No one could. But the colonel couldn't have been taking any of this seriously.

"This morning in Wraith's End," 5-90 said. "When he interfered with your order and prevented me from testing the civilian. His hand passed through my flame and touched my arm. I couldn't determine if he'd suffered injury from it, so I set an internal appointment to inspect him when we had stopped at the next settlement. Due to the dragon causing me damage, I was unable to do so until after my functions were at one hundred percent. That didn't occur until two o'clock this morning. Upon my inspection, Private Contreras's hand had no injuries, so I determined further testing was necessary. You know I cannot lie. And you also know my systems are sensitive enough to record when something has come in contact with either my body or my ammunition."

Everyone was looking at the tank now. At me.

"Contreras," Calhoun rubbed the back of his neck and stepped into the snow. "Come on out of there and we can get this whole mess cleared up. Just show us your hand. Even droids make mistakes sometimes. Reynolds can wrap it up and then we can all get a few more hours of sleep."

He was seriously taking the droid's side on this one?

I looked all around me for somebody to help, but it was just me inside a tank.

A tank that could move faster than they could run. One that packed some serious firepower... if I ever figured out how to operate it.

I began to tremble. If I went outside, I was dead. At best, if by some fucked-up cosmic joke I turned out to be a smoke eater, I'd be locked away somewhere in Big Base and experimented on until I *was* dead. That's what I'd heard they used to do to smoke eaters the Army captured on the road.

The other option would be just as bad, even though it would give me a little more time. I'd be killing everything I'd been working toward the last year. It was also the only choice that offered any hope.

"Did you hear me, Private?" Calhoun called. "Don't make yourself look bad. You proved yourself today. Get out of that tank right goddamn now."

I backed the tank up and turned it toward the road.

"What the hell are you doing?" Calhoun shouted.

I hit the button to move forward but I must have done something wrong. It was moving at the same pace I would have walked.

"Stop him!" Calhoun shouted.

Lasers began pelting the tank from every direction. The view screen lit up with multi-colored streaks. Tank 1 supposedly had great armor but I didn't know how well it would hold up against a continuous attack like that. Given enough time, lasers can cut through anything and I was still moving at the pace of a one-legged Wyvern. My vision started going blurry. I could hear my pulse pounding between my ears. Breathing felt like inhaling through a strainer.

But good training always takes over in situations like this, and I'd been trained to return fire when I was attacked.

I engaged the tank turret.

"Cease fire! Cease fire!" I could hear Calhoun shout once the lasers quit. "You dumbasses, that's the only tank we have. He's only going two miles per hour. Get on top and open that hatch."

On the screen, crosshairs blinked, top half yellow, steadily filling to all red as the power charged. I spun the viewer around. 5-90 was coming for me, not so much at a run but a slow, inevitable jog. The rest of the platoon followed at a distance. Tank 1 was in autopilot and steadily gliding along while I put 5-90 in my sights.

I know droids can't smile, but I will swear to my dying day that his metal cheeks rose with glee. Maybe it was the tilt of his head as he closed in. The sergeant brought his arm across his chest and engaged his flamethrower, but this time he'd shrunk the cone of the flames down to a fine torch.

A chime sounded inside the tank, sounding – weirdly enough – like an egg timer. The turret was charged.

I fired.

5-90 blew apart. I didn't even see where most of his pieces went. A starburst of black char covered the ground where he'd been standing.

Calhoun hadn't left his spot in front of the cabin. He had a pistol in his hand now. Raising it toward me, he shouted, "Surround him!"

They knew I'd need another few seconds for the turret to recharge, and maybe they knew a deeper truth – I wouldn't fire on them. Destroying an asshole droid was one thing, but even though every one of them had treated me like gum on the bottom of their boot, I didn't have it in me to kill a human being. I'd joined the army to slay dragons. But that didn't lift the noose from around my neck.

Where was the goddamned acceleration control?

I turned the viewer back to the road. Several soldiers had rushed ahead and gathered in a blockade attack position. The ones in front were on their knees while those in the back were standing. They all had their rifles aimed and ready. Reynolds stood tall in the middle of the rear section. She looked sad, angry, and disappointed all at once.

"Sarah," I said, though I'd turned off the speaker.

"Contreras," Calhoun shouted. I couldn't see him. He probably hadn't moved from the cabin, letting the grunts do the dirty work. "This is your last chance. I don't know if you've lost your damn mind or if you have something to hide. I frankly don't give a shit. We need that tank but don't think for one second I won't order this whole platoon to fire upon you. We can survive the road without it if we need to. Because, unlike you, we aren't lazy cowards. We know how to tough it out.

"We'll take out the turret first. And judging by how slow you're going, all we'll need to do is ride on top until we've cut our way in. Save us all that grief and you'll make it easier on yourself."

Yeah, that was bullshit.

But he had a point. They'd just surround me and keep at it until I was dragged out into the snow, whether I'd been filled with laser holes or not.

I hung my head. A headache was worming its way into my skull. The glowing controls lay in front of me and

I didn't have the time to learn them all. But I saw one I'd been looking for earlier, much earlier, when I'd been riding with Calhoun to Waukesha. When my eyes had passed over it before, I thought it was just a blob with two small circles in it, but now I could see it was the image of a traditional-white-sheet ghost.

Well ain't that something.

"I'm going to give you the count of three," came Calhoun's strained voice.

He began counting but I didn't get all dramatic and let him get to the last number. He'd made it very easy for me. I released the wraiths.

I wasn't able to see exactly how they came out. There was a sudden popping at each side of the tank that felt like the metal rods had ejected. Then came an eerie white glow and undead moaning. Soldiers all around began swearing and screaming and firing their lasers. None of the lasers came anywhere close to Tank 1.

The blockade in front of me scattered.

Reynolds was the last of them to run. She took one last look at the tank and I could see how terrified she was. I felt horrible about it. I could never fire on another person, but I guess releasing a bunch of murderous ghosts wasn't much different. They had more of a chance this way. You could outrun a wraith... if you tried hard enough. Hell, I would have offered Reynolds a ride, but I knew she wouldn't have taken it.

As she ran toward a cabin, a wraith flew past the viewer. It had its claws dug into the underside of a soldier's jaw. Blood poured down his uniform. He screamed and flailed as the ghost dragged him away.

What had I done?

I finally found the acceleration control, but first I muted the horror show going on outside. I couldn't take it, hearing the screams.

The tank zoomed forward and I felt how much power the thing really had. I went from tortoise to hare in two seconds. The view screen was dark, as if it had been turned off, but no. That was just the night and the lonely road ahead. And that's why they make night vision. I found the appropriate button and engaged it.

Still, seeing where I was going didn't make me feel any safer.

CHAPTER 5

It took me longer than necessary to find the correct control, but I'd been wise enough to set Tank 1 to autopilot, heading southeast, before shutting my eyes for a few seconds. A few seconds became a few hours until the blare of early daylight jolted me awake.

I was disappointed to see I was still in the tank and that I hadn't dreamed the whole thing.

Through the view screen, the sky ahead was clear. All sunshine and blue sprawl. Spring was around the corner and that usually meant good things were coming; my whole mood changed around March. Not anymore. Spring now meant more dragons would burrow out of the ground, making more wraiths and more scalies. Besides that, the thought of spring at that moment didn't do much for me.

I'd murdered my future with the New United States Army, betrayed the one person who seemed to give any kind of shit about me, and I had no supplies. I'd left with only the clothes on my back, but all I had was a cold, damp robe.

Peoria, Illinois was the only place I'd ever called home, so that's where I was heading. Calhoun, or somebody closer he could radio, would probably look for me there first. I figured I could stop in and leave before any of them showed up. A short window of time, but I had to see my parents, get some clothes and food for the road. It wouldn't take me long, not in the tank, though I'd eventually have to ditch it for something less conspicuous. My Uncle Pedro could get me a ride. All the more reason to head for home. I just had to find out where the hell I was.

My holoreader was back in Waukesha. Otherwise I would have pulled up a map. The dragons had destroyed most everything, but satellites were still circling the earth and GPS would outlast us all. But you had to be able to use the technology for it to be any good. I was sure the tank had that capability but I'd already made a bad headache worse by searching the controls.

I checked the position of the sun before realizing that wasn't going to do shit for me.

My abuelo once told me there used to be gas stations back in the day, and if your mobile device ever ran out of battery, you could pull over and grab a soda and chips while asking for directions. My abuela chimed in and said that it didn't matter because anytime that would happen my abuelo refused to stop and get help. Male pride.

After E-day, when the dragons "Emerged" from beneath the earth, I asked him if he missed roadtrips, if he would have stopped and asked for directions if he'd known they'd be a thing of the past. He just shook his head, said, "Nah!" and chugged the rest of his beer.

Well, *this* Contreras wasn't too proud. I rotated the viewer slowly, counterclockwise. There had to be something out here that would give me a sense of where I was. So far all I'd seen was snow and cracked asphalt. There weren't even trees to look at.

A warning signal sounded. Something was blocking the road ahead. I began turning the viewer back to the front to see what it was. The tank took measures to avoid it, veering sharply to the right before thrusting back to the center of the road. Whatever had been in the way was no longer a problem, but the maneuver threw me from my seat. I hit the cold floor and was suddenly struck with the urge to pee, and nowhere safe to do so.

My wrists ached as I picked myself up, my knees ached when I sat back down.

Autopilot is a wonderful thing. You can avoid all sorts of obstructions in the road without having to do the steering yourself. But when you have the vehicle flying at a hundred miles per hour, you'd better buckle up.

This time I did. I also slowed the speed of the tank a little.

The view screen was in the same position from when my finger left the controls. I was about to start turning to search the horizon again, when off in the distance I noticed some kind of settlement.

Well, it wasn't a cluster of buildings. It was a wall. A long gray thing that didn't look like it belonged out in the wilds of Wisconsin. There had to be a settlement on the other side. People don't build walls like that for no reason. I decided it was the best I was going to get. A Drake in the hand is worth two in the ash or however the saying went. If the wall turned out to be nothing, I wouldn't be that far off the road.

I cancelled the tank's autopilot and turned toward the ominous wall. The field I crossed through might have been farmland at one point. Then again, you could have said that about anywhere.

As I got closer I saw it wasn't just a wall. The majority of the gray bricks had been built around another structure made of off-pink stone. This original building was made to look like a castle. It had one of those tower things that looked like a dragon's claw scraping at the sky. I never knew the exact name for it, but it looked like the rook on a chess board.

It *was* a castle.

I stopped the tank a few feet from it. Sitting there, staring at it, I thought, *Sure. Why the hell not?*

If dragons were roaming America, why not have a castle in the middle of nowhere?

Something hit the tank. Then again. One ding after another. It sounded like hail on a metal roof, but it was sunny outside and the strikes were too infrequent. I raised the viewer toward the tower. People stood all along the wall and they were throwing rocks. An older man stood on the rook tower and he was mouthing something angrily as he pelted a big chunk of concrete. It struck right beside the viewer, wobbled the screen.

Great. I'd found a settlement all right. A town full of nutjobs.

Remembering I'd turned off the speakers when I left Waukesha, I opened the feed to hear what had the old man so riled up.

"… 'cause I've got rocks for days. Stones and pebbles, too. If you don't answer me, we'll bring out the big fucking guns and make you sorry you ever came near. You hear me in there you slimy sonsabitches?"

He sure had a mouth on him.

I opened the PA. "Sorry. I had my speakers turned off."

The old man turned to the others with his eyebrows

squished together. I don't know if he was confused that
someone had actually responded or that I was being polite.

He turned back to me and began yelling again before I
had a chance to explain myself. "I told you to turn off that
tank and exit out of the top hatch slowly. We've got rifles
trained on you and some worse things you wouldn't like. I
know exactly how those spider tanks work. If we hear that
turret warming up, we'll blow your ass to Chicago. If you
don't do as we say within the next ten seconds, we'll blow
your ass to Cincinnati."

Any sane person would rather be blown to anywhere
but Cincinnati. I had the worst urge to tell him I was better
off warming up the turret. Instead, I said, "Sir, I don't mean
any of you any harm or trouble. I'm just on my way home
and wondered if you could help me find my way. Also,
maybe some food and clothes I might barter for?"

I didn't know what I'd barter. A robe and a story was all I had.

The old man made another confused face at his cohorts,
then spit off the tower. "Ten!"

The rest of them bent down and brought up rifles and
aimed them at me. They were obviously not playing around.

I turned the tank back toward the road. Whatever they'd
throw at me, I could outrun. I was just about to press the
acceleration button when a wave of energy hit the tank
and everything went dark.

Yelping, I patted my chest and sides. Still here. Still
breathing. I hadn't been blown to godawful Cincinnati.
The tank had simply shut down. I unbuckled and fiddled
around in the dark, finding the power button and slapping
it with the palm of my hand. Nothing happened. Poking at
the controls didn't do anything either.

Shit.

With a heavy sigh, I found the ladder leading to the top hatch and threw it open. "Don't shoot!"

"We might and we might not," the old man called. "That's up to you. You going to try something funny?"

"No," I shouted. "I'm just glad you didn't blow me up."

The man laughed. "Well, I think any Nusie who'd rather run than shoot deserves a little compassion. But you better come out if you want more good grace. How many of you are in there?"

"It's just me. One guy."

"Bullshit!"

"I'm telling the truth!" I said.

"We'll see. Put both of your hands out first. When we see they're empty, the rest of you can come out."

I did as he said. It was difficult raising my hands out into the open while balancing on the ladder. I had to lean on the lip of the hatch.

"Okay," the old man called. "Now you can crawl out of your hole."

I did my best to keep my hands visible while I shuffled upward. But it got too difficult and I had to grab onto the top rung to pull myself up. Standing on the spider, I turned to face my attackers. I held my hands up and tried not to shiver against the wind blowing my robe open.

"Shit," the old man said, lowering a big bazooka-like weapon. "You're just a kid."

"I'm twenty," I said. I shifted my legs together. The urge to urinate hadn't left me; it had only gotten worse.

"Why are you wearing that?" the man said. "Where's your uniform?"

"I had to leave the house in a hurry."

He made a *hmph*. I don't know what gave him any right

to judge my attire. He was wearing an old t-shirt and jeans held up by suspenders that sparkled with either glitter or fake gemstones. I couldn't tell which from where I stood.

"Your tank is ours now." He patted the side of his bazooka. "It's no good to you any more. We hit it with an EMP dart. Good thing you came along. We needed the parts."

"Hey!" I hadn't gone so little a distance, after giving up so much, just to let my only way to Peoria be taken by these mongrels. "Are you serious?"

"Do we look *not* serious?"

I didn't know how to respond. Everyone standing on the wall looked like cocktails of suburbanites and road warriors. They wore turtlenecks and war paint, spiked armbands and Milwaukee Brewers ball caps. They were the most ridiculously serious looking bunch I'd ever laid eyes on.

The old man in the rook tower flashed his teeth as if he wanted to scorch me with his smile. "It's a bad day to be in the Army."

"I quit the Army. I'm going home."

"Where's home?"

"Peoria." He moved his jaw but said nothing. The silence was getting me nervous so I added, "Illinois."

"I know where Peoira is. And I like liars even less than Nusies."

I don't know how they synchronized it, but everyone on the wall, who were already aiming their rifles at me, moved their arms enough to cause their weapons to make slight clicking noises. I think they were reaffirming I could be filled with holes in half the time it took to exhale. I didn't need reminding, but the urge to piss had most of my attention.

"Look," I said. "You have me at your mercy. Just... do you have somewhere I can..."

"Can what?" the man said.

"You know." I twirled a hand at waist level. But that didn't seem to help him understand. "Take a leak?"

The old man lowered his bazooka to the ground then hummed to himself. "Lower the gate. Let him in."

A younger woman turned to him and began arguing in sharp whispers.

The man turned back to shout at someone on the ground level behind the wall. "Get the tractor and pull that tank inside, quick as you can. They'll be looking for it." Back to me he said, "What's your name, kid?"

"Guillermo Contreras."

"Okay, Gilly," he said.

My eyes nearly popped from their sockets. Who the hell did this guy think he was? "Only my family calls me Gilly."

"You get a bathroom pass into our little kingdom, then we'll turn you loose. You don't talk to anyone but me and I'll be stuck to you like stink on shit. You break that rule, you can piss in your robe all the way to Peoria," then, under his breath, "Fucking Illinois."

The center of the wall came down like an old castle drawbridge. It was a hidden gate and it had done a damn good job. I hadn't spotted it. The gate's exterior was made of the same brick, lowered by concealed hinges and wires.

"Wait," I called up to the man.

A woman on a tractor puttered her way out toward the tank.

"If I'm only allowed to talk to you," I said, "shouldn't I know your name?"

The old man looked over his shoulder as he made his way off the tower. "You can call me Seabee."

CHAPTER 6

The woman on the tractor, a real thin lady with a squinty eye, began hitching chains to Tank 1. I tried not to take too much time to look back at it. It was bad enough wondering how I was going to get five miles down a dragon-infested road, let alone the whole way back home.

"Follow me," Seabee said.

He'd left his bazooka behind in the tower and had rolled up the sleeves of his long, forest green coat. His forearms were as big as my thighs. He had a military-style haircut and the short stubble was as gray as a storm cloud. I would have pegged him as a soldier if he hadn't spouted so much hate for the Army.

Yeah, it all checked out. Seabee must have been former Navy.

The inside of the settlement looked like most others I'd seen, but someone with the freedom to be artistic had used paints and chalk to make the fronts of all the ramshackle buildings look like a typical Main Street USA from different time periods. There was a grocer and a blacksmith and even a store called IKEA. And they were placed beside a jazz club and a saloon from the old west.

I didn't know if these buildings functioned as their

facades indicated or if it was just a way to make it all look more pleasing to the eye. People probably just slept in them. I wondered who had pulled the short straw and had to live in the IKEA.

Everyone came out and watched from the side of the street as I followed the old man through the snow.

The ground was cold as fuck.

"I guess you believe me now?" I asked him. My teeth began to chatter.

"Believe what?"

"Uh... everything I told you."

A fountain stood in the center of the town, but it held no water. A name had been chiseled into the stone: Sherry.

Seabee hurried on. "When I saw you in that bathrobe, I knew you were alone. Everything else you said still remains bullshit in my eyes."

Three small shacks had been built side by side in the back corner of the town wall. Pointing a lazy finger toward them, he said, "Pick one."

The shacks were basically outhouses, but I'd relieved myself in worse places.

I entered the one on the far right.

When I was done with my business, Seabee was leaning against the wall and staring at the ground. He didn't bother lifting his eyes. Some rock on the ground had his interest.

"Are you really going to put me back on the road with nothing?" I asked him.

"We could shoot you instead."

"Come on, man. I'm as good as dead out there without that tank. And I didn't have much of a chance *with* it. I just want to see my Mom and Dad one more time before I go on the run for good."

"Peoria?" Then he looked at me. "That's where you said you were headed? Yeah?"

"Yeah. Born and raised."

He came at me like a hover train, shoved me up against the nearest outhouse and put one of those big forearms against my throat. I couldn't breathe, but I could still somehow smell whatever had blown up in the shithole behind me.

"I think this is some Trojan horse shit one of your superiors put you up to." Seabee's face turned red. He had the eyes of a psychopath. I kept thinking I was glad at least to have gone to the bathroom before this maniac strangled me to death. "Why are you here? No one's ever come to our gate, and all of a sudden I'm supposed to believe some Mexican in a bathrobe stumbles on our town in a spider tank and all he wants is directions?"

I coughed and screeched enough to say, "I'm... not... Mexican, you... fucking... dick."

He released his arm. I fell to the ground.

"Why are you here?" He was yelling now. "You can tell me or I can stomp your fucking brains out."

I rubbed at my neck, where his arm had been pinned. I'd been doing a lot of neck-rubbing lately. I stayed on my knees but looked up at him. The sun had him in shadow. "You hate NUSA? Well, so do I. After I joined up, I found out they were a bunch of assholes, but I tried to make the best of a shit situation. My droid sergeant dragged me out of bed last night and tried to burn me 'cause he thought I was a smoke eater. I stole that tank and left my platoon to get ripped apart by wraiths. I meant what I said. I'm just trying to get back to Peoria."

"Your sergeant was a droid?"

"Yeah," I said. "5-90."

Seabee shook his head. "You're lying."

"Why would I lie about that? You can't make that up!"

"You're heading to Peoria?"

"That's where my family is."

"Peoria is ashes now."

Everything went still. I'd heard the words he said, but they didn't make sense.

"What?" It was a good thing I was already on the ground. My legs felt rubbery. I said it again, "What?"

Seabee looked at me, and I don't know what he saw, but it caused his face to slacken. "Peoria was overrun by dragons about a month back. One of the worst attacks since E-Day. You should have known that. Everyone knows about it. If some hicks in the sticks like us know, any common Nusie should, too. Peoria had been requesting the Army to come save them. They sent out signals for days before the city went under. Damn Nusies never responded to the call. You had to have known."

I fell back from my knees and onto my ass. My throat tightened, eyes stinging. The world went blurry from tears welling in my eyes. "I'm going to... need a minute."

I buried my face in my hands and cried.

I tried not to think about how it happened, but the thoughts fought their way through and made me cry harder. I saw dragons burning my family alive, eating them. Tearing their flesh. I saw my house cave in and bury my abuela in a pile of rubble. My mind, the sick son of a bitch, showed all my younger cousins in a corner in some back alley, surrounded by grimy bricks, trapped by scalies of different shades of evil. The dragons crept closer and closer as the kids cried and screamed for God, anyone, to save them. Then teeth snapped and claws slashed. Fire, acid, blood, and smoke engulfed my brain.

I wanted to die.

"Hey, kid," Seabee said. His voice went softer. "Listen... umm..."

"The whole city?" I raised my soaked face to him. I tasted salt. I couldn't believe it. This was a dream, a nightmare. This wasn't real. This old man had his information wrong. "No one got out?"

"I... uh... aw shit." He helped me stand as I kept crying.

I let him drag me through the center of town. Nothing mattered anymore. I didn't care where I was. I didn't care about anything. My world had been burned away or torn to bits. The only people who loved me were dead. They'd suffered terribly. At least, I was sure they had.

Not knowing seemed worse than if I had a complete report of how they perished. My mind went to dark places to torture me. I couldn't do a damn thing to stop it.

I craved closure. I was at the mercy of endless possibilities.

When I took the time to look up, I saw I had been brought inside one of the painted buildings. Seabee laid me on a twin-sized mattress and stood over me for a second before rushing out to fetch one of the townspeople. He came back with the younger woman who'd been arguing with him on the wall. Then the old man left again with an exasperated shake of his head, leaving me with her.

She was wearing an old fire helmet, with the face shield pulled down, as if I had some disease she didn't want to catch. I kept looking at her because she had a kind look on her face, even though she was wearing knee and elbow pads with nails driven through them. And all of that was made scarier by her puffy, pink coat.

"Can I get you anything," she asked, after watching me bawl my eyes out for a while.

"Kill me," I said.

"Goddamn."

"There is no God."

"I don't have an opinion on that one way or another, but my dad asked me to take care of you so that's what I'm here to do. You want to talk about it?"

I buried my head into the pillow. No. I didn't want to talk about it.

To add a twist of weird to my trainwreck of thought, I kept remembering Reynolds. She was all I really had left in the world, but all she really had was the Army. She was just as gone from me as my parents and cousins and...

The heaving cries came again.

"Hey, I get where you're coming from," she said. "I lost my mom not too long ago. I still cry sometimes. Well, more than sometimes."

Why was this person bugging me? These people didn't even want me here. But now that I was in a depressive fit, they felt they had to keep someone around me? It probably had nothing to do with my emotions and everything to do with me being an outsider, a soldier, a Nusie. No one gave a shit about anybody anymore. At least, no one gave a shit about me – no one alive anyway. They'd died while I was off trying to do the right thing with the wrong people. And the bastards like Calhoun, if they knew, and according to Seabee they sure as hell did, hadn't told me anything about it. The thought brought on another bout of crying.

"I'm Bethany," she said. "You're Gilly, is that right?"

"Guillermo," it came out like a yell, but I was crying and couldn't help it. "Contreras."

"Oh, my dad said your name was Gilly."

I sat up, angry at everything. I was especially mad at myself for devolving into such a blubbering mess. I also knew it was justified. These weird townies would just have to deal with a sadsack of an AWOLer until they kicked me back out into the wastes.

"You can call me whatever you want," I told her.

"Gilly it is." She had jet black hair and a face that had no business being so radiant in such times.

"Can't I get some clothes or shoes or something?"

"My dad is looking into it." She tilted her head and gave me a sad smile. "You want to talk about what you're feeling?"

"No."

"It might be good to talk about something else then, anything else, just to get the pressure off your heart. That's something my mom used to say."

I wiped my eyes with the back of my wrist. Shit. I was leaking gallons. I began to shiver. "Like what?"

"I don't know. What do you know a lot about? You got a hobby or some other interest?"

I opened my mouth to speak. Closed it. I shook my head. "You'll just think I'm stupid or crazy."

"No I won't. We've been off the grid for a long time out here behind these walls. Unless you like to play Jenga with severed body parts, I think I'd be very interested to hear about it."

She was trying to make jokes. I didn't feel much like laughing. Okay. She wanted to know what I was interested in? I'd tell her.

"Smoke eaters," I said. Her smile fell away. "I know just about everything non-confidential about the smoke eaters.

I look up to them, still, even though they're gone. I know about their power suits, how they were an offshoot of the fire department. All their equipment and how it works. They were basically fucking superheroes. And they were there exactly when we needed them until NUSA broke them up. I especially know about Captain Naveena Jendal out of the Parthenon City department. It was out in Ohio. She was my favorite. I mean, she had more recorded dragon kills than anyone in the world. But nobody knew about it until after the smokies were over."

Bethany was wearing fingerless, black gloves. She began fidgeting with them and didn't stop, even after I'd quit talking. "What about Cole Brannigan? Know anything about him?"

I leaned forward. My breath got quicker. Bethany had been right about talking about something else to get my mind off my family. At least for a moment. I couldn't believe there was someone else who knew about the smoke eaters, and especially the ones out of Ohio. "Chief Brannigan? He was a legend. A little gruff for my taste, but he was the oldest rookie out of any department. Helped to completely transform the smoke eaters, even in other cities around the country. When we still had a country. How do you know about him?"

She shrugged. "I just heard some stories. Wonder where he is now."

"Oh." I sank back onto the cot, dropped my head. "Guess you don't know. He died. Sacrificed himself to kill the Phoenix that attacked Parthenon City a few years back."

"A Phoenix?"

"Yeah. I think it was the only one. I don't know much about it besides the news reports I could find. It liked to eat the dragons. Maybe if they'd left it alone Brannigan would still be around. And so would…"

Bethany must have seen me sulking, thinking about death. She was determined to steer me elsewhere. "So I guess you know a lot about dragons, too?"

"I try. They're amazing. It sucks they always try to kill us."

"What's your favorite type of dragon?"

"This is starting to sound like you're talking to a four-year-old. I'm probably older than you."

"You might be. You sound like an old bastard if you don't even have a favorite scaly."

I hummed, put two fingers to my lips. "I like the majestic nature of Golden Drakes, but I also think Jabberwocks are creepy in the coolest way, but… hold up. You keep asking the questions. Why don't you tell me about who you are and how you're all out here in the middle of nowhere in a fucking castle?"

Her smile returned. "No can do. You're still a Nusie and I didn't even want to let you through the gate. That was my dad's decision. Man's got a soft spot for fellow weak bladders."

"So I'm supposed to tell you everything and get nothing back? That feels more like an interrogation than a conversation."

"That's life."

"Do you think I could get some food at least?"

"We already had breakfast. You'll be gone before dinner."

"Can you at least tell me where I am?"

Bethany laughed, obviously getting a kick out of denying me answers. She shook her head.

"What about your mom?"

Her face went slack, maybe even a little paler.

I felt my nose running and had no other option but to use the sleeve of my robe. "You said you lost her. What happened?"

"She died out on the road, when a bunch of Nusies did a shit job of trying to take out a scaly."

Maybe if I hadn't known I'd lost my own family, my lips would have frowned in pity and I would have told her how sorry I was. We just ended up staring at each other, listening to some secret song only people like us could hear.

Finally, I said, "The Army. They fucking suck."

"They? Don't you mean you? You rolled up to our gate in a Nusie tank."

"I ran away. Went AWOL."

I noticed Bethany was wearing some kind of old Kevlar vest under the pink coat. It was official. I dubbed her apocalyptic attire as "punk sniper". All she was missing was an anarchy symbol painted onto the front of her fire helmet.

She slid a thumb under one of the vest straps. "I thought I was only smelling the wet funk coming off your robe." She sniffed the air, squished her face in disgust. "But I seem to be catching the wisps of bullshit."

Wow. The suspicious apple didn't fall far from the tree. She thought I was a liar. Her dad thought I was a liar. Maybe if I started waddling and quacking they'd roast me for Easter.

"It's true," I said. "I thought I was finally doing it, being a good soldier. The platoon forced my hand. I had to run."

"And why would you do something like that?"

"Because other than you, the last people I talked to about the smoke eaters were a bunch of kids and somehow that led to me being threatened with fire and accused of being a smokie."

Bethany stood and moved toward me. I flinched a little, moving farther back onto the mattress. I didn't have much of anywhere to go.

"Are you?" she asked.

"Am I..." I smiled, showing lots of teeth. My eyes tensed. I'm sure it looked crazy. It felt crazy. My rational brain seemed to be far away in a Peoria that didn't exist anymore. I laughed. "Am I a smoke eater? If I was a smoke eater... oh why am I even talking to you about this? You're just going to kick me out once your dad gets back."

She leaned in close, squinting her eyes a little. She was inspecting me. Her gaze drifted down to my feet then all the way to the top of my head and then back to my eyes. "Yeah, there's no way you're a smoke eater."

Who the hell did she think she was? "And how would you know?"

She opened her mouth to answer.

The door burst open and a metallic creature bounded in. It stopped in the middle of the room. With its digital eyes, it took several glances between Bethany and me. Its rubber tongue hung from the side of its rectangular mouth. Spots had been painted all over the robot's body. It was a droid dog.

"Dodaeche nuguya?" the dog said, then jumped onto the mattress and began licking me. It felt and smelled like a soft tire being shoved in my face.

I yelled and flailed my arms, falling flat on my back, thinking they'd sicced the thing on me. Bethany started laughing. After I realized the droid wasn't trying to kill me, I started laughing, too. I'd never seen a real dog – they'd been gone since E-Day – and my family couldn't afford the mechanical substitute.

The robo-dog barked. It sounded like a static-laden recording of a real canine.

I heard the door slam shut. Seabee stood there with a pair of old boots and a small stack of clothes in his arms. He didn't look charitable. He looked pissed. "Kenji, get off of him."

The dog turned toward the old man, then jumped off the mattress and laid down at Bethany's feet.

Seabee tossed the clothes onto the mattress. "Hurry up and get dressed."

"What's wrong?" Bethany asked.

"We have a problem." He glared at me as if I already knew.

"What?" I said.

The old man dug into his coat pocket and pulled out a small, silver device, about the size of a hover car's key fob. Seabee held it between his fingers. A tiny red light blinked in its center.

Bethany beat me to asking the obvious question. "What is that?"

"Merv and the others started taking the tank apart. Found this bolted next to the core distributor. Wanna tell us what it is, Gilly?"

He stared at me as if I'd killed someone. I looked from Bethany to her dad, confused. "How the hell should I know? I barely even know how to drive the tank."

"It's a tracker," Seabee said. "Had it encased in the underside of the tank. EMP can't do shit to it, but even if it could the Army already knows you're here."

CHAPTER 7

As I got dressed they waited outside. They were trying to argue in hushed tones but I could still hear them clearly. They'd taken the dog with them.

Seabee had given me a pair of mismatched socks, forest-green cargo pants, a black denim jacket, and a generic fire department t-shirt with a Maltese cross. All of it was too big for me but the boots weren't too bad. I'd probably get blisters on the back of my heels but it was better than losing a foot to frostbite.

"Merv wanted to smash the tracker with a hammer," I could hear Seabee say on the other side of the door. "Sure as hell glad she didn't. That would mark us as the final location for that tank."

"So we should send the tracker somewhere else, keep us off the map."

"Yeah, that's my thinking."

"Okay," Bethany said. "Then how do we do that?"

"If I was an asshole–"

"You are an asshole."

Seabee groaned. "Well, if I was a real asshole, I'd send the kid down the road with the tracker, but there's no way he'd get far enough fast enough. Not on foot."

"You could always give him the tank back," Bethany said.

Now that was an idea. I could thank Seabee for the clothes and the unwelcome but valuable information about Peoria, then be on my way somewhere else.

"I'm going to have to take him," Seabee said.

"Absolutely not!" Bethany was struggling to keep her voice low. "We're already deeper into this than we should be."

"In for a penny..."

"Why is it every time some chance to be a hero comes along, you have to run right into it? It's not your job or your problem. This town is your responsibility."

"And that's why I'm going to do what I have to so this town remains right where it is. Look, I can drive him someplace far enough to avoid you all getting spotted, but close enough I can be back by tonight."

"I'm all for getting that tracker out of here," Bethany said, "but there's no reason we have to take boy wonder anywhere. I feel bad for him. I do. Those were real tears he was crying in there. But my gut says he's here for information. Only he got some he wasn't expecting. We should keep him locked up before he runs back and tells them all. He's got no family any more. Where else would he go?"

That was something I hadn't had the time to consider. I had nowhere to go.

"They can't all be assholes," Seabee said.

"Since when have you ever heard of any of them growing a conscience and ditching their platoon?" Bethany asked. "You don't really trust him, do you?"

There was a beat of silence.

"Seriously?" Bethany said. "He's probably got the Army a mile out and closing in."

"I don't get that sense from him," Seabee said. "He looks like a dumb kid that got wrapped up in some shit and stumbled out of it onto our doorstep. The Army doesn't know about us. But they will if you keep slowing me down with this bullshit."

Rocks were kicked across the ground. "He was talking about smoke eaters. Said he knows all about them. Looks up to them like they're heroes from old fairy tales. Said he was accused of being one."

"Yeah," Seabee said. "He told me about why he ran off. Didn't know he was a self-proclaimed expert."

Now that was just unfair. I never claimed to be an expert.

"Don't you think it's fishy that an Army private shows up out of nowhere and starts pulling on our heartstrings? He's playing the sympathy card. But take sympathy out of it. Think about it for a second. He says he was on his way to a city that got torched. Now everyone will feel sorry for him. Welcome him with open arms. 'Oh, how horrible you almost got killed for being a smoke eater!'

"Soon enough someone in town will admit they're a smoke eater, too. Share a cup of Merv's shitty booze with him and chat it up about the good old days.

"Then boom. Army shows up to cart off the smoky and the rest of us are punished and put on the itinerary for their supply collection. Only problem is he didn't plan on us finding that tracking device."

Damn. If it wasn't so far-fetched I would have been impressed. That would have been the smartest and most devious way for a smoke eater hunter to go about it. But the Army wasn't that calculated. And she was making it sound like they had something to worry about. She made it sound like a smoke eater was living in their town.

Was there?

A real-life smoke eater? No. No way. Bethany had to be embellishing. She was just concocting a scheme that neither I nor the Army had even thought of.

The way it was looking, I'd be lucky if I was forced out of town on both legs and not tossed out on my head.

"You come up with that grand scheme all by yourself?" Seabee asked.

Bethany sighed. "I can see it in your face. You haven't changed your mind one damn bit."

"When have I ever changed my mind once I've set it?"

"Oh my God! Could you be a more typical geezer?"

"I can add prunes and Geritol to the scavenging list."

"Dad." Bethany's voice went softer, sounded like she was about to cry, "I'm serious. I've heard the stories. If they find you, they'll send you to that camp in Ohio. They'll cut you open and stick you with wires and needles. You were born to fight dragons, but you have a shitty sense about people."

Wait. What?

Bethany was saying something about how she'd already lost her mom and couldn't lose her dad, too, but I couldn't contain myself any more. I pushed through the door and stared at Seabee in awe. "You're a smoke eater?"

Kenji ran toward me, did circles around my ankles while barking, and ran back to sit beside Seabee.

Bethany flipped her rifle around and pointed it at me. "Stay where you are. I'll shove that tracker up your ass and toss you into Lake Michigan."

I stretched my hands as high above my head as they would reach.

"Calm down," Seabee said. He put his hand to the barrel of Bethany's rifle and moved it toward the sky, slowly.

She let him.

The old man turned to me. "How long have you been listening?"

"Um." I bit my lower lip. "The whole time, I guess."

"See?" Bethany said. "He's a spy."

"I'm not a spy," I said. "I'm not here on some crazy mission. I'm not with the stupid Army anymore. I tried to do the right thing yesterday and all it did was take what little I had and rip it away. All I wanted to do was get home. I don't know what I have to do to prove it to you."

She glared at me. "So your people thought you were a smoke eater, huh? Why don't we test it ourselves? We can throw you in a box and fill it with smoke. Or we can just roll you over a fire like a kebab."

"For fuck's sake," Seabee said. "We don't have time for that medieval shit."

"You're really a smoke eater?" It slipped out of my mouth. I couldn't help it. I felt like a kid meeting their favorite professional running back. Depression and grief had no hold on me for the moment, not with a smoke eater standing in front of me. "What department were you with?"

Bethany threatened the rifle. "Quit talking, fan boy!"

Again, Seabee pushed her weapon away. When he exhaled, it came out like a balloon hissing air through a pin prick. He turned to me and crossed his arms. "You want to prove yourself to us?"

"Of course," I said.

"Because we have good people in this town counting on us to protect them. If I go off on a dumb mission to help your ass out, I have to know it's for good reason."

"Yeah," I said, "I get that. You already took my tank. I just want to be able to do okay out there by myself.

Bethany was right when she said I have nowhere to go, but I promise, I never wanted to screw things up for you or this castle."

Bethany groaned. "It's not a castle. We built this place around a store called The Cheese Castle. And just like your story, it's not fucking real."

"Whatever," I said. "Just tell me what I've got to do."

"Answer this question," said Seabee, "and you'll be good in my book."

"Dad!"

"Stuff it, Bethany." Seabee leaned in close. His eyes were ocean green and they had me locked in paralysis. "What's the smoke eater motto?"

Bethany groaned and walked away a few steps, grumbling about how stupid this was.

"That's it?" I asked. "That's the question?"

"Can you not answer it?" Seabee cocked his head to the side as if he hadn't heard me well. "Do you want my daughter to shoot you?"

"Sink or swim," I said. "The smoke eater motto is sink or swim."

Kenji barked. His eyes showed digital fireworks going off.

Seabee nodded, grunted. "Come with me."

Bethany watched us walk away. I turned to look at her. Not to rub it in. Just to see what she would do. She watched us for a second, her mouth open in disbelief, then she followed.

"Can you answer my question?" I said, struggling to keep up with Seabee as he chugged ahead. "What department were you with? I've only studied Washington and Ohio. They stand out more than the others because they had such big dragon attacks to deal with."

"Shut up and walk," he said.

I didn't see more than twelve other people in town but I was sure there were more. They'd been going about their business but stopped to watch us pass by. Everyone seemed to have a job to do. Some of them had been welding metal parts together. Others were washing a pile of clothes with a tub and a brush.

Behind me, low enough her father couldn't hear, Bethany said, "If the Army does show up, I'm going to kill you first."

I looked back over my shoulder. "Are you still at it?"

She shrugged.

The building Seabee led me to was less of a housing unit and more of a large garage. Nothing more than bricks around a roll-up door. The outside had been painted to look like an old school firehouse. It even had a dalmatian sitting by a fire hydrant. I touched the Maltese cross emblazoned on my shirt. All the obvious signs had been there. I just hadn't picked up on them. This guy had history.

Seabee walked to the center of the garage door, bent over, grabbed the handle, and with a thrust of his arm, threw it open. It rose, clanking on rusty tracks. Inside was something I never thought I'd see.

"Oh, man." My legs wobbled. It had been a rough few days, but even at my healthiest I would have quaked.

A slayer truck sat in the garage. Its spherical, glistening windshield reflected my image, and on the other side was a cabin laden with cushy, gray interior and buttons ripe for the pushing. On the roof and running along each side were purple and white emergency lights. The slayer's body was painted mostly black, with just enough streaks of violet throughout. The tires were even shiny. This truck might not have been used in a while, but somebody had been taking good care of her while she was out of commission. Most of the lettering had been torn off – only a P, an N, and a couple vowels remained – so I still didn't know what department either Seabee or the slayer had served.

"How…" I couldn't find the words. "…How do you have this?"

Seabee opened the slayer's driver side door. He climbed in and started her up. It hummed. All the lights turned on, twirling and sparkling wonderfully. A slight whine of energy came from its center, but otherwise the slayer truck was silent. It rolled out of the garage and there, out in the open, I got a really good look at it.

According to the diagrams and reports I'd read, a slayer like this was thirty-five feet long. Each bin contained different tools and weapons the smoke eaters had utilized. I started to reach out a hand to touch it, but quickly forced myself to drop the arm. I didn't feel worthy. Plus, Bethany was watching me and I didn't want to give her more reason to shoot me.

Seabee left the truck running and jumped out of the driver's seat. "Are you shitting your pants yet, Guillermo?"

"I might as well be." I couldn't take my eyes off the vehicle.

"Let's get suited up," Seabee said. "In the wastes I want you to be protected as much as possible. Because we're both too old for me to hold your hand. You were a soldier so I'm going to assume you can handle yourself out there."

"Sure I can. I killed a dragon all by myself yesterday." Shit. Was that too cocky? I wasn't trying to be arrogant.

Seabee blinked. "You did, huh? What kind of dragon?"

I stumbled over my words. "Uh, it was, you know, just some acid dragon."

"A Kilgore?"

"No," I said. "We thought it was a Wyvern, but it ended up being more of a Drake. I never read about that kind of scaly."

"Nice." He gave me a nod before walking off. "Sounds like it was Maleer."

"Dad," Bethany called, but he was already walking to the first big bin at the side of the slayer truck. "Dad!"

"Wait," I said. "What did you mean we need to 'suit up'?"

Seabee lifted the bin door and holy fucking shit, out came an actual smoke eater power suit. It was the armor they wore to fight dragons. Nothing the Army had could match it. Its green metal glistened like undisturbed swamp water. A dragon skull was carved into the chest. Its boots and gloves held lights that would glow orange when someone stepped in and turned it on.

"Oh, man," I walked over to the suit.

"Go on," said Seabee.

I reached out and touched the dragon skull emblem. Its metal was cool to the touch and rough enough I worried I might cut myself. I wondered how many battles the thing had been put through.

"No," Seabee said. "Don't just touch it. Push in that skull emblem."

My breath caught, but I managed to push where he'd said. The suit opened like a broken egg.

"Slip on in." Seabee nodded toward the suit.

I felt like I was going to hyperventilate.

"Dad, you can't leave." Bethany stomped over and grabbed her dad's elbow. "We need you here. We can figure out something else to do about the tracker. About... *him*."

"Baby girl, I've been cooped up behind these walls for too damn long," Seabee said. "I want you to run things while I'm gone. You're the only one I trust to do it right. And, like I said, I should be back by tonight. Gilly and I will get far enough away, toss the tracker, then we'll find the kid some transportation and send him on his way. Easy peasy."

This caused Bethany to shoot back a retort and they began a muffled daughter-father argument. I wasn't listening anymore. The power suit was waiting.

I stepped up and slipped my arms and legs into the appropriate holes. The lining inside the suit was made of a soft, absorbent fabric. It felt good. Sturdy. Once my fingers were in the metal gloves, my feet secured inside the boots, the suit closed and sealed around me. The fabric inside tightened, but only enough to where it was secure but still comfortable.

Seabee patted his daughter on the shoulder while she was mid-sentence and walked toward me, smiling. "Smoke eaters always had the best toys."

I stepped off the truck and got a sense of the power suit's weight against the snow on the ground. I looked at my feet and, sure enough, the tips of my boots were glowing orange. I raised my head and laughed. My breath puffed steam into the air. I lifted two fists and shouted, "This is the greatest day of my life!"

Also the worst.

But I'd forgotten, for a few moments at least. Later, I would think back to that moment and wonder why I was behaving like such an idiot. Like such a kid. Emotions are screwy things. They'll take you to the lowest depths and then rocket you to the loftiest highs, using the same momentum.

What was the saying? Any port in a storm? Some people couldn't help milking a depression, let it drown them. My mind always sought any distraction it could dig its hooks into. My family was dead, I'd lost my tank, the Army was coming for me, and all I wanted to do was play smoke eater. Maybe acting like a kid was a lot less painful than accepting reality like an adult.

Seabee moved to the end of the slayer truck and opened another bin. I watched in amazement as he donned his own armor. He grabbed a smoke eater helmet from the same bin and secured it with a chin strap. Turning, he walked toward me smoothly, as naturally as if the metal was his own skin. The image was striking. I felt like I'd seen him before. Some old video on the Feed, an old book. He had a look I couldn't place.

"Who are you?" I asked. "Really?"

"I'm just your chauffeur for a couple hours. Get in the truck"

"Come on," I said. "I have to know."

"Get used to disappointment."

I pointed to his helmet. "Well, can I get one of those? You said I need to be fully protected."

He laughed as he pushed past me. "You have to earn a helmet. And you don't even know if you're a smoke eater. Get in the truck and wait."

"I might be," I called to his back.

He didn't respond.

I walked around to the passenger side of the slayer, but stopped to peer around the front, to see what the old smoke eater was doing.

Bethany knelt next to Kenji, petting his metal head and staring at the ground. Seabee said something to his daughter, but she refused to look at him. He got down on one knee and kept trying. I couldn't hear what he was saying but it was just as well. It wasn't any of my business. She looked up and tears were in her eyes. She leapt forward and allowed Seabee to catch her, hold her. How could I blame her for acting the way she was? If I had any family left, I'd hold on tight and never let go. I wouldn't care if they were trying to help some punk kid or saving the world.

The old man put an armored hand at each side of his daughter's face. Whatever he said next caused Bethany to lift her chin, sniff, and wipe the tears from her eyes. They both stood and walked toward the center of town.

"Everybody," Seabee shouted. "Emergency meeting. Gather 'round."

The townspeople we'd passed earlier stopped their work and walked over to meet the smoke eater and his daughter. A little boy and a middle-aged couple walked out of crops growing along the far wall. Others filtered out of the painted buildings.

"Whoa!" the little boy ran up to Seabee and touched his power suit. "Cool!"

Seabee put his hand on the kid's shoulder and spoke to the rest of them. "I have to leave for a little bit. Bethany is in charge while I'm gone."

They flooded him with questions.

"Why?"

"How far are you going?"

"What are you going to do with that Army guy?"

"Why the hell are you dressed like that?"

"Listen," Seabee said. "That tank we brought in here had a tracker and I'm going to take it and the Nusie far from here. This isn't any different from when we go out and scavenge.

It's to keep us going. I'll be back by tonight. Worst case, tomorrow morning."

Bethany turned to stare at her father. She kept silent.

"I just wanted to keep all of you informed," Seabee said. "I might come up against some scalies so that's why I'm taking my old equipment. But more than likely I won't see more than a few snowflakes. You have nothing to worry about."

That didn't stop their questions. It only gave them more.

Seabee raised his hands and turned to walk back toward me. "I don't have time. Just keep things going as usual. Do what Bethany says."

They all watched him walk away.

I hurried into the slayer, closed the door behind me. The inside of the cab held a faint smell of smoke and I wondered if I was breathing in the same molecules that had originated inside a dragon. The thought both excited and scared me. I began studying the slayer's controls. I imagined a crew of smoke eaters sitting there, pushing those same buttons. A captain had ridden exactly where I was. This should have been everything I'd dreamed of, and it was, but it was like chasing a happiness I could never grasp. I should have felt more.

Seabee climbed behind the wheel and slammed his door shut. The slayer moved forward and the townspeople split apart to let us through. With one hand on the wheel, the old smoke eater blew a kiss to his daughter. Bethany caught the imaginary, flying smooch and put the closed fist against her chest. My stomach twisted and my throat tightened. My eyes began to burn so I dabbed a metal finger at their corners.

"This is the apocalypse," Seabee said. "We don't have time to be depressed."

"Didn't you grieve your wife?"

He punched the accelerator. Someone had lowered the town's gate and it felt like we sped through it at a hundred miles an hour. Seabee didn't say anything, but I could sense the anger radiating off of him like an inferno. I thought he might hit me. He didn't.

"Sorry," I said.

"No, it's a good point. *I'm* sorry."

We were coming up onto the road. I didn't know if he'd turn left or right, farther from where I'd left the platoon or back toward them. But something else was on my mind.

"Why are you helping me?" I asked. "Not that I don't appreciate it. But letting me wear this suit, helping me find a vehicle. It's not just the tracking device. Most people would have killed me or thrown me to the scalies."

"I'm not most people."

"No, I guess you're not."

He sighed. "Look, kid. If what you say is true, the other Nusies think you might be a smoke eater. And if you don't really know if you are or not, I don't blame you. I didn't know I was until way later than most. So if you are, I'd feel like shit if I didn't help out one of my own. Plus, you looked so pathetic in that stupid robe and then when I told you about Peoria... Well...

"Aside from that, I've been itching to get the fuck out of that town and do something interesting for longer than I can remember. Hell, Bethany wasn't even a tween when we started that place."

"What's the town's name?"

"Doesn't have one. Towns with names are towns that want to be found."

He turned southwest.

"So what's the plan?" I asked. "We gonna throw that tracker into Lake Michigan?"

"Nope. It would just stay in one place and the Nusies would see it was in the water. Besides, if they do find the tracker, I want them to find some trouble along with it."

I looked out at the flat, gray world and tried to think of what his plan might be. I came up with nothing, so I just decided to ask him. "Where are we heading?"

"Chicago," he said.

"What the fuck? Are you crazy? Even the Army knows to stay away from big cities. And Chicago? That's got to be the worst one."

"It'll kill two birds with one stone," he said.

"Yeah, if you mean we're the two birds."

"Chicago is far enough from my town and it's going to be the best place to find a car that runs."

I considered arguing the point but I was at his mercy. "I guess it would make them think twice about looking for me or the tank. So we get into Chicago, find a car and drop the tracker in the street somewhere?"

"Nope."

"Look, man. I'm not a mind reader. Do you think you can help me out here?"

"Like I said, I want the Nusies to have trouble when they find the tracking device. I also want the thing to be on the move in the meantime, make it look like you're still driving the tank. I want to make those Nusie bastards work for it."

"Why do I have the feeling we're not just going to strap it to a remote control car or something?"

"Something."

I leaned away from the old man, but kept my eyes on him.

He was crazy. I didn't realize just *how* crazy until he gave me a wide grin and said, "We're going to get a scaly to swallow it."

CHAPTER 8

"We're going to get a scaly to swallow it." Sachko said. He was speaking to Farmington, who jogged beside him along the edge of the lake. Both of them were several lengths ahead of me, too far for me to catch up. They'd stolen my rifle.

Technically, it had been Sachko who'd stolen it, this thin, dark-haired prick with a unibrow. But Farmington had no problem being an accessory. As far as I knew, Sachko and Farmington had never spoken a word to each other before that day. Their alliance was a random and singular chance to fuck with me and share the experience.

The platoon had stopped somewhere outside of Osceola, Iowa, near West Lake. It was a hot August 24th and we'd been given a short leave. I remember the date because it's my birthday. The break from duty and the theft of my rifle had nothing to do with me turning twenty. No one knew about my birthday: no one had ever asked, and the NUSA isn't the type of organization to stop and have cake for every grunt's special day.

I was just happy to have the chance at some alone time. No one yelling at me, no washing the tanks. I could just sit by the water and not think for a while.

Farmington met me on my way. Whatever he used to shave always left a horrible razor burn on his neck. Every time I saw him he had one of his hands up there under his chin, clawing away, scratching, scratching. It was enough to make anyone lose their shit. When Farmington crossed my path, he was itching away, and smiling. It wasn't a friendly smile. Anyone who's been bullied or harassed knows the kind of smile Farmington wore. It was like a Leviathan when blood hits the water. Pure delight at inevitable destruction.

I diverted my eyes to the ground and saw that my right boot's laces had come untied. *Perfect*, I thought. I dropped to a knee, set my rifle down, and began tying. The hope was that Farmington would keep walking and leave me be. He might have done that.

But Sachko ran up from behind me. He grabbed my rifle from the ground, slapped the back of my head, and took off toward the water. "Got your gun, fatty!"

When I looked up, Farmington's smile had grown bigger and he was turning to run after Sachko. For the last six months I'd been marching everywhere. I wasn't used to running, but these two assholes weren't giving me a choice.

Anger must have been fueling me. Normally I wouldn't force myself into a state of tight lungs and burning legs. But I was more worried about what 5-90 would do to me if I didn't get that rifle back.

I didn't know exactly how far I ended up chasing Sachko and Farmington but when I finally caught up to them I felt like I'd finished a marathon. The first one. Where the guy died.

Farmington and Sachko stopped at the water's edge, at a spot out of sight from the rest of the platoon. They turned to watch me bend over and dry heave.

"God*damn* are you worthless," Sachko said.

"Come on, man," I said. I was out of breath. "I need my rifle."

"Uh-uh." Sachko raised the weapon above his head. "You have to earn this, big boy. What are you willing to do to serve your country?"

What fucking country? I thought.

"I already joined up," I said. "Why are you guys always fucking with me?"

Farmington stood beside Sachko. His smile had gotten wider on the jog out here. "There had to be a mistake when we picked you up, Contreras. You don't deserve to carry this weapon."

"No, no." Sachko turned to Farmington. "His name is pronounced Fatty. Or Lard-ass."

"I think it's *gordo* in his native tongue," Farmington said.

"Yeah!" Sachko said. "Gordy. Gordy ate too many tacos growing up. Gordy couldn't even run a hundred yards without having an asthma attack. Tell you what. You come put your lips on my ass cheek, I'll give your rifle back."

"It's against NUSA code to take another soldier's firearm," I said. Mistakenly, I thought laying out some protocol would appeal to their logic.

They laughed.

When I coughed, it came out like a wheezy trumpet. "How old are you guys, fucking twelve?"

"Bitch, I'm twenty-three," said Sachko. "And we don't give a damn about code. Not with you."

"Our word against yours," Farmington said.

"Can't be our fault if a dragon eats your rifle," Sachko said. "Shit like that just happens sometimes. You're the scaly expert right, Gordy? Fucking know-it-all, what kind of dragon would live in this lake? How can we get one to come take a nibble on your rifle?"

Farmington caught the weapon and dipped the barrel into the water. "I bet this would do it."

"Stop!" I shouted.

"I think you have to throw the whole rifle in," Sachko said. "Give it here."

Farmington threw the rifle back to Sachko.

The water behind them exploded with several splashes. They screamed and jumped, raising their hands in front of their faces. But when the water spray subsided, there was nothing there, and a slight echo of laser fire filled my ears.

A woman's laughter came from around the bend. "Why so jumpy?" Reynolds had her rifle in her hands, sauntering toward us on the path. Her helmet sat a little crooked.

"What the fuck, Reynolds?" Farmington shouted. "If you ever shoot at me again–"

"You'll what?" Reynolds said.

Farmington didn't finish his statement. He went back to scratching his razor burn.

Reynolds' eyes suddenly went squinty. "What are you doing out here?"

"Just having a little fun with Contreras," Sachko said. "Getting him some exercise."

"Really?" Reynolds said. "And I guess in all your dicking around, you must have forgotten 5-90 will have your ass if you fuck with another soldier's gear."

"Must have slipped our minds," said Farmington.

Reynolds nodded to Sachko. "Give it back to him."

Sachko's look was filled with venom, as if Reynolds had said something unsavory about his mother. "You going to bat for this fat fuck?"

"I'm going to bat for the platoon," Reynolds said. "And last I checked, that included Contreras."

"I'm heading back." Farmington threw his hands up and began walking to where the platoon had set up camp. There was no reason for him to hang around any more. The fun was over.

Sachko turned to me. "You want your rifle back?"

I nodded.

"Can't hear you," he said.

I sighed. "Yes."

"Yes what?" He held the rifle out to me.

I reached for the weapon. "Please."

Sachko twisted around and tossed the rifle into the lake. "Then go get it, fatty."

"I'm going to kick both your asses!" Reynolds charged at them.

Sachko and Farmington, new best buddies, laughed and ran off. In ten minutes time they'd be sharing what they'd done with the rest of the platoon. They'd be celebrated.

I kept my eyes on the spot in the lake where I'd seen the rifle sink. My helmet fell to the ground as I broke into a run. I dove into the water.

Back on shore, Reynolds was screaming, "What the hell are you doing, Private? Stop! Get out!"

I didn't realize how shitty a fully-clothed swimmer I was until fully submerged. You couldn't really see anything down there but puke green water and a few beams of sunlight. But I saw my rifle. At least, the blinking red light on the butt.

I felt myself sinking. Shit. What the hell had I done?

I reached for the rifle, but my fingers grabbed more puke green water. The gun was drifting away. Arms pulled me up as I tried one last time to grab my weapon. Then we broke the surface. Reynolds had a good hold of me, but I still flailed because I knew I wasn't going to be able to swim with all that uniform on. Plus there was the rifle. It was in my hand and I couldn't even doggie paddle like that.

"Quit moving," Reynolds shouted in my ear.

"I'm trying!"

"Try harder. You're going to get us killed."

I saw something rise out in the lake, just enough to crest the surface. The ripples were moving toward me and Reynolds. I didn't think it was a catfish.

"Swim!" I shouted.

"We'll be faster if you let me do the swimming."

She managed to drag me onto the lake shore. I lay there on my side drenched and weighed down. Thank God Reynolds had been around. I'd been stupid to jump into that lake.

"You're stupid as hell for jumping in that lake." Reynolds shoved me. I rolled onto my back. "It could be infested with dragons."

She was in her bra and panties. I blinked. Was I really seeing this? We'd never spoken before, and I only knew her as the platoon medic. Now she was standing over me, dripping and half naked. But if she'd kept her fatigues on, she would have been just as drowned as me.

My leave should have been way more quiet than this.

"Shit!" Reynolds hissed and turned from me. She was staring at her hand.

"Are you okay?"

"No, I'm not okay. I cut my hand on the damn rocks saving your dumbass." She shoved her hand at me. A slash ran across her palm, steadily seeping blood. "I'm getting my med bag."

Water blasted from the lake, showering us both. A huge shape surged onto the shore. All I saw was tusks and dark gray scales, this huge mouth coming to swallow me. Then something bumped into me and Reynolds was there, blasting her laser rifle into the big mouth.

"Sweet leaping Christ!" I back peddled away from the monster, now dead and stinking like penguin shit on the shore. "I knew I saw something in the water."

The dragon had a wide tail, like a whale's or a dolphin's. Its body was fish-shaped until you got to its forelegs and webbed claws.

"It's a…" I studied its long snout and huge tusks. It didn't have reptilian teeth like most other dragons. The eyes were open and frosty blue. "It's a… well, fuck I don't know what the hell it is."

"It's dead," Reynolds said. She scooted back to sit beside me again. I think we were both still in shock. We watched the dead scaly for a minute. She kept her rifle aimed at its head, where a few laser holes were still smoking. Finally she pointed to my leg. "It got you."

A big hole had been torn through my pant leg. Underneath, a long cut was bleeding and mixing with the lake water.

"Damn," I said. I wouldn't need stitches, but it would scab like shit. "Hey, thanks for saving me, Reynolds. I think I'm just starting to realize what happened."

"I saved you twice," she said. Then, after a hesitation, "Call me Sarah."

"Gilly. And yeah, I guess you did save me twice."

"You owe me now." She stared very seriously into my eyes. That close, I noticed that her eyebrows were a shade darker than her hair, and she had a light sprinkle of freckles across the bridge of her nose.

She slapped her cut palm against the gash in my leg.

"Ah! What the shit!"

"It's official now," she said. "We're linked by blood. You owe me a life debt twice."

"Aren't you a medic?" I squirmed under her grip. "This isn't very sanitary."

She shrugged, smiling at my discomfort. But it didn't bug me like Farmington or Sachko.

"Maybe," she said. "But you gotta take this seriously. Say it. You owe me a life debt."

"You want to get dressed first?"

"Quit changing the subject. Say it."

"Jesus, all right. I owe you a life debt."

"Twice."

"*Twice.*"

"Good." She released her hand and walked over to where she'd thrown her fatigues and med bag.

The scratch on my leg started hurting when I stood up. I backed away from the dragon, but I kept my eyes on it, really admiring how large and sharp those tusks were. The look of its jaw made me think it could snap a steel beam in two. I really did owe it to Reynolds. That would have been a painful death.

I'd never seen anything like this dragon on the Feed. It wasn't uncommon for new species to pop up every now and then. Usually they were named by the first to discover them, like celestial bodies. If that meant me, I didn't know what to name it. But I had an idea. "How are we going to report this?"

"Oh, that's not happening," Reynolds said. "No, no, no. This is going to stay between us three: you, me, and the Gilly dragon."

CHAPTER 9

The ground rumbled as it moved across the lake shore. It took a leisurely gait and why wouldn't it? There was nothing that would threaten something so big.

Big? More like titanic. About three stories tall from what I could estimate. Even a three-headed Behemoth would be dwarfed. The sunlight hit it at just the right angle and lit up its golden scales, casting just enough of it in shadow to make it look majestic and mysterious and everything I thought it would be when I ever encountered one.

What a day.

Most scalies had a sinister look. Slithering tongues, sharp spikes along the back, teeth that showed even when their mouths were closed. You knew they would try and kill you just by looking at them.

Golden Drakes, sometimes referred to as "Luck Dragons", had more peaceful faces and even their horns were curvy and smooth, decoration over decimation. They usually kept to themselves, from what I'd read. But if they were provoked, or if another dragon encroached on their territory, GD's were worse than any dragon on record.

It wasn't just their size – though being as big as a skyscraper could do cataclysmic damage, even by accident.

Golden Drakes flew at incredible speeds. Whole towns could be ripped up in two flaps of its wings. Given its size, the GD was as destructive as an F5 tornado to anything within a decent range. A tornado all right; a twister that breathed fire. It hadn't been studied enough to determine whether its breath burned hotter than other scalies or if the flames were just so big it didn't take as much effort.

If someone ever had the misfortune to piss off a Golden Drake, it really wouldn't matter. Once the dragon went into attack mode, somebody was going to die. They were like hornets in how they attacked. It was like temporary psychosis or rabies. They might as well have been called "Jekyll and Hyde" dragons.

But somehow they got the "luck" label. The books and Feed documents said it was because of their regal and magical appearance. Their rarity caused some to believe they were like shooting stars you could make a wish on. I was more convinced it was because, if you ever saw a Golden Drake, you were lucky if you survived the experience.

We were driving the slayer truck along the western shore of Lake Michigan as we watched the dragon. Soon we'd be in Chicago city limits.

The Golden Drake had its wings tucked close to its sides. The sunlight lit them up like colorful, stained-glass windowpanes I'd only ever seen in churches. Its huge feet created small, frothy waves as it ventured into the lake. The scaly lifted its head toward the sun and chirped a song that sounded like a combination of nails on a chalkboard and a thousand people burning alive.

I couldn't think of anything to wish for.

"Shit," Seabee said. "If they were all that calm, we wouldn't be driving through ashes and I could stop to get a beer."

"Please tell me we're not going to feed the tracker to the GD."

"Hell. No."

The Golden Drake continued moving into the water and we drove past, letting live and living. What used to be the Windy City lay a few miles ahead. It looked more like a bunch of crumbling rocks from that distance. Towers of gnawed-on coal.

At the corner of my eye I could tell Seabee was taking glances at me. "You okay, kid?"

"Yes and no."

"What do you mean?"

"I don't know. Life has a bad way of giving you the good shit and the bad shit all at the same time so you can't fully enjoy either."

"I think you just defined what life is."

"Doesn't mean I have to accept that definition."

"Let me tell you something. I tried my damnedest to settle down with my wife and relax for the rest of my days, not once but *twice*, and each time Life grabbed me by the balls and dragged me off the path. This last time I really got reamed by Life's big, veiny dick. I lost my wife, and all my plans didn't mean shit. So yeah, I agree with you. Life, existence, whatever you want to call it, it's a bitch. But you can either keep going, to spite the cunt, or if you don't like what you're seeing you can always..." He made a gun with his hand, held it to his temple and made *pew, pew* noises.

"So Life has both a dick and a... 'c' word?"

Seabee laughed.

He'd told me there was no time for grief. Maybe that was true. But how the hell did you get through the day, let alone the next minute?

"Hey," Seabee said. "What I said before, about my smoke

eater days? I changed my mind. You can ask me whatever you want."

I perked up, slightly.

When we'd left the cheese castle, I'd been hoping to pass the time on the road with great conversation. I wanted to hear all of Seabee's stories. The old man had quickly squashed that. Now, something had changed.

He raised a finger to my face. "But if I don't feel like answering something, I won't. And you can't push the issue. Deal?"

"Gee, thanks," I said. "You know, your timing could have been better. I could have asked you all kinds of stuff earlier. Now I've got five minutes before you tell me to shut up."

"I'm just trying to get your mind off other things, and it's not entirely selfless. I need you focused. In the present. We'll *both* get flambéed if your mind is all..." he moved his hand to make it look like it was talking, blabbing. The armored fingers of his power suit clanked.

We passed an overturned hoverbus on the overpass. It had been burned so badly it looked like a papier-mâché model that had been scorched and then pissed on.

"Here's a question," I said. "When you were a smoke eater, did you do the same kind of crazy, stupid shit we're about to do?"

He laughed, checked the side view mirror a few times. Must have been an old habit. "Once a smoke eater, always. And yeah. We used to do dumb shit all the time. Sometimes it was the only option besides letting a bunch of good people die. And did I detect a note of smartassery in your question? Shouldn't this be a dream come true for you? You're in a slayer truck, wearing a power suit, and on your way to find a horde of fire-breathing scalies. Right?"

He playfully shoved my shoulder. "Right?"

A smile crept onto my lips. He kept shaking me until I'd answered him four times. "Okay. All right. Yeah. This is pretty cool."

"We have to get you talking like a smoke eater. This mission isn't 'pretty cool,' this is fucking badass!"

I laughed. "Not all smoke eaters talk like you do."

"Oh no? And what other smokies do you know besides me?"

"I mean… none." A mishmash of faces ran across my mind. None of them had been smoke eaters. "But I read about a few of them."

"Yeah? Like who? Who do you know the most about?"

"Captain Jendal?"

"Naveena?

I sat up and turned to face him. "Did you know her?"

He shrugged. "I might have met her a couple times."

"Are you serious? What was she like?"

"Damn, kid. Do you have a crush on her or something?"

"Not everything involves Ds and Cs, old man. No, I just really look up to what she did. She killed the Behemoth, rode an ice dragon, had the most confirmed dragon kills out of any smoke eater in the world. Then when Ohio stopped slaying and did the whole tranquilizing thing, she still nabbed the most scalies."

"Yeah, well… smoke eating is a team effort…"

"And saying I have a crush on her, I mean come on. She's like ten years older than me."

"…and they said *I* was a loose cannon…"

"No one knows where she is, but I've heard stories–"

"Stories?" He'd been babbling, off in his own world, but now I had his full attention.

"Yeah. Whenever I thought I could get away with it, I'd talk to people in whatever town my platoon had stopped in. Other secret smoke eater fans. I had to barter a lot of my shit, but some of them had great stories to sell.

"Plus, you know, the Army had probably robbed the same Swiss Army knife from the guy I gave it to for a few believable rumors. So, I didn't even care if they were lies. But that's the thing about stories and especially the people telling them. You never know if they're true.

"One thing I heard was that she was going around the country finding all the smoke eaters in hiding, collecting them like a militia to take down the Army. But a lot more people think she's at Big Base and being experimented on."

"Big Base?"

"Yeah, it's what the Army calls their headquarters. Just outside the place Parthenon City used to be. I've never been there."

"Yeah, I've heard of it. I just have a different name for it. Anyway, these storytellers, none of them ever said she was dead?"

"No," I said. "That would be most likely. But who wants to hear that? We want to think our heroes are still alive… if no one else. Hey! Why are you getting to ask all the questions?"

He pointed ahead. "We don't have time for any more jaw jacking."

I couldn't see the lake any more. Towering ash nests rose above us. The remaining chunks of skyscrapers seemed to shift like labyrinth pieces and seal any escape. Was the sky getting darker or was it just me? It was always disorienting speeding along the road, seeing a city in the distance like a mirage, and then suddenly finding yourself in its belly. Even more so when there were monsters crawling the streets and sewers to swallow you in a more literal sense. Welcome to Chi Town.

"This is bullshit," I said.

"Don't worry, kid." He sighed. "You'll have plenty more opportunities for memory lane. We're going to be spending more time together than I thought."

"What makes you say that?" I asked.

"Because, once again, Life is yanking on my balls." He turned the slayer sharply to the right. We flew off the road onto rough terrain, mainly ash. A crooked sign grazed my window. We were going too fast. In the blur, I thought it said SUBWAY.

A giant hole burrowing into the earth lay ahead of us.

"Holy shit we're gonna die!" I grabbed the closest handholds I could find.

Seabee just laughed.

CHAPTER 10

The slayer's headlights revealed an endless tunnel. Seabee worked the steering wheel left and right as if he knew exactly where he was going. We were inside an ash heap, but it wasn't made out of the same cinders you'd find at the bottom of a campfire. The scalies knew how to compress and sculpt the ash however they wanted. They'd scorch it to make it harden. The end result was as tough as a concrete wall, but no structure lasts forever. The ash heaps could topple like sandcastles given the right circumstances.

Every new curve in the tunnel would make the truck bounce or skid. I would tense up and squeak through my teeth. Debris would rain onto us and I would imagine the whole nest caving in. Seabee would just turn on the windshield wipers. We continued deeper into the nest.

I didn't want to say anything to throw off his concentration. I was glad he was driving and not me. Then again, if I were behind the wheel, we wouldn't have been speeding through a hole underneath Chicago.

The tunnel sloped down then opened into a wider area, but it wasn't much taller. If we'd been in a smoke eater cannon truck and not the standard slayer, we wouldn't have been able to fit.

Seabee parked and left the high beams shining on a shape embedded into the ash wall ahead. It looked like a dragon's claw print, but it was too smudged to know for sure. From where we were, the tunnel branched off into additional paths of different sizes, going in different directions. I counted three of them. There might have been more.

To our left, a structural beam was buried in the ash like an archaeological ruin. Most of its tiles had fallen off, but it still held a sign telling us we were on the Red Line.

"Stay here." Seabee reached for his door.

"Wait a minute." I unclenched my teeth. "What are we doing down here? This is worse than being on the street."

"I've got to find a dragon and make it swallow this tracker." He waved the device at me then put it in one of his power suit's metal pockets. "Waiting for one isn't an option. We don't have that kind of time and we don't want something showing up that I can't handle. Stay inside the truck. I shouldn't be long."

He turned back to the door.

"How did you know this nest was here?"

Huffing, Seabee took his hand off the door handle. "People out in the wastes have to scavenge to survive. We can't just go rob someone like you Nusies. I scoped this out a few months ago on one of my outings."

"You came to the city? By yourself? Does Bethany know about that?"

"No. I mean, yes. Damn it, it's none of your business one way or the other!"

"What use am I just sitting here?"

"Keep your voice down." His voice dropped to a whisper. Before that, he'd been talking even louder than me. "Are you a smoke eater?"

I didn't reply. We both knew the answer to that one: a big, resounding "I don't know."

"This isn't where we find out if you are," Seabee said. "If something happens to me, you can take the slayer back to my town and tell them the gory details. Or you can drive this thing all the way to Calabasas. I'd be dead so what the fuck would I care?"

"Go back? I don't even know how we got down here."

"Just follow the tunnel to the street."

"How long should I wait? What if I leave, but you were right there and I should have waited a little longer? What if something gets me when I'm walking around to get in your seat?"

"Goddamn," Seabee said. "You're worse than my daughter. Hold on."

He jumped out of the truck. I stared past the door he'd left open, into the dark of the dragon nest. A cloud of ash dust blew by, floating through the dim light above the door.

What if a scaly slithered in before Seabee got back? What if there was something down here big enough that it didn't even have to infiltrate the cab, it could just swallow the truck whole?

I heard Seabee's steps crunching against the ashen floor, moving farther and farther away. One of the bins opened with a metallic *clank*. I could hear him rustling around back there.

I could feel something watching me. Maybe more than one something. The tiny hairs on my body rose. I'd always thought that was just a dumb expression. Normally I would have shaken away the eerie feeling, my mind playing tricks on me, but the last time it had happened a droid dragged me from my bed to be burned.

Seabee climbed back into the cab and shoved something at me. I looked down at his hand. He held a smoke eater helmet.

My breath caught in my throat. "But you said–"

"I dub you an honorary smokie." He waved his arm around like a drunk priest blessing me with the sign of the cross. "Now shut up."

I was too stressed out to be offended.

The helmet was heavy. I could already feel the strain on my neck. Turning to look in any direction felt awkward. The metal was cold, rough. The inside of the helmet smelled like ass sweat and stale smoke. I loved it.

"I'm going to cast my radio signal to your helmet," said Seabee. "That way we'll be able to stay in contact. Don't fill the traffic with your endless stream of damned questions. Only talk if it's important. Fuck that. You'll think everything is important. Only talk if you're in danger of being eaten or something."

"I just say 'cast' to transmit and 'end cast' to turn it off, right?" I asked.

He stared at me for a few seconds. Was that pride I sensed in his face? "Yeah. I guess you read that on the Feed?"

I strained to balance the helmet as I nodded.

"I'm pretty sure this is a Flapper nest, so it could go either way. If you lose contact with me, count to five hundred. Then haul ass out of here. You see a horde of 'em coming toward you, haul ass out of here. If I tell you to haul ass out of here–"

"I haul ass out of here," I said. "Got it. But what if I need to defend myself. Is this a gun suit or a sword suit?"

"It's a sit there and wait suit." Seabee turned to leave.

"Come on, man. I'll just start pressing buttons if that's how you're going to be."

"You're going to wear me out before the dragons do." He leaned back in his seat, sighed. "You have a laser sword just like mine. You engage it by pushing the button between your glove's thumb and forefinger."

I held up my arm and spotted the button. I moved my thumb toward it.

"Not in here, dumbass!"

I dropped both arms. "You don't have to be rude."

"If shit goes down and you have no other option, fine, use the sword. But outside of that and bailing out of here, you're going to let me do my thing so we can get you a car and send you on your merry way. Don't fuck up and slice your leg off." He hopped out and closed the door before I could ask him anything else.

I watched him walk away, softly cursing under his breath. His shape faded at the end of the headlight's reach. Soon he disappeared down one of the tunnels.

"Can you hear me?" His voice came from the speaker in my helmet.

"Cast," I said. "Yeah, I can hear you. What are you seeing?"

"Same shit you are. Just ashes and darkness. Don't touch anything in the slayer."

I sat there waiting for him to say something else. A minute passed. Maybe another five. I ended my radio cast and drummed my armored fingers against the door. The hum of the slayer's engine made me nervous. It wasn't loud, but a scaly was sure to hear it. The high beams were also going to attract unwanted attention, but the thought of turning them off and putting myself in total darkness was worse.

I heard my mother's voice, *You'll never have to worry while*

I'm around. When I was a kid too scared of the dark to fall asleep, she would always say the same thing as she leaned her head inside my bedroom door. *You'll never have to worry while I'm around.*

But she *wasn't* around anymore. I was alone in the dark.

My nerves felt like they were on fire. I suddenly had a ball of erratic energy bouncing around inside me with nowhere to go. Anger, defeat, despair. I didn't know what to call what I was feeling. It was all of them. None of them. I wanted to slice a thousand dragons in half, stuff my face with canned peaches, and curl up to cry all at the same time. I needed to do something!

I told myself to push it down. Bury it. Bury it. Think of something else.

"There are some eggs here," Seabee's voice crackled. "Looks like they hatched a while ago. No wraiths around, so that checks out. These eggs look different. Don't ask about them. I'm just talking out loud and letting you know I'm not dead."

I gave him a "10-4" because I didn't know what else to say that wasn't a question.

I remembered that smoke eater helmets had a cool feature and ran my fingers along the side to find the button. It took me a few passes but when I pressed it, dark lenses ejected to sit over my eyes. The tunnel lit up in a thermal view. Everything was pixelated in different colors and a number in the bottom right showed the temperature of whatever I looked at. The smokies called these thermagoggles. Not very inventive, but what else would you call glasses that allowed you to see heat signatures in the dark?

"Wow," I whispered to myself.

That indented shape in the ash wall was still ahead of me. It was indeed a dragon's claw print.

Didn't Seabee say this was a Flapper nest? Or had he said Popper? I couldn't remember. I wasn't up on my knowledge of Popper anatomy but I knew they were short, round diggers with no wings. They didn't have huge claws like this one. Poppers were mostly mouth and teeth with a big shovel-like horn at the end of their snout. Flappers were all teeth and wings. They were the size of a dog but you never only saw one. They hunted in dense packs like flying piranha.

This wasn't a Popper *or* a Flapper nest.

Was that a snarl?

I looked down each tunnel. Their walls were warm but I saw no slithering tails or any other movement. Under the slayer cabin, the truck engine shone bright gold. I could see all the truck innards moving and giving off heat, like I had x-ray vision. But something else drew my eye.

Under the truck, deep below the ash, something was digging its way up. It showed red in my thermagoggles, starting off small, barely a dot. But it grew and I knew that meant it was getting closer. It meant it was much bigger.

I casted to Seabee, "I think I have a problem."

"Didn't they teach you radio etiquette in the Army? You just say the thing. There's no preamble."

The red blotch took on more of a shape. It had a body the size and length of a freight train. Its head reminded me of a tyrannosaurus. The scaly broke the surface and slammed into the slayer's undercarriage. I flew out of my seat as the whole truck lifted and dropped back down. Ash poured onto the roof like sand out of a broken hourglass.

I screamed into my helmet. "A big, fucking dragon just came out of the ground and hit the slayer. What do I do?"

"Hold on, kid. I'm coming. Don't leave. What is it? Did you get a good look at it?"

"I don't know!" I looked at the ground. A red-lit tail was slithering off. I followed it and saw the dragon was heading away from me, under the ash. "Some big dinosaur snake. I think... I think it might be leaving."

"I'm headed your way. Do me a favor. Turn the slayer around to face the way we came."

"Man, I don't know. What if that thing comes back?"

"Then we'll have more of a chance to not get eaten if I don't have to waste time pulling a u-ey."

I mumbled, "Should have turned it around before you left."

"What did you say?"

"I said–"

"Oh shit!" A laser buzzed furiously on Seabee's end. "Shit!"

"What?" I said. "What's going on?"

"Poppers!"

I began to shake. The old man was putting up one hell of a fight. Each of his grunts were accompanied by an electric slash of his laser sword. He was calling each dragon every swear in the book. Whether he made it back or not, I was going to have to reposition the truck.

I scanned the area with the thermagoggles one more time to make sure that big snake bastard wasn't anywhere around. When I saw it was clear, I retracted the goggles and grabbed the door handle. I hesitated. It felt like I was covered in chum and about to jump into shark-infested waters.

My Uncle Pedro came to mind. He would always get drunk at a barbecue or other family event and try to get us to do stupid dances or pull some prank on one of the other adults. I would always resist and he would always slur and stretch the vowels of three tiny words to goad me into going along: "Let's doooo iiiit!"

All right, then. Let's do it.

I opened the door and slid out onto the ground. I put my back as close to the truck as possible without grinding the metal and shuffled around the front, keeping one hand in contact. I thought I heard the flapping of wings. Seabee was making so much noise through my helmet speaker I couldn't focus on my immediate surroundings. I stopped in front of the slayer, between its headlights. The beams tried to stab the dark but the fallen ash made it look like I was shrouded in fog.

I squinted but remembered I had a better way to see. When I extended the goggles, an angry, orange cloud was rushing toward me from one of the other tunnels. The sound of a hundred leathery wings grew louder.

Poppers shouldn't have sounded like that. They sure as hell didn't look like that.

Back to using my bare vision, I stumbled toward the driver's side door. I kept going the way I had been, my back against the truck, only much faster this time. I could have run for it, but I didn't want the scalies to attack and not see it coming. That was one thing I learned from the Army. You always kept a scaly in front of you.

I held up my right arm, moved my thumb to the button on my glove, pushed it. White hot light sprang out. It was wider than it was long, but it was clearly a blade. It had so much power I thought my arm was going to fly off without me. I kept moving.

I'd just made it to the other side of the truck when the Flappers found me.

They pelted into the slayer like hailstones. With the

hook-like claws on their wings, they latched to the truck and began skittering all over it. Some of them flew to the other side of the slayer and attached to the wall just in front of me. One of them bent its neck back, saw me, and opened its long, toothy jaws to hiss.

A stream of flames leapt from its mouth. I leapt out of the way and left the slayer door to be scorched. There were three Flappers on my side of the truck and they attacked as one, beating their wings around my head, biting at my helmet. If I bent the wrong way they'd be able to get to my neck. I flung my arms around in a panic, forgetting I had the laser sword engaged. The hot blade found one of the Flappers' necks. It's head, sliced off, dropped to the ash, quickly followed by the rest of it. The other two Flappers backed off, hovering above me like demonic hummingbirds. They tilted their long heads toward the heap of dragon flesh on the ground and grieved their fallen sister with a rippling squawk.

They turned their glistening black eyes to me. Their fire would come next.

"Oh shit." I jumped and slashed at them.

They rose out of my reach. I could hear the other Flappers clawing along the other side of the slayer. I'd have more scalies to deal with if I didn't kill the two above me and escape into the slayer truck.

The two in the air screeched and circled me.

I lost it. A burst of anger exploded in my gut. It felt good to dump my internal shit into something productive. These fuckers weren't going to get me. *"Chinga tu madre!"*

I squeezed my hands into fists. What I didn't realize was that I'd pushed the button in my left glove. The power jump. I flew into the air, grazing the nest ceiling with my helmet.

There was an instance of confusion and dread, but when I saw I was at the same level of the Flappers, I sliced in one big swing.

I'd like to think I saw fear in those Flappers' beady eyes as I cut them in half.

I landed on my feet and stumbled backward. The slayer caught me before I fell. Hissing came from above me. An entire horde of Flappers, too many to count, lined the roof of the truck, leaning over to inspect their intended kill.

A noise reverberated in my ears. It must have been my own short, mumbled shrieks. Whatever Seabee was doing, I'd quit listening a while ago. I had my own problems.

I reached for the door handle to the driver's seat. The laser sword was still on and pierced into the slayer's metal. "Damn it!"

I disengaged the sword and used my other hand to open the door. The Flappers began dive-bombing. Several missed, others bounced off my helmet and the shoulders of my armor, but one latched onto my arm. I grabbed it by the tail and used every bit of strength to pry it off. I jumped into the driver's seat and slammed the door shut on the Flapper's neck.

The bastard could stay there and struggle till it suffocated to death. I wasn't opening the door again.

The other scalies took flight and glided as a flock around the truck. One at a time, they smacked against the windshield. When the fourth or fifth Flapper smacked against the glass, a thin crack appeared.

"Seabee," I called through my helmet.

There was no response.

Give him more time, I thought. He probably couldn't hear me because he was too busy dealing with an entirely different scaly problem.

Or because he was being digested.

I put the slayer into drive and put the nose into the lip of the tunnel ahead. The Flappers flew off for another round. This time they went for the driver's side window. Their breath fogged the glass. Dragon spittle ran down. The scaly caught in the door spasmed every few seconds. I could feel its tail hitting my leg.

My boot crushed the accelerator as I put the slayer into reverse and cut the wheel all the way to the right. I struck the ash wall behind me. The Flappers quit their aerial routine and landed on the windshield. With their sharp beaks, they began chipping away at the glass. It wouldn't take them long to get inside.

I punched the truck forward and turned it as far as it would go. There was no time for a twenty-point turn, but it was hard to maneuver such a big machine in such a small, dark space. I slammed on the brakes just before I hit the wall in front of me. The Flappers didn't budge. They had too good of a hold on the windshield. There were so many of them, I could barely see the mass of scaly bodies.

"Get off the truck!" I yelled.

Like that would do anything.

I had to reverse one more time before I was even close to driving the slayer out of the nest. The Flappers continued to chip away at the windshield. How it had held up till that point was a credit to the propellerheads who designed and constructed smoke eater equipment. And that wasn't a euphemism for the scientists working alongside the smokies: they were officially called propellerheads. And they should have been given equal credit for every dragon bagged and tagged.

"Hey, you ugly fucks," Seabee's voice came through my helmet.

The Flappers on the windshield turned their heads in odd angles to look toward the tunnel to my right. They flew off like one disjointed body. I heard laser slashes from my helmet radio and directly outside the slayer truck.

My door was pulled open and the dead Flapper fell to the ground. Seabee stood there. His face was covered in dark liquid and chunks of ash.

"Get in the jump seat in the back."

When a man covered in blood gives you an order, you tend not to ask questions.

The Flappers swarmed the slayer but were giving us a few feet of distance for the moment. I hopped out of the driver's seat and crawled through the door behind. I didn't know which one was the jump seat. Seabee got behind the wheel and began driving us out of the nest, back the way we came.

We had to use our helmet radios. It was otherwise too loud to hear each other. "Which one of these is the jump seat?" I asked.

"The one facing the rear. The one with the gun."

"Slayer's don't have guns on the inside," I said.

"This one fucking does. Now get in it and buckle up."

I held onto a handle to keep myself from falling. Sure enough, there was a seat right in front of me with a large gun bent down with its barrel facing the floor. I got into the chair and buckled up.

We were flying through the tunnel. The ash wall flew by my window at what felt like a hundred and fifty miles per hour. Seabee had turned on the emergency lights on the outside of the slayer, and the only reason I could see why he'd do that was to light the way as much as possible.

"Ah, fuck," Seabee said.

"What now?"

"You know that big dinosaur snake thing you told me about?"

"Yeah?"

"It's called a Basilisk."

"How do you know?" I'd never gotten around to reading about them, but I had a bad feeling I knew what Seabee was going to say next.

"Well," he said, "it's right behind us."

CHAPTER 11

The slayer shot out of the tunnel and onto the sunlit Chicago street. Seabee turned us toward the center of the city, not back toward the safety of the wastes. We were surrounded by more and more ash heaps and rundown buildings.

I was about to tell him he was going the wrong way, but then he yelled, "Hold on!"

Something clicked behind my back. Loudly.

The door beside me opened on its own. My chair flew out and I began screaming. I was jolted to a stop. The jump seat's gun released, rose and bobbed, and was now pointed toward the rear of the truck. Below me, asphalt rushed past in a blur. My chair was now extended six feet to the side of the slayer by a metal arm.

I grabbed the two handles at each side of the gun in front of me but I hadn't stopped screaming.

"Will you shut the hell up back there!" Seabee shouted.

I closed my mouth, but that just turned my scream into a nervous hum.

Something exploded behind the slayer. In a flurry of ash and fire, a horde of Flappers, Poppers, and one very large and angry-looking Basilisk burst from the ash heap.

It looked like we'd kicked open an over-sized wasps' nest. The earth continued to regurgitate dragons as the Basilisk led the charge. It didn't take them any time to spot us. The slayer's flashing lights made it easy.

"You said it was a Flapper nest," I said.

"I guess I was one-third right."

Seabee jerked the slayer into a sharp right turn. My power suit's elbow grazed the side of a building and caused the jump gun to bounce around. Out of all the buildings in Chicago, the old man had to find the only one with glass still attached in the windows. Broken shards flew all over the place, bouncing off my helmet.

The dragons came around the corner. The Poppers in front skidded in the turn but kept their footing. Their swollen bodies humped along as their big horns seemed to carry them ahead. A few of them shot balls of fire toward us but the shots died mid arc and fell to the ground well behind us. The Flappers came next, turning spirals in the air as if they had choreographed it beforehand.

The Basilisk wasn't so graceful. The big snake's bottom half kept going past the turn though its head was pointed at us. The momentum pulled it into the same building I'd grazed with my elbow. Glass, metal, and brick crumbled under the scaly's weight. It took a few seconds to right itself, but soon it was back on the chase.

How the Basilisk had appeared in my thermagoggles wasn't too far off from accurate. It had a head and snout like a Drake but without the horns. Everything else was pure, giant viper. The Flappers scattered as the Basilisk roared and broke through them.

"What am I supposed to do?" I shouted to Seabee.

"Shoot 'em! Shoot 'em all!"

"All of them?" I'd been in the Army. How much different could it have been to point at something and shoot? I found the triggers under each gun handle and squeezed. Lasers tore through the air. It took all my strength to keep the gun level. My first shots took out a couple of Flappers but missed the Basilisk by a mile. I put the barrel lower and grounded some Poppers as they ran down the street. The Poppers in the back saw what I'd done and dove into the ground, digging below the surface with those big horns.

The wind blew against my cheeks. It made me feel less secure, another way to remind me I was out in the open and zooming haphazardly alongside a truck driven by a demented old man.

I aimed at the Basilisk.

It was close enough to try a bite at me. I'd be an easy snack, dangling off the slayer like a kabob. With its mouth splayed open, I got a good view of its two long fangs and the weird way its throat came to a thin slit. That's where I put my shots.

The lasers, golden yellow in their light, pounded into the Basilisk's throat. It reared back, stopping in the middle of the street as the Flappers continued forward. Poppers erupted from beneath the ground like cresting dolphins. They were closer than before.

Seabee swerved the slayer twice, first left, then right, all within half a second. Fighting dizziness and the sun now in my eyes, I looked away. We were racing along the Chicago river. I saw a half-sunken tourist boat and then something big and sharp-finned cresting the surface of the water before it disappeared.

Oh, please, I thought, *keep your big ass in the river.*

A cluster of Flappers appeared in my periphery. I turned

and blasted them. They scattered but I followed each one, leading my shots. If they'd been smart they would have given up on chasing us, but their hunger was their death.

The ground burst open. A Popper flew out and landed on the metal arm connecting me to the slayer truck. The dragon grunted as it looked around, using its bulging green eyes to take in its surroundings. I saw it looking at Seabee inside the truck. It ran its fat, sloppy tongue over its jaws. If it went after him, we'd both be screwed.

"Hey!" I shouted at the Popper.

It turned its tubby body toward me and began grunting like a cat hacking up a hairball. I spun my chair and knocked it off with the barrel. The Popper hit the ground and exploded in a ball of fire. I must have hit it just in time, right before it spat its flame wad into my face.

"Hold on!" Seabee shouted.

He hadn't even seen that I'd saved his life. "What do you mean hold on? I've been holding on. You've got me dangling out here like a worm on a hook!"

"We're going to have to cross over."

Those words brought to mind images of wraiths going from this plane of existence into the next. That was terrifying enough. But Seabee had meant we were going to cross over in a different way, a worse way. I turned my chair around to face forward. We were heading for a bridge just ahead. At one point it had connected one side of the Chicago River to the other, but as it stood now, the middle of the bridge was gone and what was left looked to be crumbling.

"Don't do it!" I yelled.

As if that would have stopped him.

A roar straight out of hell thundered at my back. It's

possible it made my chair shake on its arm. It definitely made my spine spasm. I turned the gun. The Basilisk was back, and right on top of us.

Seabee said, "Shoot it!" as he turned the slayer onto the bridge. The slayer's engine revved as loud as the Basilisk's roar.

The big snake was so close I could smell it: rotten eggs and turtle shit. I'd have gagged if my stomach wasn't already in my throat.

Dark flames sprang from the Basilisk's mouth in a high-pressure cone.

I felt the slayer leave solid ground and sail into the air as I yelled, "Fuuuuuuuuuuuuuuck!" and pulled the gun triggers. Lasers ripped into the Basilisk's body, tearing off small chunks of flesh. It wasn't enough.

The dragon's flames engulfed the back of the slayer, from the bottom of the airborne tires all the way to the top of the rear emergency lights. My hands tensed against the trigger. Lasers flew all over the place. I'd quit trying to aim, expecting the fire would take me too. The flames didn't reach that far, though I could still feel them. The heat was almost enough to burn the air entering my lungs.

The slayer slammed into the ground on the other side of the river. With a sound like cannon fire, the rear tires burst. Sparks flew from the bare wheel bearings, the flames spread, and none of Seabee's fancy wheel spinning stopped it from turning over.

My stomach should have gotten a gold medal for all the flips it did. I was thrown to the side and then into the air, hanging sideways. The slayer rolled onto its passenger's side and skidded fifty feet. I was so freaked out I forgot to release my hold on the gun's triggers. Lasers flew into the sky above us. I was sure every dragon within twenty miles would see the accidental signal and come rushing.

But the Basilisk had gotten there first.

The lasers suddenly stopped and no matter how hard I squeezed the triggers, nothing was happening. The back of the slayer still burned. I looked to the nearest emergency light. It didn't flash. The engine had died. No power meant no lasers.

From the other side of the river the Basilisk had watched us wreck. Now it watched us burn. With a low growl, it curled around the underside of the broken bridge, slithering around and around, crossing the gap between one broken end and the next. The Basilisk twisted slowly closer. It knew it didn't need to rush.

It kept its eyes on me, almost like it was gloating.

Along the opposite bank, the Poppers watched. It didn't take them long to decide we weren't a meal worth fighting for. Besides the bigger dragon, there was no way they could have dug under the river without the chance of getting themselves drowned in the process. They made subtle chirps before burrowing into the street, leaving us to the Basilisk.

"Seabee," I said.

He didn't answer.

The Basilisk uncurled from beneath our side of the broken bridge. It rose up tall and pulled the rest of its body onto the street. Moving from side to side, it looked like the big dragon was doing a dance to the music of our final breaths. Seabee may have already been dead.

From where I hung in my seat, the street below looked a thousand feet away. In reality, it might have been twenty to thirty. That was still a long drop. I grabbed the side of my chair, made sure I had a good hold of it. The Basilisk's growling didn't do a damned thing for my nerves but I had to concentrate.

I took two deep breaths and took the belt buckle into my free hand. I pressed the release button. My body swung down and the weight of it pulled at the arm clinging onto the chair.

The power suit was great for taking hits and heat, but it was shit when it came to preventing dislocated joints. It didn't add any superhuman strength so I had to rely on my own weak arm to keep me from dropping. I was going to fall one way or another. I just couldn't make myself take the initiative.

The Basilisk made the decision for me. All fifty-plus feet of the scaly rose over me. It was so big it blocked the sun from view. It reared back, ready to strike.

I let go. My knees and back took a lot of the impact, even though I tried to roll out of it. Tears formed at the corners of my eyes as I got to my feet. The Basilisk went for the empty chair. In one bite it took off half the cushion and metal bracket.

I stumbled over to the truck's windshield and looked inside. Seabee hung from his seat belt. His eyes were closed. I couldn't tell if he was still breathing.

The windshield was cracked but remained mostly intact. I engaged my laser sword and pierced the glass. The Basilisk made a rasping noise high above me. I heard its heavy body rubbing against the ground. It was getting closer. My whole body shook but I focused on the job. Any distraction would slow me down. With a few more cuts, I made a hole big enough to crawl through.

I squeezed inside the cab and crawled over to Seabee,

put my ear to his mouth. His breath puffed against my cheek.

All right, old man, I thought. *We've made it this far.*

A giant reptilian eye filled the window next to Seabee.

I hit Seabee's belt buckle and caught him as he fell from the chair. The Basilisk's snout broke through the window. I covered Seabee's face with my arm as the glass fell onto us. I hoped it was enough.

The dragon's slimy forked tongue flicked to and fro inside the cab, slobbering over the driver's seat, the pedals, the steering wheel. I had no doubt the scaly was strong enough to wrap that tongue around one of us and pull us into its jaws. But it couldn't reach us. Not yet. If I didn't get us out of there soon the Basilisk would try with its fire breath.

Speaking of fire, the damn truck was still burning. The smoke began to surround us.

I grabbed Seabee under the arms and scrambled backwards. It was like pulling a cement block. My head made it through the hole in the windshield. The Basilisk was still busy trying to snatch us through the window. My muscles burned. Every fiber of my body begged for me to stop but I couldn't. Maybe there was another way.

I wrapped my right arm around Seabee and hit the power jump button on my left glove. We flew from the slayer truck like a skipping stone. But the noise of my power suit's thrusters caught the Basilisk's attention.

Seabee coughed and blinked his eyes open. "What happened?"

There was no need for me to tell him. The big snake slithered around the truck and bent over us. It hissed, then breathed in as it curled backwards. Dark and fast, its flames would turn us to ash, like everything else around.

A bright blast of blue energy struck the Basilisk's head. It fell to the ground, shrieking and flopping, its tail flicking heavily over our heads. Blood spurted from its wound, splattering my face. A siren wailed. To our right, the ashes crunched underneath something heavy as it ground to a stop. Purple and white lights flashed from its roof and all along its sides. The black paint was faded from use and neglect and boasted a few dents and scratches. Way bigger than the slayer, it wielded a huge gun barrel on its roof, like fire department aerial ladders.

Holy-fucking-shit, it was a smoke eater cannon truck with a number fifteen slapped on its side.

A black woman in a power suit jumped out of the truck's passenger side and leapt into the air toward the Basilisk. The dragon writhed against the ground as the woman hit it with a blitz of lasers as she sailed down, landing on its neck as if she intended to ride the scaly. But the dragon stayed down, barely able to raise its head to bite at the woman. It puffed out a blast of fire, but the woman shot a wad of foam into its throat with her other arm.

From the back of the cannon truck, a big man stepped out and opened one of the bin doors. He walked toward the Basilisk with a big metal rod resting against his shoulder. When he was halfway to the dragon, he pushed a button on his pole. Laser light sprang from the end and formed the shape of an axe blade. The large man didn't bother with leaping onto the dragon like the woman. He walked over to its head, dodging a few bites from the jaws, and buried the laser axe into the scaly's skull.

The Basilisk went still.

"Eat that, bitch!" said the woman standing on the scaly's neck. She jumped to the ground and joined her partner as they walked over to us. "You boys from out of town?"

The man helped Seabee up with an easy tug of his arm. The woman grabbed both of my hands and helped me to my feet. When she turned to Seabee, she backed away a few steps and stared at the old man with angry eyes and a mouth that hung open in disbelief.

"Hey, Tamerica," Seabee said to the woman, with a guilty hang of his head. He turned to the enormous smoke eater standing at his side, saying, "Afu, you look good, man."

Tamerica stomped over to Seabee, she swung a fist and cocked the old man across the jaw. Seabee dropped onto his ass and stared up at his assailant, but he didn't seem to have a shred of surprise on his face. He rubbed at the red mark on his chin with the tips of his armored fingers.

"You motherfucker," Tamerica said. "Cole Brannigan, if you weren't already dead, I'd kill you myself!"

CHAPTER 12

The Basilisk and the slayer both lay dead. There was no reason to drag them anywhere and we didn't have the means to do so anyway. You know who else was supposed to be dead?

Cole Brannigan.

"What did she just call you?" I stared down at the old man sitting in the ashes.

He rubbed at his face and looked up at those of us who'd gathered around him. I couldn't believe it. There was no way this was the same guy who'd overseen the Ohio smoke eaters. The woman who'd punched him had to be mistaken. It was just a big misunderstanding.

The man who'd been driving the cannon truck rushed over. "T, what are you punching that old man for?" He skidded to a stop when he saw Seabee on the ground. "Ch… Chief? What the fuck?"

Afu helped Seabee onto his feet. "I knew it. I knew you weren't really gone."

"That's right, go ahead and help him up, Afu," Tamerica said, "so I can knock his ass right back down again."

"Hold up," I said. I blinked, squinted, widened my eyes, anything to compare the face of the man in front of me to the photos I'd seen on the Feed. "You're Cole Brannigan!?"

The old man blinked at me. "I was called that at one time, yes."

"Wait, you said your name was Seabee..." No. That's not what he'd said. It was his initials: C.B. Not Seabee. Cole Motherfucking Brannigan.

"Holy shit." I stumbled backward, putting my hands on my thighs. This was like meeting Abraham Lincoln years after the incident at the Ford Theater. I turned to the woman grimacing beside me. "And you're Tamerica Williams. That guy over there is Afu Kekoa." I turned to the driver with red eyes. "And you're?"

"Shit," he said. "I guess I didn't show up in whatever rap sheet you memorized. I'm Chris Renfro."

"The smoke eater with Dragon Eye?" I said.

Renfro shook his head. "There's a lot of other things going for me besides that."

"Who are you, kid?" Tamerica removed her helmet and let her thick, black hair blow in the wind. Chunks of ash flew into the curly strands. She was exactly like I'd seen her in photos. Stocky and formidable. I'd heard her attitude rivaled Chief Brannigan's.

"He's with me," Brannigan said.

"That doesn't tell me shit," said Tamerica. "Why should I listen to a dead man?"

"I'm Guillermo Contreras," I said.

They didn't seem to hear me. Brannigan and Tamerica locked eyes and the other two watched them like time bombs about to go off.

"I know you're mad at me," Brannigan said, "I can explain everything. But first, I want to know what you three are doing in Chicago. This is some serendipitous shit."

"We live here," said Afu.

I blinked at the big Samoan man. Besides the fact Cole Brannigan was alive and well, that was the craziest thing I'd heard all day. "You what?"

"Maybe we should move this conversation into the truck." Renfro walked between us, looking from left to right as if he could sense something we couldn't. His red eyes could see in the dark, after all. Maybe they could see more than that in the daylight hours. "I don't like being out in the open like this for too long."

Tears welled in Tamerica's eyes. They began to flow like streams down her cheeks as she ran toward Brannigan. I flinched. Brannigan raised his hands to protect himself. Tamerica wrapped her arms around the old man in an embrace. She stood there sobbing with him tight against her. He patted her back. The sound was like two steel swords crossing.

"You motherfucker," Tamerica mumbled against the old man's shoulder.

"Seriously, though," said Renfro. "Let's get in the truck."

Brannigan pulled Tamerica from him, holding her at arm's length. "Come on. We'll talk some more in the rig."

I followed behind them. I felt like an outsider. Not even a smoke eater, but wearing the same armor, riding in the same vehicles. It was like playing at a dream that had ended long ago for everyone else.

We all crawled into the cannon truck and Renfro rolled us down the street, staying at a decent speed in order to swerve around debris, but still arrive at the destination before any scalies got wind of us.

Tamerica synced all our helmet radios together with a few voice commands. She did it so casually, too. As if it hadn't been years since they'd worked a paid shift. As if they'd all seen each other the day before.

"So, where do I start?" Brannigan said. He was in the middle seat while Afu and I were on opposite ends in the back of the truck.

"How about you tell us how you didn't disintegrate when the Phoenix exploded," Afu said.

"Shit," said Brannigan. "That's easy. You know those jet packs we can put on our power suits? We used them back when we jumped out of Jet-1 in New Mexico."

"You jumped off the top of that building?" Renfro asked.

"I sure as fuck wasn't going to hang around," Brannigan said. "After I barred that roof door, I dodged the Phoenix and got to the edge of the building. All I had to do was release the wraith and jump."

Afu shook his head. "I'll be damned."

"You knew the whole time what you were going to do," Tamerica said. "Why'd you hide it? Why didn't you at least come find us and tell us you weren't dead. Fuck, I've been depressed for years."

"She really has," said Afu, with a nod.

Tamerica turned around in the captain's seat. Her glare could have shattered bricks. "Boy, shut up."

Everyone had heard about the Phoenix. The smoke eaters had killed it by regular means a few times but the bird would resurrect and become stronger with each new life. In a rush, the propellerheads had figured out a way to keep the Phoenix in ashes. No one knew how they'd done it, but the result was a giant explosion at the top of Buck High-Rise Estates, and Brannigan scorched to particles. The prevalent rumor I'd read on some Feed forums suggested the smoke eaters had sacrificed Brannigan to appease the firebird. They were all whack-jobs, but it showed how easily people could be influenced. That's why it was so easy to end the smoke eaters.

"I wanted to tell you," said Brannigan. "But fuck, I'd been trying to retire to a quiet life since before I ever became a smoke eater. You know how Naveena and Donahue, rest his soul, basically forced me into this shit. I saw my perceived death as the way to get out and let better people take over. Y'all didn't need me anymore."

"That's bullshit," said Tamerica. "We needed you more than ever. After the Phoenix, the mayor put an end to us. She let the New United States Army take over. Same shit happened in every other city in the country. It was like a pandemic of green boot bastards taking over. They let everything go to shit. I am so fucking mad at you!"

Brannigan nodded. "I guess it's not a good time to tell you Guillermo here used to be a Nusie."

My eyes nearly popped out of my head. "Why would you tell her that?"

Afu laughed. "You must be new to Chief Brannigan. He has no filter or give-a-damn. Hey, though. Were you really in the Army?"

"Yeah," I said. "But I really hated it and I ran away."

"Kid showed up at my settlement in one of their tanks," Brannigan said. "He said he stole it and went AWOL. My town commandeered it. Bethany is probably using the parts as we speak."

"How are Bethany and Sherry?" Renfro asked.

Brannigan looked out the window. "Sherry isn't around any more. Army and scalies saw to that."

No one said anything for a few seconds too long. Desolate Chicago flew by my window. I tried and failed to recognize any significant point of interest. It was all just ashes and ruin now.

Afu cleared his throat and pointed at me. "Why are you wearing a power suit?"

"It was my idea," Brannigan said. "Anyway, that's why we're here. We found a tracking device on the spider tank. I brought Guillermo here to find a car and get rid of the tracker."

I turned to Brannigan. "So you were still able to put that tracker in a scaly? I hadn't even thought to ask."

"Damn right I did." He waved his armored hand at me like it was nothing. "I shoved it down some Popper's throat before I got back to the slayer."

"You brought an Army tracker with you?" Tamerica turned in her seat to look at Brannigan. "Into *my* city? Why would you do that?"

"Well, what the fuck?" Brannigan said. "I didn't think anybody would be living here, let alone you three. I figured the Army would steer clear of the city, or if their nuts swelled up and they decided to come look for it, they'd find teeth and fire to thin their numbers. Either way, I thought it was a good plan."

"You and your plans," Tamerica said. "You're more dick than brains and you ain't got much dick to begin with."

"Why'd you have to bring genitalia into it?" Brannigan said.

"It wasn't a bad idea," I said. Why was I defending Brannigan? He'd nearly gotten me killed. "The Army has a general rule of staying away from metropolitan areas. They won't come here."

"They would if they had a good reason," Tamerica said. "There's something neither of you are saying. Why would you come all the way to Chicago to get rid of a tracker, just to throw the Nusies off your trail? Why not just toss the tracker into the lake and be done with it?"

"That's what *I* said!" My voice went too loud through everyone's helmet speakers. Feedback made us all cringe until it faded away.

"We also came to get him a car." Brannigan shrugged.

Tamerica puffed air into her cheeks. I'd seen a few Lindwyrms do the same thing before breathing fire. She turned to me. I flinched. "Why would the Army want to track you down anyway... uh... What was your name? Guillermo?"

I nodded, but Brannigan spouted, "I call him Gilly."

"Only my family calls me that," I said.

"Whatever," Tamerica said. "He's one soldier. Couldn't have been more than a private. He stole a tank. Big whoop. Tell me why you really came to Chicago."

"Well the tank he stole was the only one the platoon had left," Brannigan said. "And he killed his sergeant with it."

"You killed a guy?" Afu asked. He looked me up and down.

"He wasn't a guy," I said. "He was a droid."

"Your sergeant was a droid?" Afu's bottom lip wobbled as his mouth hung open.

"That's what *I* thought!" Brannigan pointed at Afu.

Tamerica shouted, "Why were you in that nest, Brannigan?"

"All right, damn it," Brannigan said. "The Army thought Gilly was a smoke eater."

Everyone in Cannon 15 turned their head toward me. Even Renfro, who was steadily driving the truck through tight squeezes and around stacks of overturned steel and dust, kept taking glances over his shoulder.

"Is he?" Tamerica asked.

"Can all of you stop talking about me like I'm not here," I said, "or that I don't speak your same language?"

I doubt they heard me. Everyone started talking at the same time.

"I don't know if he is," Brannigan said.

Renfro whistled. "A Nusie smoke eater."

"What makes them think he's one of us," Tamerica said.

Afu's cheeks jiggled as he shook his head. "A robot superior officer?"

"...that's why we came to Chicago..."

"...figured they would have tested for smokies before they joined the Army..."

"So you just threw him in a power suit and hoped for the best?"

"Couldn't you just turn the droid sergeant off if he starts giving orders?"

"If he was a smoke eater, we would have found out in that nest. If he wasn't, he'd just be another dead Nusie and I could live with that."

Everyone closed their mouths and turned to Brannigan.

My breaths came and went quicker and more shallow. "Wait a minute. You took me into that nest hoping I'd get burned or smoked out?"

Brannigan moved his jaws but no words fell out. I guess he couldn't slither out of this one. He must have said more than he'd intended.

The air in my nostrils burned. "We never had to go into that nest. Did we?"

"Kid, look–"

"Don't call me kid!" I said.

"I owe you my life," Brannigan said. "I was wrong about you."

"You're goddamn right you were wrong. What was the idea? You were going to put me in the middle of some dragons and see how I did? Is that what sink or swim means?"

Brannigan clenched his lips and sat back.

For a moment, I'd shut up the old man. I didn't want to waste the opportunity. He'd been calling the shots till then and I'd gone along with him until I found out I was nothing but scaly fodder. I had a decent amount of anger that I'd shoved down. This just gave me a reason to spew it all out.

I said, "I'm sorry about your wife. I really am. But I didn't do that. I wasn't there. I'm not in the Army anymore. Jesus! I used to look up to you. Smoke eaters are supposed to protect people, they're not like the fucking Canadians. Was that it? I was a sacrifice? You were going to see what the dragons would do to me? Really? What if they'd bitten me in half? Not even a smoke eater can withstand that! Or was it that you were jonesing for some adrenaline, and so filled with hate and vengeance you were willing to risk my life so you could get your fix? And what if I turned out to be a smoke eater? Would that have been proof enough for you that I'm not lying?"

"You're right, Gilly." Brannigan hung his head. "I'm sorry."

"Don't call me Gilly either. It's Contreras or Guillermo. Only my family calls me Gilly. And you're sorry my ass." I shook my head. "Stop the truck. Let's get this over with."

I was tired of being judged and distrusted. The thread eventually snaps.

I'd considered suicide a few times while in the Army. Not seriously, of course. The thoughts just came and went:

jumping off a bridge we'd march past, or throwing myself under one of the spider tanks. Nothing real. Wisps of smoke. I wondered if I had the guts to do it. I didn't. But it worried me the ideations had shown up at all.

I wasn't worried anymore.

"You heard me," I said. "Stop the truck. Let's find out once and for all. We can find a real smoky dragon. I'm sure there could be a few Wawels slithering around here. I'm tired of hem-hawing around. Let's get this–"

Several large, dark shapes dropped out of the sky and landed heavily into the street ahead of the cannon truck. Renfro slammed his foot into the brake pedal. The entire truck shifted and spun. A screech from the tires filled my ears as the world outside lost focus. The icy road could have snagged us and tossed over like a can of soda at any second. But we stopped safely, the length of the truck stretching across the street. My window faced the way Renfro had been driving. I saw what had fallen out of the sky.

Five dragons stood side by side in the middle of the street. Two were Fafnirs: one red, one green. Another was a yellow Lung dragon, which I'd only known to live in China and Korea. The Lung had long curly tendrils coming from above its top lip like a weird antennae moustache. The other two scalies were Silver Razors – twins. You never saw one without the other.

The red Fafnir was the scaly in the middle, and from its neck Colonel Calhoun jumped to the street. Every dragon in front of me was fastened with the same sort of saddle. Atop each of these saddles sat a New United States Army soldier. If the dragon was big enough, a black rope ladder hung from the saddle for each rider to climb. The other soldiers dismounted their dragons and walked over to stand beside Calhoun. While the other soldiers wore their issued helmets, Calhoun only wore his maroon beret. The grunts pulled rifles off their backs and aimed them at us in the cannon truck.

There was still a soldier on dragonback.

"Oh fuck," I whispered to myself.

Reynolds rode the yellow Lung dragon. I was glad to see her. I was glad she was okay, but I couldn't believe what I was seeing, and the squirming in my guts told me I was in a world of shit. The dragons didn't stir. They sat there patiently. They didn't try to eat the soldiers in front of them, and the Nusies didn't so much as look warily over their shoulders at the large scalies behind them.

Calhoun had something in his hand. When he raised it to his lips, I saw it was a small megaphone. He barked into it. "Turn off your vehicle and step out onto the street with your hands straight up above your heads. You have thirty seconds before our dragons tear you and your illegal truck apart and burn what little remains. Thirty..."

CHAPTER 13

"Twenty-nine!" Reynolds was bending over me. Her auburn hair hung in thin, stringy strands, and there was so much of it that the few times I looked up from my place on the ground I couldn't see her face.

My hands were squishing into the dirt. Sediment would get under my fingernails and I'd be up until three in the morning scraping it out. But I'd stopped worrying about that around push-up number twelve. They weren't coming easily. Hell, they weren't even coming at a decent rhythm.

"Come on, man," Reynolds barked. "Just give me one more."

I grunted, gritted my teeth. I really hated this kind of shit. "I... can't."

"You give me a full thirty push-ups and we won't run the perimeter again."

Wow, she really wanted me to get one more in. I really wanted it, too. She'd been wearing me out all morning. Two laps around the perimeter already, five sets of five burpees, and I forgot how many crunches it took for me to roll over and dry heave. I'd do anything to avoid more of that. A single push-up was an easy price to pay.

I'd been holding in a plank position and lowered myself to the ground.

"That's it," Reynolds said. "All the way down."

I wanted to make it count, I really did. I made sure to press my chest into the dirt. There'd be evidence all over the front of my fatigues if she tried to say it wasn't a full push-up.

But once in that position, I couldn't push myself back up. My body had given out. I tried to hype myself into doing it. I told myself about the running to come if we didn't rise. It didn't seem to matter. I gave a hard shove to the ground, but it felt like every bit of energy was sucked out of me. I dropped onto my face.

"Damn good try." Reynolds was laughing. "I salute your effort. But, unfortunately…"

"Come on…"

"Our deal was thirty or another lap. So…"

"…I'm going to die."

Reynolds rubbed her hand through my hair. I felt bits of dirt fly everywhere. "You're not going to die. Get up."

Things didn't just ache. They refused to work or twitch any more. My lungs felt tighter. Coughing didn't help. Somehow I got to my knees, feeling exhaustion even in my gums. "I hate this."

Reynolds pulled out an old compact mirror and cleaned the front of her teeth with a finger. "Then why did you join the Army?"

I stood and immediately felt the urge to vomit. Bending over helped my head quit spinning. "Why are you wasting your time with me?"

"We're only as strong as–"

I straightened my stance and pointed a finger at her face. "Our weakest link? Is that what you were going to say? See, you think of me the same way the others do. I don't

know who you're trying to fool with all this spending time
with me bullshit. We don't even talk, we just do exercises.
I didn't ask for a fucking personal trainer."

"I'm just trying to help."

"Why? There's no point. I don't belong here. But I'm
the dumbass who signed my life away, so I'm stuck here
in hell. I'd appreciate it if you made my sentence easier
by just leaving me alone." I turned away. Life only gives
you so many opportunities to stomp away from a short list
of people and I knew for sure this had been one of them.
Reynolds ruined it.

"Excuse me, Private Contreras," she called at my back.
"I said one more lap around the perimeter and I'm going
to get it."

I turned, just to see if she was fucking with me. I didn't
think she was. She wasn't smiling, but she wasn't angry
either. Her face was neutral and still.

I fell into a run and brushed past her. "This sucks."

Reynolds easily sped ahead of me, even turning to run
backwards, which was still faster and more spring-heeled
than my forward stumble. "You wanna know why I spend
so much time with you? Because you make me feel safe."

And like that she was turned the other way and booking
it at least a hundred meters ahead.

Wait, I make her feel safe?

No boost of speed came upon me, but my curiosity kept
my feet moving. How did a crumb like me make her feel
safe?

Reynolds turned the corner on the other side of the
town, taking the path that led up. The people called this
place Stonehaven. They'd erected it in the middle of an old
rock quarry, and must have thought it would be safer from

dragons. As far I'd heard, they'd been right. It was just too bad the NUSA found them instead.

"Where... the hell... are you going?" I shouted. Reynolds didn't hear me. I followed her up.

There was no way I could continue running up that steep climb. It must have been thirty minutes later when I finally crested the top of the rise and found Reynolds looking down at the town with hands on both her hips.

"This... is not... around the perimeter." Slowly, and with a lot of effort, I came over to stand beside her. Every crevice of my body was collecting pools of sweat. Reynolds didn't turn to look at me, she stared down at the town as the wind played with her hair. "What did you mean back there?"

"Look below us," Reynolds said.

"I can see it," I said. It was just some dwelling boxes and a few people milling around. Some guys from our platoon were leaning against Tank 2 while they laughed and stared at one of the old men of Stonehaven passing by.

A smile came to Reynolds' face. It was a little weird. Lately, she seemed to be all over the place. Was she seeing the same thing I was?

"Down there," Reynolds lowered her head slightly. "Those tanks, those guys in fatigues, even that metallic sergeant, wherever he is. That's *my* platoon."

I didn't understand her pride. I'd considered more than once that she had nothing else and that's why she was so gung-ho. Maybe she had no family back home, maybe not even a home back home. But you could have said that about every grunt in the platoon. I wished she would have talked about it more.

"I'm pretty sure it's Calhoun's platoon," I said.

"He leads us, sure," Reynolds said. "But we're all in it together. We're one unit. That's my platoon. Don't you think I was treated the same as you, if not worse, when I signed up?"

She looked so deeply into my eyes I thought she would dive in. I didn't notice my exhaustion so much anymore. Her stare was intense. I had to look away, but I didn't know why. Maybe I just couldn't figure out where I landed with Reynolds.

"But I changed my thinking."

"Your thinking?"

"Yeah. I thought I had been sucked up by the NUSA and bouncing around with everyone yelling at me or making fun of me. Then I realized that I was a part of this thing. I wasn't being dragged along. I took ownership. I saw it as *my* platoon. You have a good heart, Gilly. And the persistence of a Jabberwock. I think all you need is a little ownership in this service. So look down there, find a tank or another grunt and say, 'That's my platoon.'"

I looked down there, but all I saw were those same soldiers, one sticking out a leg to make the old man trip and fall. Laughing, laughing. The world was full of filthy fucking hyenas. I wouldn't claim them. They disgusted me.

Reynolds put her hand on my shoulder. "Go on. Feel it. Say it as many times as you need. Say, 'That's *my* platoon!'"

"This is stupid."

"Say it."

"Reynolds."

"It's just three words." She was really squeezing my shoulder.

"Sarah, I don't–"

"Say it, *Gilly*!"

"That's my platoon." I said it to myself in the back of the cannon truck. I stared in awe at Reynolds astride the bright yellow Lung dragon. Back in Waukesha, I'd left Calhoun and the others on foot in the middle of the night with several wraiths to fight off. They shouldn't have been alive let alone anywhere near Chicago. How had they gotten here on the backs of dragons?

Everyone inside Cannon 15 turned to stare at me. Their looks could have bored holes into my flesh.

"What?" I said. "I didn't know anything about this."

Tamerica looked back outside the window. "These motherfuckers just rode some dragons right on top of us. You're telling me you had no idea they could do that."

"I didn't know *anybody* could do that," I said. "I was a private. They barely ever told me what town we were in."

"We don't have time to argue," Brannigan said.

Outside, the red Fafnir raised its head and gave a few grunts from deep inside its throat. It sounded like old horn blows from the dark ages. Biblical times. When they used to make music with goat horns and shit. But the scaly didn't have to rub it in. We all knew we had only a few seconds to make a decision.

"We've got two choices," Brannigan said.

"Run or fight," Renfro said. "I'm good with either."

"We can't outrun them," Afu said. Worry filled his thick face.

"We can sure as hell try." Renfro gripped the steering wheel. I could tell he felt more at home behind the wheel than in front of a dragon. There was nothing wrong with that. I was shit at both.

"It's your call, T." Brannigan said. "Your rig, your crew."

Tamerica looked at him as though she'd been hoping

he would have taken over the responsibility. She sighed and said, "I've never dealt with anything like this. Five dragons at once? And Nusies with rifles too? We don't have a chance."

"Sure we do," said Brannigan. He patted the top of his helmet. "It's just a few scalies and some assholes in the way."

He was full of shit. There was no way we could survive this. I had to shove some sense into this conversation.

Outside, Calhoun had reached nineteen in his count.

"Give me up," I said. "They might be lenient if you give them a reason to be thankful. They're probably more pissed at me than any of you."

Brannigan and Tamerica spoke at the same time, in sync, "No fucking way."

"We don't give people up." Brannigan nodded. He said a lot with that tilt of his head. He was sorry for how he'd treated me. He didn't want to repeat the mistake.

"Besides that," Tamerica said. "There's no way those Nusies are going to let four confirmed smokies go freely. We're going to have to lay them out."

"Knuck if you buck!" Afu jumped up and down in his seat.

"Guys," I said, "you don't have to–"

"Didn't you hear me?" said Tamerica. "We're fucked either way. I'd rather go out fighting. How about you, Contreras?"

I would have rather not "gone out" at all, but I blinked, then slowly nodded. "Yeah."

"Renfro," Tamerica said. "Back the truck up to the last intersection. Set the outriggers, raise the cannon, and blow away anything that isn't in a power suit."

"Sink or swim." Renfro popped the truck into reverse and we were flying backwards. He careened the back half into a tall blob of concrete, but soon we were in line with the street.

I didn't know what number Calhoun had reached by that point. It didn't matter. I saw through the windshield all the soldiers were climbing back onto their dragons, except Calhoun, who remained standing there in front of his red Fafnir. He was yelling some order to the rest of the platoon.

The dragons spread their wings and roared.

Fuck me, I thought.

"The rest of you," Tamerica said. "Use the buildings at each side of us. Am I the only one with a laser gun?"

"Yeah," Brannigan said. "Me and Guillermo have swords. You, too, Afu?"

The big man nodded. "You know I can't aim worth a damn."

"Then I'll hit them from a distance," said Tamerica. "We need to separate them. Don't take on more than one at a time."

I didn't know if she meant scalies or soldiers.

"Go, go, go!" Tamerica shouted.

I followed Brannigan out of the truck. Tamerica and Afu leapt out of their side and bolted across the street into the adjacent ruin. The Nusies fired their lasers at us. The beams flew over my head, struck the ground near my boots, but Brannigan and I made it into a crumbling building before any of the shots could hit us.

We entered a small room with no ceiling.

Brannigan leaned against a gouge-filled wall and slid onto his ass. "We're going to have to split up."

"Are you sure?" I dropped to a knee and flinched at

every laser blast that hit outside the opening we'd just run through.

"Our best plan is to let Renfro blast a few of them. The rest will scatter after that. I think."

"You think?"

"You fought alongside these Nusies," Brannigan said. "You should know how they operate."

He engaged his laser sword, stood up, and ran out of the tiny concrete room we'd been huddled in.

"What the hell?" I shouted after him.

His voice entered my helmet. "Relax, Gilly. We still have radio contact."

"Same here," Tamerica's voice came through. "That green bitch and her rider are flying over me, trying to find a way inside here. Looked like a Fafnir. I need to give Renfro cover."

"I'll come help get that scaly off of you," Afu said.

"Y'all better hurry." Renfro's voice shook.

Not wanting to wait around in that small room forever, I pushed further into the building. I didn't care which turn I took; I just went whichever way felt best. When I found a stairwell, I went up. I figured the least I could do was give everyone a bird's eye report of what was happening on the ground.

My breath and legs were beginning to give. I stopped on the twelfth floor, which had been gutted, missing the entire outer wall so that it looked like a cliff. Wind and snow and every other element had had its way with the interior.

I walked past lumps of ash that seemed to resemble filing cabinets and other office accoutrements until I reached the edge of the floor. I looked onto the street below. Lasers streaked across like coked-up fireflies. One of the Silver Razors was clawing against the building across from me. I didn't see its twin. Both of these scalies looked like walking mirrors. It was a way to distract their prey. Light would reflect off their shiny hides and dazzle whatever they were looking to swallow. They either sliced flesh to ribbons with their dagger-like teeth, or used their short, but high-heat, breath to scorch the same flesh.

"One of those Silver Razors is trying to get into the building across from me," I reported into my helmet.

"Great," Tamerica said. "I thought I only had the green one to worry about."

I spotted her in a broken window. She shot lasers toward the cannon truck, where Calhoun's red Fafnir was slowly creeping toward Renfro, who stood at the controls in the back. The second Silver Razor crawled from the back of Tamerica's building and slithered onto the roof. It lay under the sunlight, reflecting beams like a homicidal disco ball. It was sending out a beacon to the others.

Air fluffed up over the edge of the floor I stood on. Ashes flew over my boots. A rhythmic flapping grew louder and soon yellow horns and tendrils rose from below me. Reynolds' beautiful but angry face appeared. She had a cut across her cheek that hadn't been there when I'd left her in Waukesha with the wraiths. Of course I blamed myself.

"Gilly," she hissed.

There was a device running from her ear to the side of her mouth, almost like a microphone, but it stuck to her skin like a bandage. I would have gotten a better look at it, but the Lung dragon sang its bright song right into my face. It was like being attacked with a thousand wind chimes.

"Sarah," I said. "I'm so sorry. Please–"

"Shut up! I almost died because of you. I tried to warn you. You never listen to me."

I held up my hands. "It wasn't my fault."

"It never is." She rubbed a hand against the Lung dragon's head.

The scaly flapped its large yellow wings to stay afloat, raising its head to purr at its rider.

"How are you doing this?" I asked. "Since when can you ride dragons?"

Reynolds flashed her eyes up to me. She inhaled deeply through her nose and answered, "Huxi!"

I'd read enough meditation books to recognize the word she said. It was Chinese for "breathe."

The Lung puffed up its chest. I saw the light burning under its scales before the flames ever left its mouth. I turned and headed for the stairs. My shadow grew against the concrete floor as yellow light flashed at my back. The first inklings of heat pelted against my suit. It started as a small envelopment of warmth, then grew as if a wildfire was chasing me. I fell down the stairs and slammed into the wall at the bottom. Lying on my back, I looked to the floor above. Everything was golden fire, dancing and rippling. The scaly had flooded the floor with flames. Normal fire dissipated after a dragon finished breathing it, but these flames remained, floating above me like fatal clouds.

I scrambled to my feet and brought out my laser sword. All around me the air was dark yellow, filled with floating bits of ash. I couldn't see more than shadows a few feet in front of me.

The Lung dragon's head broke through the fire above me. It snapped its teeth, and although its moustache tendrils slapped across my helmet and my suit, it couldn't get close enough to bite me.

"You asshole!" Reynolds screamed.

Hell hath no fury like a woman scorned and with a dragon to ride.

I slashed my sword toward the Lung but I didn't want to get too close to either the teeth or the fire. I stayed against the wall. My first swipe caught nothing but air, my next had me stumbling into the wall to my left. When the scaly flicked its yellow head to try another bite at me, I cut into one of its tendrils, leaving the rubbery thing to drop at the ground between my boots.

The Lung dragon pulled out of the fire, yelping and roaring in pain. A slice of its wings split the flames open. Reynolds and her dragon dropped from the building, twisting toward the street. The scaly must have gone berserk when I'd sliced off one of its lip tentacles. Reynolds couldn't control it. All she could do was hold on and hope throwing up or losing consciousness in the force of the dragon's spin was the worst that would happen to her.

I felt horrible. But Reynolds had been the one to attack me. She'd chosen the Army over common sense. And she'd never said a damned thing about being able to ride the scalies.

The Lung's floating fire evaporated and I could see my surroundings more clearly. I climbed back to the floor above and got a view of the street. Calhoun rode atop his Fafnir and clawed along the top of Cannon 15. Renfro placed the cannon barrel on them and fired. The colonel took his dragon to the air as a blast of blue light flew just under the Fafnir's claws.

The red scaly began to hover around the truck. Renfro tried to follow them with the cannon but it would only be a matter of time before Calhoun found an opening and dove in to take Renfro out.

Lasers whipped out of the building across the street, shattering glass as they flew from the top window and tore into the midsection of the Silver Razor that hung from the side. The dragon whined and leaned away from the shots. The sun shimmered across its reflective scales. It couldn't escape. The soldier riding the Razor's back whipped the reins in his hands to no effect. The Silver Razor was already dead and dropped from the building. It landed against the street on its back, squishing its rider into red goo.

The green Fafnir flew past me. A smoke eater dangled from its foreclaws with both of their hands gripped onto its ankles. It was Brannigan. He was screaming but his voice carried over the street sounding joyful. The old fuck was having the time of his life.

"I'm going to need some help," Renfro called through my helmet.

"What's going on out there?" Tamerica said.

Renfro couldn't answer. He was having trouble just keeping the cannon aimed close enough to the Fafnir so Calhoun wouldn't divebomb him.

Calhoun's red Fafnir had begun to blast down streams of fire as it circled the cannon truck. The colonel then began taking shots at Renfro with his rifle. The colonel didn't look too confident in the saddle, and he was having a hard time aiming properly. But one of his wild shots would eventually hit its mark.

"It's Calhoun," I radioed back. "He's trying to take out Renfro."

"Our priority is to protect that truck," Tamerica said. "Everybody head back."

"I'm hanging from this green one," Brannigan said. I could see green wings through the middle of two ruined buildings in the distance.

"Then let go and come help defend the truck," Tamerica said. "It's the only one we have."

Calhoun found an opening to attack. He yanked on his dragon's reins and they fell out of the hovering position. The Fafnir stuck out its hind claws as if to snatch Renfro, but the smoke eater had the cannon barrel spinning at full throttle. The barrel knocked the dragon in the head before it could touch him. For extra measure, Renfro dug into his power suit and threw something small and black into the air. Laser light flashed and spun like a propeller, cutting the Fafnir along its side. I smelled burned meat.

The dragon roared and twisted its wings at an odd angle. Calhoun slid sideways. His weight tugged at the reins, pulling the scaly even farther away from Cannon 15, flying like a comet toward the edge of the building where I stood.

As with all events beyond my control, two words slipped from my mouth: "Oh, shit."

Fully grown Fafnirs weighed an average of seven tons, and this big red bastard was probably a few pounds over that. The structure I was standing on had already been a wind gust away from crumbling to ash. When the scaly crashed into the building, it was like a wrecking ball had hit it. I fell forward, then down. Nothing was holding me up any more.

I landed on the Fafnir's back, though I didn't realize it until I'd quit screaming and saw I hadn't fallen to the street. My bones hadn't broken. My innards hadn't popped out like spaghetti from an overfilled water balloon. The only thing that hurt was my face, where it had smacked against the Fafnir's rough, red scales. When I looked up, Calhoun was ahead of me and bent forward steering the dragon out of the trash-yellow cloud left by the demolished building.

"Holy fuck," Afu said through my helmet. "That Guillermo kid is riding the red Fafnir!"

I felt dizzy. Some of the concrete dust and ash had flown into the back of my throat. I gagged and tried to clear it from my mouth with slobbering coughs.

Calhoun turned in his saddle.

"You!" The whites of his eyes stuck out bright against the brown, powdered debris caking his face. "I should have let you freeze to death."

He turned the Fafnir to spin us through the air, trying to shake me off. What Calhoun didn't know was that it would take the very fingers of God to pluck me from the back of that scaly. Aside from freezing and drowning, falling from a high place was the last way I wanted to die. Even if I had to dig my armored fingers into the dragon's back, I wasn't getting off until I was back on solid ground. But how the hell was that going to happen?

A surge of vomit threatened to rocket from my mouth, but it had been a long time since I'd had those canned peaches. Dry heaves wracked my body. My grip began to loosen.

"It's just not your day, soldier." Calhoun stretched an arm back, pointing his rifle. He wasn't handling the weapon by Army regulation; it weaved all over the place, but as close as we were to one another it would do what he intended. He fired. The Fafnir dived and it bucked the colonel's aim. My eyes filled with bright red light. I had to blink a few times before my eyes adjusted back to normal. The red laser had grazed the side of my smoke eater helmet.

Calhoun gripped the dragon reins tighter while trying to get a better bead on me. Keeping tight to the scaly's back, I slid my hand toward my right glove. I pressed the button and dug the laser sword into the Fafnir's flesh. The dragon screeched like a baby wailing to death. It really fucked me up. I felt strangely horrible for having caused the beast pain, but I didn't get a chance to feel bad for long. The dragon pitched toward the earth.

What the fuck had I done?

Calhoun's rifle fell from his hand. He whipped the reins to no avail, shouting, "Fly, you bastard!"

There was no way my shallow sword plunge had killed the dragon. It hadn't even gotten close to any vital organs. Still, we were free falling.

At the last second, the Fafnir caught the air in its wings and landed into a four-legged stumble against the street. My head bounced to the rhythm of the Fafnir's cavorting. My neck felt like it would snap in two. The dragon twitched to and fro, tensing its muscles and scratching its hind claws at me like I was a flea.

I threw myself to the street, tumbling across the ash and snow. Calhoun barked wobbly-voiced orders at the bucking Fafnir, but the scaly wasn't listening. I guess whatever power the Nusies had over the dragons wasn't enough to combat a laser sword to the ass.

We hadn't landed too far from the cannon truck. I could see Renfro at the controls on the back of the truck just down the street. Afu and Brannigan ran over to the truck and put their backs to it. Their laser swords glowed at their sides. Afu pulled his axe from the back of his power suit. From a broken window two stories above the truck, Tamerica launched out, using her power jump to coast safely to the ground.

I ran toward them.

"Are you okay, Gilly?" Brannigan's voice came through my helmet.

"I'm good," I said. "What are we going to do?"

Shadows moved above. As I ran, I looked up. I wished I hadn't. Reynolds and her Lung dragon circled in the air while the green Fafnir and the remaining Silver Razor clawed along a building at either side of us. Soon they leapt off and joined Reynolds, widening the death circle.

The wind was picking up, lifting ash and snow into the air. It created a haze around us. I knew Chicago was the windy city, but this seemed unnatural. The dragons flying above were having a hard time staying upright.

I made it to the cannon truck and bent over, catching my breath. My stomach wasn't ready to settle down yet, and I was afraid it would find something to regurgitate before I could put up a fight. Several chunks of slushy ash flew into my mouth. I gagged.

"Where's the red one?" Tamerica said.

"Down the street," I said between gasps. "It's giving Calhoun trouble."

A roar came over our heads. The red Fafnir flew in and flapped to stay just above us. Tamerica raised her laser arm.

"Don't even try," Calhoun said through his tiny megaphone. He was a little too proud of that thing. "You might get a few shots on me, but there are enough of us here to end you all. You can make this hard or easy, it doesn't mean a thing to me which way you go."

"It didn't give him enough trouble," Brannigan said.

We looked at each other. On the truck, Renfro looked down at us. He was tired, and the cannon was pointed the opposite way. If he started to move it, Calhoun or one of the others would just attack the rest of us and get him last.

"Give up now, and you can keep breathing."

"I'm not going to be a goddamn experiment," Tamerica said to us through gritted teeth.

"I'd rather be dead," Brannigan said.

"Of course you'd say that," said Afu, "you're not that far from dying anyway."

"Fuck your old jokes," said Brannigan. "I haven't seen you in ten years and you're still spouting that bullshit."

"I'm sorry, you guys," Tamerica said. There was a sad acceptance in her voice.

"No," Brannigan said. "It's my fault. I had to fuck everything up."

"You're right," Tamerica said.

Brannigan squished his eyebrows together.

"You guys can't give up," I said, even though I felt like permanently falling to the ground. "Sink or swim, remember?"

"We're not quitting," Brannigan said. "We're just accepting."

"That sounds the same," I said.

They had less to worry about than I did. They might have been kept as prisoners and experimented on by the Army scientists, but I was the one Calhoun had a personal grudge against, as well as Reynolds and every surviving soldier in my platoon. The NUSA might have wanted to eradicate smoke eaters, but I was a traitor and that was worse. I'd be lucky to get a firing squad.

"No," said Tamerica. "Accepting means we'll slash and shoot till the end. They aren't taking us alive."

Using his natural voice, Calhoun shouted, "Form up on me."

The other soldiers dropped their dragons out of the circle to hover next to Calhoun and his Fafnir. The air pushed them around like struggling kites.

"I'm done waiting," Calhoun said. "Fry these

abominations. I don't wanna even see bones left behind. And don't let up. They don't burn like normal people."

The soldiers breathed in to give their dragons the orders. The smoke eaters beside me readied to jump into glory. I was too tired to move.

The wind suddenly grew stronger. My helmet threatened to leave my head. Tamerica lifted an elbow to block the gust from her eyes. Afu grabbed hold of the back of the truck and Renfro squatted low behind his controls. A roar came down the street, from the sky. Hell, it was coming from everywhere, all around us. It was the loudest thing I'd ever heard. I squatted and closed my ears with the tips of my armored fingers.

Calhoun and the others flew higher to get out of the wind, but they couldn't escape it. The scalies bumped into each other, forcing the soldiers to spread out to avoid colliding with one another.

Reynolds looked up and shouted, "Oh shit!"

She made her Lung dragon dive toward the ground. A golden-scaled body filled the air above the street, soaring over Reynolds's head. The giant dragon plowed into the Nusie who'd been hovering next to Reynolds; it snatched the soldier and his green Fafnir in its teeth and kept flying.

I turned to follow the scaly. When it got far enough and turned for another pass above the ruined buildings half a mile away, I saw what it was. The Golden Drake.

Buildings began crumbling around us. The wind never let up. I saw the Golden Drake flap its wings and then a few seconds later a violent gust racked my body and caused me to stumble backwards.

Calhoun's orders came out as garbled shouts. If his soldiers heard him at all they weren't obeying. There were only three of them now. Reynolds had flown off somewhere to avoid getting chomped and the guy riding the Silver Razor was buzzing around like a one-winged fly.

"Everybody get in the truck!" Tamerica shouted over the wind.

Renfro bedded the cannon and jumped off, not bothering with the ladder steps. The rest of us piled into the cab. The doors wobbled so hard I thought they would rip from their hinges. It took both me and Brannigan to shut the door on our side. Afu got his closed before us, but Renfro was already speeding us down the street by the time Tamerica sealed herself in.

I kept turning to take glances through the windshield. Ash and snow flew everywhere – it was like driving through a foggy tornado. Just ahead, a shadow crept across the street, hunkering low against the wind. It was the Lung dragon, wings pulled in close, claws struggling to grip into the street. Reynolds lay against its back from within her saddle. Renfro didn't let off the accelerator.

"We're going to hit that dragon," Tamerica said.

Renfro gripped the steering wheel. The hum of the engine didn't soften.

"Renfro!" Tamerica grabbed his arm.

Reynolds yanked on her reins and pulled the Lung into a jump. They both disappeared into the debris as the wind took them away.

"What was that about?" Tamerica asked. She hadn't let go of Renfro's arm.

"I knew she was going to move," Renfro snapped.

Brannigan took off his helmet and wiped sweat from his gray head. "Hell of a time to be playing chicken."

"She's a good person," I said, shaking my head. "*Was* a good person. I thought."

"She's a Nusie," Brannigan said. He patted my knee but it didn't make me feel any better. I hadn't forgotten he'd tried serving me up to the scalies. He turned to Tamerica. "We need to get out of Chicago."

"Not yet," Tamerica said. She was about to say more, but Brannigan interrupted her.

"Why the hell not? We've got a ride. We'll just need to find somewhere to hide out for a day or so, then we can hit the road. If you need a home, we can go back to my town and–"

"Hey!" Tamerica shouted. "You really think it's just us three living here? We've got other people depending on us."

"Oh," Brannigan said. "Well, what are we going to do then?"

"*We*, huh?" Tamerica said.

Afu and Renfro chimed in at the same time, saying, "Yeah, *we*."

Tamerica took off her helmet and smiled. "So the gang's all back together, then?"

They all nodded. I did, too, though I felt out of place.

"All right," Tamerica nodded as she spoke, "I'll tell you what we're going to do. We're going to get our people out of the city and then we're going to figure out how the Army is riding dragons."

Renfro hit a bump in the road and mumbled a "sorry."

"You kidding me?" Brannigan said. "If it wasn't for that Golden Drake, we would have been crispy critters. I nearly got my arm blown off by a laser rifle. What are you going to do? Walk up and ask them how they're doing this scaly cowboy shit?"

"So now it's *you* and not *we*?" Tamerica asked.

"You know what I mean," Brannigan said. "Short of capturing one of them, we won't know how they're doing it."

"We won't need to capture one of them." Tamerica turned back to me.

"I already told you," I said. "I never knew anything about that."

"Maybe not," Tamerica said. "But you might help us crack into this."

She pulled a holoreader from her suit's pocket and see-sawed it in her hand.

"Where'd you get that?" Afu said. His long hair was dripping with sweat and coated in ash.

"Took it off the asshole who was riding the Silver Razor," Tamerica said. "I didn't have much time to look, but it's got a password on it. I'm thinking only Nusies know it. So, Contreras, think you can help us crack it?"

None of the soldiers used any connected system. There was no Feed anymore. The guy who'd owned the holoreader probably had his own password for it to protect his porn or action movies. But I wasn't going to tell Tamerica that.

"You take me with you and help me get out of the city, I'll help you with the holoreader." I tried not to blink as Tamerica stared me down.

"That sounds like a good deal to me," Brannigan said.

I huffed and rolled my eyes.

Tamerica snorted a small laugh before turning back to face the front. "You got a deal, kid. Renfro, how's it look behind us on your side?"

"They aren't following us. No GD, either."

I thought about abbreviations and how that sounded short for goddamn. Which, funnily enough, was what had been going through my head when the Golden Drake showed up. Then I looked at the man I'd been calling Seabee and wondered how anybody could put up with such an obnoxious blowhard. He wore a smug smile like he was happy how everything had turned out so far.

I turned to look at the wastes outside my window. The wind was still turbulent, but had died down from hurricane-level. "Where have you guys been staying around here anyway?"

Afu laughed and said, "You like baseball?"

CHAPTER 14

They'd turned Wrigley Field into a redneck version of the Pentagon.

Metal sheets in various stages of rust had been welded at the top of the stadium along the outfield. A roof enclosed the rest of it. The famous red sign that hung on the Field's corner at Clark and Addison was still there, but the digital square had been smashed. Words had been laser-slashed over the part that had read "Chicago Cubs." The sign now read "Wrigley Field Home of Ash Kickers."

"Jesus Christ," Brannigan said. "Are you guys Cardinals fans?"

"Cleveland all the way," Afu said, his eyebrows tilted downward, serious as a heart attack. "But we didn't do most of this. After the Nusies took over, the city turned the field into an emergency shelter or something. We've had to replace a few of the outer sheets, but it's mostly as is. They dug up a whole level of bunkers and stuff under the diamond."

"Goddamn," Brannigan shook his head sadly as he looked out the window. "This place used to be one of the wonders of the world. Sherry dreamed of playing here when she..."

The old man drifted away from his sentence and I decided to change the subject. "How do you get in and out?"

"It's right here," said Tamerica. "Didn't spot it before, did you?"

I still didn't spot it.

Renfro turned left toward the building and stopped on a sharp decline. Ahead of us was a wall of those metal sheets. I wondered if we would just barrel through with the cannon truck. Renfro hit the yelp siren briefly, and ten seconds later the door rose outward on hydraulic lifts.

A thin man with long hair and glasses stood on the other side. A dimly lit, tile-lined tunnel reached into the depths behind him. The man wore a long-sleeved forest green shirt over a band tee – one of those black metal bands whose illustrated name looks like every other black metal band's illustrated name. His jeans were black and his boots were brown. He looked like a roadie, but the brainy kind who worked the lights and pyrotechnics.

Renfro pulled the truck inside Wrigley. While the door closed behind us, the man in the metal shirt walked around to Tamerica's window.

"Hey, man," Tamerica said, leaning out on her arm.

"You guys have a good outing?" the man said. I couldn't see him from where I sat.

"We got a lot more than we bargained for," Tamerica said. "Hop in and we'll give you a ride back home."

"All right," the man said, lazily, as if she'd offered him a potato chip. The door beside Afu opened and the man climbed in. He sat beside Brannigan and gave the old man a nod. He looked at me and did the same. "You guys are new. You smoke eaters, too?"

"I don't know," I said.

"Yeah, we are." Brannigan's voice had entwined with

mine. It earned the old man a few points towards getting off my shit list. I felt included.

Renfro drove.

"Cool," the man in glasses said. He then sat back in his seat and would have probably stayed silent for the remainder of the ride if Brannigan hadn't spoken to him.

"Who are you?" Brannigan asked.

"Oh." He sat up and pushed his glasses closer to his face with a thin finger. "I'm Lot."

Brannigan turned to me, and with a hand to the side of his mouth said, "Well he doesn't look like much to me."

Despite liking Lot on sight, and trying to remain focused on the serious situation at hand, I snorted a laugh through my nose. I always appreciated good wordplay.

"This is Lot Scynch," Tamerica said. "He was a propellerhead for the Chicago smoke eaters."

"Thank you for your service," Brannigan said, with obvious sarcasm.

"Shut up you old bastard," said Tamerica.

"What's your name?" Lot asked Brannigan.

He smirked. "You can call me–"

"This is Chief Cole Brannigan," I said. I gave the old bastard my own smirk, happy to give him a taste of his own medicine. "Long-thought dead, but not so much."

"Whoa!" Lot said. Instead of getting bigger, his eyes almost shut completely. "Good to have you back, man."

"This guy must be great at parties," Brannigan said.

"If it weren't for Lot," Tamerica said, "we wouldn't have any power, running water, nothing."

"Wish it didn't have to be that," Lot said. "I blame every Nusie for screwing up the world we had. Army my ass. You know what they are?"

"What?" Brannigan leaned forward.

"They're the new police," Lot said. "Only they don't have to hide their murderous ways anymore."

"Well," Brannigan said, "you know what I've always said about the police?"

"What's that?" Lot asked.

Brannigan turned to me and grinned. "Fuck the police."

"If I ever see a Nusie," Lot said, "I'll strangle them with my bare hands."

My breath caught in my throat. I wasn't Army anymore, but I wasn't so sure Lot would see a distinction.

"I've always wondered about that phrase," Brannigan said. "You could easily kill someone with gloved hands."

I stared at the old man, but he wasn't messing with me. He was seriously wondering about his notion as he stared off into space.

I was surrounded by psychotics.

Tamerica stared ahead through the windshield, stuck on complimenting Lot. "He's a good guy. Without Lot, we wouldn't have been able to live here for as long as we did."

"*Did*?" Lot blinked and leaned forward to see Tamerica better. "As in past tense?"

Tamerica shook her hair loose with her fingers. Sighing through her words, she said, "Yeah, we're going to have to call a quick town meeting."

I thought there would have been more of them.

We'd all gathered in what used to be the Cubs' locker room. The walls had been knocked down to make it wider, but the small wooden cubicles remained. It smelled like mint and ass. Instead of a coach giving a pregame pep talk, Tamerica stood before us, fresh out of the shower and wearing a hoodie and sweatpants.

Brannigan and I hadn't taken a shower yet, though we did step out of our power suits to cool off. This was an unfamiliar place with unfamiliar people. No one had offered me anything, and we didn't have any clothes to change into. I wasn't about to ask for anything special.

I counted twenty people in that locker room aside from myself and those of us who'd ridden in on the cannon truck. There was a baby, a few kids, but most of Tamerica's people were adults. They ranged in ages between me and Brannigan, and they were of every shade and height you could imagine. No one had introduced themselves to either of us, but they passed us with wary eyes, shielding children who clung to their legs.

"Bunch of introverts," Brannigan mumbled to me.

I shook my head. "They just don't trust new people."

"Same difference."

I glared at the old man. "That's not the definition of an intro – ah, never mind. It doesn't matter."

"All right, everybody." Tamerica's voice filled the room, causing everyone's head to turn toward her. "I have some bad news. A platoon of the New United States Army has come into Chicago. They can ride dragons. We need to leave immediately."

Brannigan's laughter came out like lightning, quick and loud.

If they weren't staring at Brannigan, the Wrigley people were whispering among themselves while Tamerica turned to the old man. "Something funny, Chief?"

"No," he said, wiping his eyes. "It's just, I appreciate being blunt, but holy fuck couldn't you have been more diplomatic with that speech?"

Renfro tensed and nodded in agreement. But he kept quiet, standing beside Tamerica, rubbing the back of his neck.

"We don't have the time," Tamerica said. She turned back to her people. "We'll leave at 0600 tomorrow morning. That should give everyone time to get their things together and get some sleep."

"Who are those two?" A middle-aged black woman pointed toward me and Brannigan.

"They're smoke eaters," Tamerica said. "Passing through from out of state. They helped us out there today."

That seemed to be enough for the woman. She nodded and tugged on the man beside her to leave.

The others started throwing questions and demands at Tamerica. I stood there feeling strange about having been lumped into the title of smoke eater with the rest. Tamerica hadn't mentioned that I'd been a Nusie just a day before. It showed good leadership on her part; saying so would have done nothing but rile everyone up – especially Lot. It was easier to say I was another smokie. I looked the part if nothing else. The way things were going, I'd be disappointed to find out I wasn't a smoke eater. The fantasy felt better than mourning my family and the empty dark of the future. Some well-meaning assholes might have told me I was just escaping, but when someone's reality sucks this much, I say hit that eject button and float amidst the unreal.

"I'm taking a shower," Brannigan said. He walked off, pushing through the people with his shoulders wide and a defiance in his steps.

Damn it, I wanted a shower, too. As I listened to the Wrigley people talk, I felt weak. My legs wobbled. I needed to find a chair... or a bed... water.

A heavy arm dropped around my shoulders. Afu squeezed me tight and spoke into my ear. "You don't look so good, bruh. Come on. I know just what you need to pick you up." He led me around the gathered people, through a side door, and out into the hall. "I'm gonna show you my favorite thing about living here."

After a few steps down the hall, he opened a door to our left and I was dragged inside.

Like every other wall in the place, the ones in this room were covered with giant red Cs and illustrated bears. Rusty metal poles rested above metal benches and metal chairs, while black iron plates of different sizes rested beside the various torture devices along the walls and in each corner.

It was a weight room.

"Afu," I said, feeling like I'd turn into sludge right there, "I'm not really up for a workout, man. That won't help me at all."

Afu sat me down on a bench. "Nah, bruh, nah. I love lifting, but that's not what I brought you in here for. Just relax right here for a minute."

He disappeared around the corner. I heard the opening and closing of a wrapper, then the clunk of a latched door, and then the hum of an electrical appliance. I soon smelled the funk of beans and meat.

It can't be, I thought.

About a minute and a half later, Afu came back and held a plastic plate to my face. In the center of the plate a microwave burrito sat steaming and partially wet. "When's the last time you had one of these?"

I took the plate. "I... honestly can't even remember."

I'd never liked microwave burritos, not when I used to have the real thing pretty much anytime I wanted.

My emotions began to rise up through my nose and eyes again. I teared up a little and took a bite out of the burrito. It burned the roof of my mouth and I had to spit it back onto the plate. "Hah... hot!"

"Oh shit!" Afu jumped up and ran back around the corner. Cabinets banged as they were opened. A faucet ran. He came back with a glass of water. "I always hate waiting for those things to cool down. If you're hungry, who has time to wait? And if you don't cook it enough, it stays frozen in the middle. Follow the directions on the wrapper, you burn your taste buds off."

I lifted the cup he'd given me and drank the lukewarm water. I tongued the roof of my mouth. It was raw and tender. "Maybe I'm not a smoke eater after all."

"Because of a hot burrito?" Afu said. "I don't think it works like that, man. I don't even think the scalies could eat one of these right out of the microwave. Besides, it didn't kill you. Flames have hurt me before. Plenty of times. But not like they would have done to regular people. We have resistance, not immunity."

"I appreciate you trying to make me feel a part of the group, but I'm pretty sure I don't belong with anyone anymore. I didn't feel at home with the Army and I don't have a home to go back to." I wiped my eyes. They'd gotten wet. "Goddamn burritos."

"Damn, Gilly, I'm sorry. I was just trying to get some food in you."

"No," I swallowed at phlegm collecting in my throat. "I appreciate it. I'm hungry as hell and even more tired. I just... I just want the world to stop for a day or two so I can get back to the way I was."

Afu pulled a rubber band out of his pocket. He held it

in his teeth as he pulled his hair back into a ponytail. He began tying his hair and said, "Brother, there is no getting back to the way you were before. The world's changed, your life has changed, how do you expect to come out unscathed yourself?"

I bit into the burrito again. It was still hot but I could swallow it without burning my throat.

"But I know exactly how you feel," Afu said. "It's like waking up in a roller coaster and some asshole has cranked the speed all the way up and then abandoned the controls."

"That's a good analogy," I said.

"I got analogies for days! My wife says I've got too many of them."

"Your wife?"

"Tamerica." His smile stretched across his face. He already had a big mouth as it was. "It took a few tries for her to say yes, but we've been married for three years coming up next month."

I took a few more bites of the burrito. My hunger was beginning to outweigh my emotions. "I can't believe I'm sitting here with you. That I'm here with all of you. I used to read about you guys. You felt made up, larger-than-life. I always felt like I was reading a comic book and not a newspaper clipping. And now that I've met you for real, you all seem so normal."

"You know what they say," Tamerica appeared in the doorway, "never meet your heroes."

She stepped into the room. Brannigan and Lot followed in behind her, but they tried to enter at the same time and got stuck shoulder to shoulder between the jambs. They glanced at each other, confused, then backed out as one.

Lot held a hand up to the doorway. "Age before beauty, man."

"Then I guess you'll be waiting outside." Brannigan walked in and sat on a leg curl machine.

Lot came in on his lanky legs anyway.

"Renfro will join us a little later." Tamerica held up the holoreader and set it on the bench in front of me. "Let's see what we can find in here."

Staring at the holoreader, I swallowed another bite of burrito, but it turned gummy in my throat. I downed the entire cup of water.

"Well," I said, with a cough, "I'll try."

"No," said Tamerica. "You said you would *do* this. We can't afford trying."

"Don't anybody say it," Brannigan spouted. "Don't use that old fucking movie quote. I don't want to hear it."

Tamerica turned to him. "What the hell are you babbling about back there?"

"Oh," said Afu, pointing to Brannigan, "you mean the thing that little green dude said in that space movie."

"Don't even think about it," Brannigan said. He leaned back with his fingers linked behind his head, frowning and daring someone to say it.

I had no idea what he was referencing.

"Anyway," Tamerica turned back to me with a roll of her eyes, "all we need you to do is look for any reports or communication that could tell us what the Nusies might be planning, how they're riding dragons, or anything else that's helpful."

I looked over at Lot Scynch, who was using his fingers to spin a forty-five pound plate around on its bar. I whispered, "Does he know I was in the Army."

Tamerica glanced over her shoulder at the propellerhead. "He knows you might have gotten the password to this holoreader. If you can't get in, he'll have to figure something out."

I was going to tell her again that I would try, but stopped myself. I hit the power button on the side of the device and a lock screen rose into the air. It was a picture of the soldier who'd owned the holoreader, the one who'd gotten squished under a Silver Razor. In the photo, he was wearing his helmet and a pair of sunglasses, making an "O" with his lips as if he'd been whooping. His arm was wrapped tight around a young civilian woman who didn't seem nearly as excited as he was. In fact, she looked scared. She wore makeup, which was strange enough for anyone nowadays, but the mascara streaked down her face and the lipstick was smeared. Her tank top hung loose from her shoulders. The front of it was especially droopy as if someone had grabbed a fistful of it and tried to rip it off. The camera's flash had turned their surroundings dark, so it looked like the two of them were alone together in a void. Him looking triumphant, and her wishing she could fly away and be anywhere else.

I felt queasy looking at it.

"Sick motherfucker," Tamerica said. "Hurry up and get this photo out of my face."

"Okay," I said.

Nervously, I poked the green digital keys floating over the picture. I tried my own password for the holoreader I'd left back in Waukesha. 5-90 had given it to me, so maybe it was a platoon-specific code: **P!zzant0**

You've entered the wrong password, the notification read.

Brannigan snorted laughter.

"Shut up, man," I said. "That was the password I was given."

"They gave you that one?" Brannigan laughed some more.

"What's so funny?" I said. "It's pizza with some extra symbols."

"Bruh," Afu said. "That basically says piss ant zero. They didn't like you very much."

"What?" I looked again at the code I'd entered. "Son of a bitch."

"It doesn't matter." Tamerica patted my shoulder. "Is there another password? Come on, man. You said you could do it."

"I..."

"Did you lie to me?" Tamerica said.

"No. Just give me a minute." I tried another code:

NUSAFirst

Wrong.

Arm33Strong. **Platoon1**. **CalhounSux**.

None of them worked.

"If you get it wrong too many times," Lot said, fiddling with a screw on one of the weight machines, "you might lock it out to where I can't even hack it."

"It's okay, Contreras," Tamerica said, though I could tell she was disappointed. "Let Lot take a look."

"No," I said. "I can do this."

She reached over to take the holoreader. I jerked it away so she couldn't. The device flew from my grip and skidded across the floor.

"Shit," Brannigan jumped to his feet. "Don't break it."

Tamerica and I both ran for the holoreader. She threw an arm in front of me, but we both ended up skidding to a stop and landing on our asses when a bright light sprang from the holoreader and began forming a shape in the air.

Someone was calling.

"First Platoon? Anyone there?" A black woman's head

hovered from the holoreader's screen. She looked almost ghostly, partly because she was a hologram head, but also because she looked so malnourished and sleep-deprived.

I'd never seen her before, but everyone else in the room whispered a swear or had their mouth hanging open. Who was she?

Renfro walked into the weight room and answered my question. "Yolanda?"

"Oh my goodness!" the hologram head said. She looked all around the room. "Guys? Is that really you?"

"It's us." Brannigan said, walking forward.

"Chief?" Yolanda squeaked as if someone had squeezed her too tight. "What's going on? Is this real?"

Tamerica looked at me. "How'd she have this holoreader's number?"

I shrugged. I honestly didn't know.

"I'm still alive, Yolanda," Brannigan said. "I'm glad to see you. We can come get you and explain everything. Where are you?"

"I'm in Parthenon City," Yolanda said. A digitized hand appeared as she wiped at her wet eyes. "All of us are."

"All of you?" Tamerica said.

"T," she said. "Oh, I'm so sorry. I know you told me to get out of town. I should have listened."

"Don't worry about that," Tamerica said. "Are you working for the Nusies?"

Tamerica got off the floor and stood before the hologram. I followed her lead.

"They forced us," Yolanda said. Shadows moved around the room as the holographic light shifted with the hanging of her head. "They took all of us. All the propellerheads in Ohio. They make us build them all sorts of strange things.

Unethical things. They don't feed us unless we get results. It's never enough."

"Yolanda," Brannigan said. "We were attacked by this platoon. That's how we got the holoreader. They were riding scalies."

"I know," she said. "That's just one of the things they had us do."

"What do you mean?" Afu said. "How's that even possible?"

"Guys," Yolanda's head jerked around, as if someone was coming up behind her and she was turning to look. "I don't have much time. How can they ride them? It's... it's a device we put in the dragons' heads. Simple really. We'd been tranquilizing them for years. We were bound to start adding tech. The Nusies wear a psionic counterpart matched to their scaly. It's a mental symbiosis of sorts."

"My God," Lot rushed forward, beckoned by tech talk. "How were you able to do that in such a short time?"

"Lot," Yolanda smiled sadly. "It's good to see you. Short time? No. We've been working on that since they took over. Only just got it working. Wait, you guys are in Chicago. That's why they had us send the dragons to Waukesha."

"They mail-ordered the dragons?" Afu said.

The smoke eaters all turned to gawk at Afu. He looked at each of them then shrugged.

"That's exactly what they did," I said. Everyone was now looking at me. I swallowed, but continued with my thought. "That's where I left the platoon, in Waukesha. They must have called Big Base and had them set the dragons to fly out to pick them up."

It sounded ridiculous when it came out of my mouth like that. I tensed and shut my mouth before anything else stupid came out.

Brannigan's laughter cracked through the room. "The Nusies can order dragons now like fucking pizza?"

"More like an air strike." Tamerica looked at me. Her face was grim.

"Who's this?" Yolanda said. Her head was so large and glowing, when she looked down at me I felt like I was under the notice of an ancient genie or sorcerer.

"Brannigan picked him up on the road," Tamerica said.

"You called it Big Base," Yolanda said to me. "Only the soldiers call it that."

I blinked. "Yeah, well–"

"You said you left your platoon in Waukesha." Lot stared at me with a tilt of his head as if I'd grown a pair of wings.

"Are you First Platoon?" Yolanda's head asked.

I looked from Yolanda to a visibly-angry Lot, then to Tamerica, who'd parted her lips to speak, but she tensed and looked away, nervously running fingers through her hair. She wouldn't be able to get me out of this one.

"It's not a big deal," Brannigan said. "This is Guillermo Contreras. He was a Nusie and now he's one of us. Let's get back to the point–"

"Not a big deal?" Lot popped his fingers one by one, glaring at me with his chin up. I thought he was going to take a swing at my face, but he pointed at Tamerica. "You kept this from me on purpose. Because you knew how I'd react. You think he's going to help us? You just murdered us all." He turned to the hologram. "Yolanda, I'm so sorry. I'll see if I can find a way to keep in contact with you, but right now I have to go."

Lot stormed out of the room.

Brannigan hiked a thumb over his shoulder. "Is that guy serious?"

"He's been through a lot." Renfro said.

I felt too crummy to appreciate the pun. The Army would be a stain on me for the rest of my life and there would be nothing I could do to prove myself. I'd be sending people stomping angrily out of rooms for the foreseeable future. Yolanda didn't seem as upset by my association with NUSA, but, just like Lot, her stay would be short.

"Guys, they're coming," she said.

"Yolanda, wait," Tamerica said. "Try to call us again when you can."

"I don't know, I don't know what's going to happen," Yolanda said. She looked on the verge of a full meltdown, though she was trying hard to keep it in. "I've missed you guys. Wait, wait, I have to tell you. I have to tell you in case I don't see you again. The Nusies, they didn't just take me, they have her. They have her somewhere down below. They have Naveena."

The hologram blinked out and she was gone.

CHAPTER 15

Captain Naveena Jendal. The woman I'd looked up to for most of my life. The Army had her locked up at Big Base, probably torturing her in all sorts of experiments, drawing her blood, slicing off her flesh, putting her through hell to see what she could endure. But she was real. She was alive. Yolanda had made it *sound* like she was still alive, but for how much longer?

"Fuck me sideways," Brannigan said. He kicked a rack of iron plates and ended up limping away, cursing. "You know what we have to do, right?"

"Did you see Yolanda's face?" Renfro said. "She looked half dead."

"We have to do something," Tamerica said.

Afu nodded. "I'm sick of hiding from these shit bags."

"We'll have to get our people somewhere safe," Tamerica said. "But after that, all of us, we're going to get her out and raze that base to the ground."

Brannigan clapped his hands together. "I'm in. You got a plan?"

Tamerica put a hand to my shoulder and moved me closer to the others. "Gilly is going to help us figure it out."

I blinked at each of these smoke eaters' faces. They were

itching for a fight. They'd been chased and ostracized for years and felt this was their return from the shadows. But how the hell could I help?

"I've never even been to that base," I said. "I've only heard about it."

Renfro and Afu's faces sank a bit.

"Doesn't matter," Brannigan said. "You know how the Nusies operate. We can get what's-his-face to hack that holoreader."

"Lot," Tamerica said.

"Yeah," said Brannigan. "I'm sure he can get a lot out of it."

I shook my head and backed away from Tamerica's grip. "I don't know, guys. I'm done with the Army and everything, but apparently Big Base is loaded with soldiers. Guys just itching to shoot something. From what I heard, there's more spider tanks and rifles there than on the road. And now they have dragons. It would be suicide."

"Then we won't pull an all-out assault," said Tamerica. "We just need to get inside and get Naveena out."

"But how?" I said. "They'll have the place guarded on every side."

"We can figure it out," Brannigan said. He lowered his head to look at me under his gray eyebrows. "If you help."

"I'm not a smoke eater!" I was shaking. So tired. I still hadn't had a shower. "I just want to go home."

"Guillermo," Brannigan said, "you would have a home to go to if there'd been smokies in Peoria. Where were the Nusies?"

"There are good people in the Army, you know." I couldn't believe what I was saying. I was thinking of Reynolds. "I know at least one of them who's probably just... confused. She actually wants to help people. I'm sure there are more like her. They can't all be bad apples."

"When you're a Nusie, you support everything the Nusies do," Brannigan said. "It doesn't matter your intentions. You should know better than anybody. You broke rank and got punished for it."

"But she wouldn't..." Yes, she would. She'd already tried to kill me. Who was she helping on the back of a scaly? I wondered if that counted as one of the life debts I owed her.

"She?" Brannigan said. He gave Renfro a look. "Okay, it makes sense now."

"It's not like that," I said.

"It's all right," Tamerica said. "Leave him alone."

Looking at me, she motioned toward the door with her eyes. She began walking and I followed her out.

"It's not that I don't want to help," I said, as we entered the hallway. "Captain Jendal is like my personal hero, it's just–"

"Shut it." She said it gently. "Your job right now is to shut up and listen. Shut up. And listen. Nod if you can do that."

I nodded.

We walked into the darker, more sparsely-lit crevices of Wrigley Field, around white walls splattered with yellow water stains. I smelled ammonia and other stale funks. The air was cooler here. As we walked my sweat grew chilled against the back of my shoulders. Tamerica led me up a series of stairs and then we stopped outside a room lined with dark-tinted glass.

She turned to me. "I want you to talk to Lot."

I shook my head hard enough to conjure up an ache. "No

way. He doesn't want to say anything to me. He's going to punch me the first chance he gets."

"You said you would shut up and listen," Tamerica said. "Remember?"

I sighed. I didn't want to talk to Lot or anybody else at that moment. I just wanted to cry in the shower and feel a little cleaner, but I decided the only way I was going to get that was to go along with Tamerica for a little while longer.

Again, I nodded.

"All right," Tamerica said. She knocked on the door.

A voice inside shouted, "Who is it?"

"Captain Williams," Tamerica said.

"Come in, I guess."

Tamerica walked in first, but extended a hand to my back to lead me in behind her. We were inside the Wrigley announcer box. It had been outfitted with all kinds of computers and wires and screens. I could see what remained of the baseball diamond from where I stood. The windows in the announcer box hadn't been covered.

Lot sat on a cot against the wall. When he saw me his face went red. "What the hell?"

"Just stop." Tamerica held up her hand. "He's not going to say anything. He's just here to listen."

"But—"

"And you," Tamerica bulldozed over Lot's retort, "are going to talk. To make him realize the importance of things. He was in the Army, yeah. But he left. He has no love for any of them. I don't blame you for feeling the way you feel, but I think you should give him a chance. I'm giving him a chance. And you know I don't give those out for nothing."

I realized I'd been clenching my teeth. I loosened my jaw but held my lips together.

"And what am I supposed to talk about?" Lot asked.

"Tell him about what happened to your brother."

"I don't want to talk about that," he said.

"I know," said Tamerica. She sighed. "How about this: you tell him about it, I'll wipe out everything you owe me from our card games."

Lot's eyes sprang open. "You what?"

"I'm being for real," said Tamerica. "Clean slate. Deal?"

Lot leaned back and lay on the cot, draping an arm on his head. He hissed out a stream of air through his lips. It lasted a long time. I looked to Tamerica but she kept her gaze on Lot. Finally, the propellerhead spoke. "It was Memorial Day. My brother Floyd had all of us over for a cookout at his place in Elgin. Both of us were out of a job, 'cause this was the year after the smoke eaters had been made illegal. Bastards turned our headquarters into a damn bank. Anyway, Floyd was a smoke eater. We weren't really close growing up – I liked quantum physics and he liked action movies – but that changed when we ended up working together. Shit, we'd see each other every shift and then off duty at least once a week. He was my best friend, and even though he was born to be a smoke eater, he always wanted to be a dad. Said he was going to share some important news with us after we all ate.

"Since we didn't have much money for the cookout we ended up grilling the chemically-grown hotdogs that taste like burnt tires. You know the ones. We didn't care, though. He had his girlfriend there at his side while he turned the franks. Our parents came over and drank their cheap wine. Couple friends were there, too. Good time.

"But everyone was out cooking that day. I mean, on Memorial Day who isn't grilling? But somebody across the street must have had an accident or something because we start seeing this huge cloud of smoke over Floyd's house. We ran to the front yard and saw the place across the street was burning down. This old man was standing on the yard, all ash-stained and delirious, screaming about his wife being trapped inside.

"Floyd just gives me this look," Lot said. "Takes off toward the house, all arms and legs. He was a lanky guy. He didn't say anything. He didn't have to. We all knew he had the ability to go into that smoking house when none of us could. Some people just have it, you know. And I'm not talking about the breathing smoke thing. Some people just have that drive to help no matter how horrible things get around them. I look over and see his girlfriend holding her stomach, with two hands. And that's when I knew what he was planning to tell us. I was going to be an uncle."

Tears came to his eyes.

Lot sniffed. "He goes into the house. Front door was open. Old man is screaming, please, please. We all watch, it feels like hours. But it was only a couple minutes until Floyd comes out with a woman over his shoulder. He lays her on the ground, checks her breathing, few pushes to her chest and a blow into her mouth and she's coughing. Breathing.

"I smiled. God, I was so proud of him. Slaying dragons is scary and noble, but there's nothing like seeing someone save another human life. It's like watching someone being born. It makes you realize how precious life is. Floyd wasn't even out of breath.

"Us and all the other neighbors tried our best to spray the flames with water, using garden hoses and buckets we'd pass in a line. It wasn't doing anything, so we just focused on cooling the houses beside it. Save what we still could. The old man and his wife held each other and cried while their place burned down. We waited and waited for the fire department to arrive. They never did. Instead, a bunch of spider tanks showed up.

"Soldiers scrambled out of those tanks like they were going to war. I couldn't understand why the Army would respond to a house fire. Maybe they thought it was a dragon. They started shouting at us like we'd done something wrong, telling us to get down on the grass. Most everyone did what they said. We were scared and confused. Not Floyd.

"He stood there with his hands up, like he could shoot lasers at them with his eyes. They pointed their rifles at him and told him to lay on the ground or they'd shoot. My parents begged him to listen, but the soldiers told them to shut up, and if Floyd was anything, he was stubborn and didn't like being told what to do, especially for no good reason.

"But he stayed calm, told the Nusies that there was clearly a fire and that we'd all been working to put it out. I think where he messed up was when he mentioned that the old woman needed medical attention. He said he'd carried her out. Then all the Nusies started looking at each other, like they had telepathy. Floyd kept talking. He said they had to tell us if we were being detained and if we were, they had to tell us why. He just wanted to clear the air, for them and for us. We didn't know what was going on, why it was happening. Everyone just wanted answers. For whatever reason, that just pissed the Nusies off."

Lot made a noise like he was going to throw up.

"It's okay," Tamerica said. "Take a second and then tell him what happened next."

"I don't need a second!" Lot sat up in a blur. I thought he was going to charge toward me, but he stayed on the cot. His face was red and filled with hate. "They shot him. No warning. No reason. They filled him with holes and let him bleed all over his front lawn. His girlfriend screamed. I still hear it in my head most nights when I can't sleep. When my dad tried to get up and go after them, they knocked him down and put a rifle to his head and told him he'd be next if he didn't stay down.

"And the whole time I went somewhere else in my head. It was like I was watching a movie. I couldn't believe it happened, didn't feel real, wasn't my brother, not my family. By the time it started sinking in, they'd put us all in resist-o-cuffs."

I'd seen the devices Lot was talking about. They were like handcuffs, except they tightened around your wrists if you squirmed or moved too much. One of the guys in the platoon said he'd seen someone's hands squeezed off because they'd been so scared they couldn't stop shaking.

"They brought all of us into my brother's house," Lot said. "I'm guessing the neighbors ran inside and were glad it wasn't their family. One by one they interrogated us at Floyd's kitchen table. Several of them dug into the fridge and took whatever they wanted. I said nothing when they brought me into the kitchen. They threatened to torture me, my parents, even Floyd's girlfriend. They didn't leave out the fact she was pregnant. It was just another angle they tried to use, but it didn't move me. I was numb. I wasn't even talking to myself in my head, so I sure as shit wasn't going to talk to the Nusies. They hauled me away and locked me in the bathroom. I lay in the tub, handcuffed, staring at a crack in the ceiling, hoping it would split open and swallow me so I wouldn't have to be there, feeling and hurting. At some point they came and got me and brought me to the living room with everyone else. I found out that my parents had let it slip that he'd been a smoke eater, so they wrapped it up as a job well done, uncuffed us, told us that they'd be back if we didn't mind ourselves, then zoomed away in that fucking bug-looking tank."

Lot went quiet and all I could think to say was, "Fuck."

"You know what happened to Lot isn't unique," Tamerica said.

"No," I said. "It's not."

Had I been just as bad? Whose fault was it that dragons had been allowed to destroy Peoria?

"I'm so sorry," I told Lot.

He lay back down and turned toward the wall away from us.

"Come on," Tamerica said.

We walked back outside and I closed the door behind me as softly as I could.

"I never..." I was trying to gather my thoughts. The man in the room had lost his brother, his whole family ripped apart, for what? "I'm not like that, Captain Williams."

"Call me T," she said. "And I know. I can tell about certain people."

"All I ever wanted to do was help people," I said. I felt like a failure in every possible way.

"You think it's too late?"

I leaned against the wall. The cheesy t-shirt Brannigan had given me was soaked in sweat and felt like ice against my back. I wanted to sink to the floor and not get up for a few hours. "I don't know. I don't know if I'm a smoke eater. I don't know where to go. I don't know what's real and true any more."

"I'll tell you what's real and true," Tamerica said. "Everybody always wants to talk about compromise and shades of gray. Everybody wants to talk about how it's not about us versus them or choosing a side, that we can all meet in the middle. The truth is that's bullshit. Because the other side is going to push their line as far as they can and they don't care who it slices in half. This, right here and right now, is your time. This is where you decide what you believe in. So what's it going to be?"

I closed my eyes and felt the burn of exhaustion in my eyelids. After a few breaths, I looked up at her and knew deep in my bones and guts and everything in between that I'd made the right choice when I said, "Sink or swim."

CHAPTER 16

The next morning Brannigan had me put on the power suit. I sleepily slid into it before riding out with the smoke eaters to search the immediate vicinity for Nusies. We ran into a pair of Wyverns digging through a wrecked candy store, but they went down without much of a fight. I didn't even get out of the truck.

We headed back to the Field and helped everyone gather their belongings. Food and water were the priority and if anyone wanted to bring anything else, they had to be able to carry it in their own two hands. Lot had designed a series of large metal hover carts that attached to the back of Cannon 15 like train cars. They looked like floating apocalyptic paddy wagons to me, but they were roomy inside and had seats, seat belts, and plenty of safety bars. Lot had been thorough.

Tamerica was nervous. I'd pass her while carrying packages of water pouches and she would be pacing back and forth in front of the truck. She didn't believe Calhoun had just decided to leave us alone. She asked me what our protocol had been in the Army and I told her if they weren't going full force at us and trying to get in, they were probably long gone. But I added the caveat of that being the case pre-dragon-riding. They could still be close. But we'd run out of time and the Nusies' assumed absence had to be good enough while Tamerica's people loaded onto the metal cars.

The sun was rising over Wrigley Field as I climbed into the truck beside Brannigan. I watched the stadium disappear behind us, saying, low enough the old man couldn't hear, "Go Cubs."

Brannigan turned to me. "What you say?"

"Nothing."

He looked to make sure Tamerica wasn't paying attention. "Hey, just between you and me, in your humblest opinion, is this rescue mission a dead end?"

"Only if we don't try," I said.

Brannigan nodded and leaned back, seemingly satisfied.

I didn't mention that I was still scared of getting eaten, burned, or shot. But I'd read somewhere a long time ago that bravery was doing what needed to be done even when you were afraid.

"What's your deal with Captain Jendal anyway," I said.

Afu, across from me, laughed.

Brannigan glared at the big Samoan, then rubbed at his wrinkled face. "There is no deal."

Afu leaned forward. "Remember that time we broke into Cedar Point?"

The truck hit a bump.

Brannigan groaned. "Yeah, I remember all of you were popping those holo pills. You may not remember the events correctly. So we don't have to reminisce."

"And you were drunk on whiskey," Tamerica said from up front. "I might have been high, but I remember everything. We got on that carousel and that old song started playing. Me and Afu were getting busy in the cushy chair and you and Naveena were riding horses side by side. I broke away from Afu and saw you both kissing."

"She kissed me!" Brannigan said. He slammed a fist against his armored thigh. "I loved Sherry. I *still* love my wife."

"No one said you didn't," Renfro said.

"I'm old enough to be Naveena's father," Brannigan said. "It's gross. She was inebriated and I slipped. We're good friends. We're *all* good friends. That's why we're going to go get her out of that goddamned base. Can we talk about that instead of one accident I had ten motherfucking years ago?"

I turned to Afu. "He's still got a thing for her, doesn't he?"

"Yup," Afu said.

"Fuck you all," said Brannigan. He crossed his arms and pouted like a four-year-old.

We all laughed.

Every so often, Tamerica would check in with Lot and the people in the back. She scheduled bathroom breaks every couple of hours and made sure the kids and older people were staying hydrated and fed. We were heading to a settlement on the Indiana/Ohio border. Tamerica had family there, and it was supposed to be secluded enough that the Army wouldn't know about it.

I spent my time listening to the smoke eaters talk about old scaly fights and unfathomable situations. I heard about the dragon worshippers in Canada sacrificing young women and how Brannigan and Naveena had tried to stop it, but ended up getting them all kicked out and banned from the country. Renfro suggested that we try to get in contact with the Canucks to help us fight the Nusies but Brannigan answered with a quick, "Fuck that."

It felt like we reached the settlement in no time. Unlike how I was treated outside Brannigan's castle in my spider tank, this town opened its gate immediately when they saw Cannon 15 rolling up. It seemed like this had all been planned for. It was impressive. I've never planned any of my meals let alone a disaster strategy.

This settlement was surrounded by shrubs and trees and vines – a veritable jungle in the middle of the ashes. I guess Tamerica saw me silently oohing and ahhing over it.

"It's fake," she said.

"What?" I looked more closely at the mass of greenery creating a canopy over the truck and all the brown, wooden buildings of the town.

"Half of this shit was taken from a garden center," Tamerica said.

I rolled down the window and poked my head out. I still couldn't tell the difference. It had been a long time since I'd seen anything close to real vegetation outside of my dinner plate, but took her word for it.

People began to trickle out of the buildings and I saw a few climb onto the roofs and swing down from the vines like Tarzan. Then I realized they weren't people at all. The town was full of droids.

"Where the hell did you bring us?" Brannigan said, squeezing beside me to look. "It looks like a goddamn tin man convention out there."

"I thought you said your parents lived here," Renfro said.

"They do," Afu and Tamerica said at the same time.

The droids watched us from where they stood or hung from rooftops and doorways. One of the bots had gotten tangled in fake vines just above a wooden house with a long, steeply pitched roof. It reminded me of ancient Viking houses. When we came to a stop, the droid hanging above us ripped itself from the vines and dropped into a kneeling position. It rose and showed us its green eyes. A smile had been drawn onto its face with what looked like red paint.

"Come on," said Tamerica. She radioed back to Lot and the doors to the hover carts dropped open. People began to file out with their things.

I followed behind Tamerica and Renfro. Brannigan took his time getting out and when I looked back to check on him, he was walking with his arms bent at his sides, looking from side to side as if one of the droids was going to try to tackle him.

I held back until he caught up to me. "What's wrong?"

"I hate droids."

"I've had bad experiences too, but they're just machines. They follow their programming. I say if Tamerica trusts them, we should, too."

Brannigan grumbled and kept walking as the bots moved in closer, curious. I hoped I was right.

Tamerica put a hand against the shoulder of the droid with the red-painted smile. "Guys, this is Happy."

"Please come in," Happy said with a flat, emotionless voice. He marched up to the Viking house's front door and pushed it open.

When we entered, a large fire flickered in the center of the room. It was giving off generous waves of heat but no smoke. As we moved around it, the flames looked flat from one angle and I knew it was a hologram.

The inside of the house wasn't what I'd expected. I thought I'd see tables covered in ale mugs and turkey legs lying on plates with a huge bite taken out of them, baskets of bread and axes, horned helmets. Instead, I saw a clean space filled with neatly-made beds and droids pouring water into a pitcher or unpacking a first aid cart.

A large machine zoomed around the corner and stopped in time to bump my armored knees. An old black man's head was sticking out of the top of the contraption. I yelped and jumped back. The head started laughing.

"Best watch yourself before you get run over!"

I stumbled backwards into Brannigan. "What the hell is he?"

"Relax," Brannigan said, pushing me back to stand straight. "This guy I *do* trust. This is Tamerica's father, Carl Williams."

"Chief Brannigan?" Carl said. "I thought you were dead! You look good."

"You don't look half bad yourself, Carl," Brannigan said. "No, I'm still kicking. Just a little miscommunication on my status."

"Is that what you're calling it?" Tamerica said.

"Tammy," Carl snapped. "Respect your elders. And come over and give me a kiss."

She walked over to him and kissed his cheek.

"Chris," Carl said to the man with the red eyes, "you look tired."

Renfro nodded. "I've been driving a long time."

"Go on and grab one of those beds over there."

Renfro gave a mock salute and began removing himself from his power suit.

Carl turned his machine toward the big Samoan next to me. "Afu."

"Hey, Dad."

"Damn it, don't call me that! You sure as hell didn't come

from my loins. Rebecca would have split right open! Hey, where's that Harribow boy at? He owes me a bag of jellybeans."

Tamerica shook her head. Renfro and Afu looked away.

"Aw shit," Brannigan said. "I forgot about Harribow. What happened?"

Tamerica shrugged. "Lindwyrm emerged right under him about two months ago. He didn't make it."

"Lord," Carl said. "He was a good kid."

Everyone was quiet for a second. I assumed Harribow was another smoke eater. Carl shook away his grief and turned his attention to me.

"And who's this? New recruit?"

"This is Gilly." Tamerica winced. "Sorry, I mean, Guillermo Contreras. He's with us now."

"Gilly?" Carl said. "You good at swimming or something?"

"It's a family nickname, sir," I said.

"Sir?" Carl widened his eyes, tightened his chin. He looked impressed. "Well, you have to be the most polite young man I've encountered in a long time. You military?"

"He used to be," Brannigan said. "He's going to help us break into the Nusie base in Ohio."

"They've got Naveena," Tamerica said.

"That Indian girl Chief is sweet on?" Carl asked.

"I'm not sweet on her!" Brannigan's voice filled the long house.

"Oh, my goodness," an older black woman gasped as she'd come around the corner, a hand held to her mouth. She wore a cream-colored dress that reached down to a pair of Jesson hightops.

"Mama," Tamerica said. The two women ran to each other and hugged. But Tamerica's mother had her eyes on Brannigan.

"You…" She broke away from Tamerica's arms and took three heavy steps toward the old man.

"Hello, Mrs Williams," Brannigan said. The way he looked at the floor suggested he knew he should have said more… or better.

"You've been alive this whole time?"

"Yes," Brannigan said.

"You've caused my baby more heartache than I've ever seen." Tamerica's mother said. Her eyes glistened, but there was more anger there than sadness. "I've hated you for a long time."

"Rebecca!" Carl said from his machine. "That ain't no way to talk to people who've been dead. Or at least those who need our help. We thought Chief got blown up. Now he isn't. So what?"

"So what?" Rebecca clenched her fists.

"It's okay, Mama." Tamerica grabbed her mother's hands and held them to her chest. "I forgive him. You should, too. He shouldn't have done it, but he did it for his family. And either way, he's here now and he's going to help."

"Help with what?" Rebecca asked. Her eyebrows tensed as she looked at each of us one by one, skipping over Brannigan.

"We're going to take on the New US Army," Brannigan said.

"Lord Jesus help us." Rebecca pulled her hands away from her daughter and held them to her own chest. "All of you must be crazy."

"Fed up, is more like it," Renfro said. "All of us are done hiding."

"It's the right thing to do, Mama," Afu said. This guy really enjoyed having in-laws.

Rebecca looked at Afu and sighed. "Afu, oh, baby. It's good to see you. Come on, all of you, let's get you fed and bed."

The droids brought us plates of tofu sausages and bags of corn chips that had expired a decade before. No one complained. Out on the road, it was a meal fit for a king. The rest of Tamerica's people were having their own dinners in their designated houses, but Lot joined us in the Williams place. Carl told us how he, Rebecca and the Ash Kickers had ransacked the droid factory in Parthenon City when things went south. They drove out to the spot we were in now and set up a settlement.

"If it hadn't been for these metal men," Carl said, "we would have died already."

"Don't say that!" Rebecca smacked the top of his machine, which Brannigan had told me was called a psyroll. Brannigan had been forced to use the same one after he'd fallen from the back of a Behemoth. After the chief had healed up, he'd given it to Tamerica's father, who'd been using an old wheelchair before that. The psyroll connected to the user's spinal cord and all Carl had to do was think of going forward, backward, or spin if that's what he wanted to do.

After we ate, the droids picked up our plates and marched in a line to the kitchen. I stood, ready to lie down and sleep for as long as the smoke eaters would let me.

"Where are you going?" Rebecca asked. "We still have dessert."

I sat but blinked at her in confusion.

Happy, the droid, came out with a large plate stacked

with a chocolate cake, smeared all over with dark brown icing.

"Is that real?" I said. My mouth was watering.

"Sure is," Carl said. "We've been saving the chocolate for a special occasion. We figured if you all were going to get your asses blown off, this was as good a time as any."

"Carl!" Rebecca said. "Language."

"I can say ass all I want. It's in the Bible."

"That's a different kind of ass."

"See! Now you said it too."

Rebecca flushed and ran out of the room, mumbling something about getting everyone fresh plates.

We all laughed.

I had two slices of that cake and there was still a third of it left after everyone had eaten their fill. I couldn't remember the last time I'd had actual, real chocolate. Or a cake for that matter. I was happy to consider it a late birthday dessert.

The year before, after our day by the lake, Reynolds had come by my pallet and lit a match. She whispered me a quick happy birthday song while everyone else was asleep. I must have mentioned it to her on the way back from the water. It was small kindnesses like that that made it hard for me to hate her. What was it going to take to wake her up? Maybe she was too far gone. Drowned in the big green camo ocean.

All of the smoke eaters picked a bed in the Williams house. Brannigan of course plopped onto the one beside me. As we lay there, Happy did a dance and played some old hip hop song from a million years ago. He kept saying, "Check it, check it," as he would pop and lock his arms and legs, and then he'd turn his head, brandishing that creepy red smile. I couldn't help but think of Sergeant 5-90, and how much worse my old superior would have been if he'd had an eternal grin.

Happy bowed and left the room.

Renfro was snoring, so we had to whisper over him.

"I'm working on a reverse patch," Lot said. "I think we'll be able to call Yolanda sometime tomorrow if it goes right. Whether she thinks it's safe to answer is a different story."

"All right," said Tamerica. "You keep working on that. See if you can get me a map of our old headquarters. Afu and I will come up with a plan on infiltrating the base."

"And what about me?" Brannigan said.

Tamerica smiled, savoring whatever she was about to say. "You're going to train the rookie."

Brannigan pressed his pillow over his face. "This serves me right, doesn't it?"

"Wait," I said, "I'm going to get real smoke eater training?"

"Who else, man?" Afu had grabbed another plate of cake and was talking with his mouth full as he lay on his side in the bed.

"And what am I supposed to train him with?" Brannigan said. "We can't go chopping all your parents' droids apart. Fun as that would be, anyone could do that. I can show him power jumping, but that's it. We don't have anything that will get him ready for what we're up against."

Tamerica's smile hadn't wavered. "When we left Parthenon City with all the droids and supplies, something told me to bring one more thing. Renfro said I was crazy or just sentimental. But now I'm glad I brought it."

"What is it?" I asked.

"You'll see."

CHAPTER 17

Happy dug his metal feet into the dirt as he shoved open the rusty shed door. I stood in my power suit beside Brannigan, waiting to see what was waiting for me inside. We were at least a hundred yards away from town and everyone had been told to give us space to train. We couldn't afford anyone getting hurt.

But I wondered where that left me.

I tapped Brannigan with my elbow. "Is there some way we can find out if I'm an actual smoke eater before we go through all this?"

"Kid, when I was recruited, they put me in a glass room and filled it with dragon smoke. When I was chief, we implemented the same test, but back then we had waivers they'd sign and emergency medical on standby in case we'd gotten it wrong. That was then. Now, we don't have that luxury, we don't have the time or a way to test it. You have combat experience. You're willing to fight. That's good enough for me." Brannigan sighed. "We need all the help we can get."

An icy pang rose in my stomach, but I nodded and watched Happy emerge from the shadows, pulling a large trailer holding something covered in a dusty, green tarp. It had no definitive shape, but there was a lot of it.

"This bastard just doesn't die," Brannigan said. He pushed in front of Happy, who backed away while the old man grabbed a corner of the tarp and pulled it free. Lying there was an enormous pile of metal shaped like a dragon. "Say hello to Mecha Scaly."

I took a step back. Even motionless, the thing looked deadly as hell. "Are you kidding me? You want me to fight that thing?"

"What else? You want to go into the wastes and see what we can rustle up? That didn't work too well in the subway. Tamerica is right. This is the best way to train you."

Happy walked up to the metal dragon and petted its side. "Good dragon."

The droid's flat, digital voice caused both me and Brannigan to turn toward him.

"What are you doing?" Brannigan asked the droid.

Happy continued petting the side of Mecha Scaly. Metal on metal, it sounded like a chef sharpening his knives. "Good dragon."

"Quit that!" Brannigan shouted. "Go make a cake or something."

"Mr Williams told me to assist you for your training session," Happy said. Given his name, I thought Carl and Rebecca might have made him sound more cheerful and less like he wished someone would pull his plug.

Brannigan sighed and stomped around to the other side of the dragon. "Fine. Whatever. Just don't get in our way or I'll personally chop your head off."

"Yes, sir," Happy said. The droid took a few steps backward and watched with his arms folded behind him.

"Fucking droids." Rummaging underneath Mecha Scaly, Brannigan banged his armored hands and arms against it, searching for something. "Where are the damn controls?"

"Controls for what?" I asked.

"For the dragon. If you get in a jam and I need to cut the power."

"Pardon me, sir," Happy said from his spot off to the side. "But there are no controls."

"What?" Brannigan said. "Don't tell me there aren't any controls. I fought this thing ten years ago and put all my rookies up against it afterward. There's always been controls. It's a safety thing."

"Unfortunately, sir," Happy said, "when they brought Mecha Scaly here, they were unable to locate its controls. Mr Williams had us repair it as best we could and though the dragon functions admirably, it can only be stopped by the same switch from which it is turned on."

"So you're saying it'll be like fighting a real scaly?" I asked.

"It has been programmed to act like a biological dragon, yes." Happy's smile was starting to piss me off.

Brannigan groaned. "Fuck it. Gilly, we'll have to make do with what we have."

"Don't call–"

"Yeah, yeah," he said. "Family only. Whatever. Listen to me. Sink or swim isn't just a fun phrase. You're going to have to do this the hard way. I'll be here to help if you need it. You'll do fine."

"I'll do fine?"

Brannigan beckoned me over. I shuffled my feet as I walked.

"Let's go over what you have," he said. "You've got a laser sword. That's going to be your bread and butter. Open your pockets."

I did. Brannigan dug into the one on my right leg.

"Ok," he said, holding up the spherical silver ball he'd pulled from the pocket. "This is a–"

"Haymo," I said. "I know."

"Oh? So you've used one?" He mocked the voice of an overly-concerned mother. It would have jolted memories of my own, but my mom had a deep voice, like passing thunder. I wasn't sure what he saw in my face, but the old man suddenly got serious. "Do you know how many seconds you have before this thing slices your hand off?"

I shook my head. "No. I don't. Sorry."

"Don't be sorry. Just listen. I know you're not completely green, but it'll save time if you just shut up and hear what I have to say."

I mimed closing a zipper across my lips. I could taste the metal of my power suit on the glove tips. Some kind of tungsten alloy if I remembered right.

"Now," Brannigan said, "like I was telling you, this is a Haymo grenade. You push the top button here to trigger it. You have ten seconds before the laser propellers come out and then they're going to slice through whatever they come into contact with. Use this only when you know you have a good shot."

He reached into my other pocket and removed a wraith remote. I hadn't even known it was there.

"You won't need this," he said, putting it back. "But keep it on you. Always check your gear when you suit up. Every time. I don't believe in gremlins but I've had shit disappear when I needed it most."

I nodded, even though I didn't think it would be too difficult to keep up with only the two items in my pockets.

"Okay, show me a power jump."

"Wait." I actually looked around to look for anyone else he might have been speaking to. "Right now?"

"Yeah, right now. The button in the left hand. You'll have thirty seconds before you can use it again. I just want to see if you can balance in midair."

As I moved my thumb to the jump button, something caught my attention over Brannigan's shoulder. Happy was making a determined march toward the dragon.

"For your efficiency," the droid said, "I'll engage Mecha Scaly."

Brannigan blinked at me. "Did he just say–"

It took me too many seconds to register what Happy was doing. The droid opened a box behind the dragon's left hind leg and shifted something inside it. A mechanical pop came like a gunshot. In the same instant, Mecha Scaly's eyes began glowing red. Pushing itself onto all fours, the dragon's claws bent the sides of the trailer as it flexed its tail and stretched out the robotic kinks it had been collecting in that shed for the last decade.

Brannigan turned around. "Shit."

Mecha Scaly raised its head and stared for a brief second. It swiveled its attention toward me, then ejected two giant metal wings that had been hidden inside its body, making it look more like an evil jet plane.

The dragon roared. Behind the rows of its metal teeth, at the back of its manufactured throat, was a glowing circle of white-hot flames, surrounding a sphere of holes that looked like a high-pressure shower head.

I braced for Mecha Scaly to breathe fire. I didn't expect jet flames to blast out of the two enormous bulbs at the tips of its wings. The turbines churned and blew like murderous wind. It caused both me and Brannigan to duck and cover our ears.

Then the fire came from the dragon's mouth, a wall of flame rushing toward me.

I flinched, and out of sheer, dumb luck my thumb had already been hovering above the power jump button. The power suit's thrusters took me into the air, soaring above the approaching fire.

It felt like my stomach plopped into my feet and my heart flew into my throat. Below me, I could see the wall of flames, a perfect conical stream of hell. Smoke curled at its edges, rising like it was chasing after me. It couldn't have lasted more than a second, but I followed the flames to Mecha Scaly's mouth. I could see its entire length, all the way to the sharp point of its robotic tail. I didn't realize I was airborne until that moment.

I fell slowly toward the ground. Screaming.

I had no clue where Brannigan was. He could have been inside all that fire, crumbling to ash. Maybe he'd been taken by surprise and didn't dodge the flames in time. It wouldn't seem fair. He'd survived a Phoenix only to be taken out by a mechanical training prop? But I'd heard of plenty of people who died deserving better.

Mecha Scaly shut its mouth with a loud *wham!* I landed on my feet and stumbled to keep standing. The ground below me was scorched. Black char crunched under my boots. There was still no sign of Brannigan.

The metal dragon moved a claw forward. I felt the ground shake, though I couldn't hear anything over the wings' turbines. I engaged my laser sword but stayed still, digging my boots into the ashes. Mecha Scaly moved another claw off the trailer, inching toward me.

Happy gave me a thumbs up.

I cast my radio. "Brannigan? Brannigan? Are you alive?"

His voice came weakly through my helmet. "I'm over here, kid."

Keeping Mecha Scaly in my periphery I dared a glance to my left. Brannigan stood far from me, over by the nearest tree leading into town.

"What are you doing over there?"

"Watching," Brannigan said. "How are you going to learn if I help?"

I raised my laser sword and shook it at the old man. "How am I going to learn anything if I'm dead?"

Mecha Scaly roared. It sounded like crashing cars and static. It broke into a full gallop and charged toward me. Ash and dirt and slushy snow flew into the air in its wake. I froze. The laser sword hung at my side.

"Contreras," Brannigan's voice crackled into my ear. "Attack or get out of its way."

His coaching didn't jolt me into action. My mouth wobbled open and shut, but I couldn't breathe. I stood there like I was glued to the ground, staring at the equivalent of a carnivorous freight train barreling down on me.

"Fucking jump on its back," Brannigan shouted, "Slash at it! Something!"

Mecha Scaly leapt. An image flashed in my mind of the dragon plowing into me, shrapneling bloody pieces of me all over the ground. Brannigan wouldn't even have to dig a grave. The crater left behind would be enough to scoop in my remains. But Mecha Scaly sailed over my head and never touched the ground. Its wing turbines revved faster. It shot into the sky, leaving behind a gust that pushed my helmet crooked and left my mouth agape in confusion. I watched Mecha Scaly fly away, becoming a tiny speck that was soon hidden by clouds.

"Where the fuck did it go?" Brannigan said.

"By the looks of it," I said, "Australia."

"You lost our training prop?"

"I didn't lose anything. It flew away on its own." How the hell was it my fault that Mecha Scaly had grown tired of fighting smoke eaters and wanted to retire to a warmer climate?

Happy walked over with his arms behind his back. "Sir, if I may. Mecha Scaly has been programmed to simulate all forms of dragon combat."

"Looks like it simulated a bon voyage," I said. "Doesn't matter. Fighting it wouldn't have helped us prepare for what we're up against. They ride dragons."

Happy tilted his head to the side. "Your enemy rides dragons?"

"Yeah," I said. "And they shoot laser rifles while doing it. How do you simulate something like that?"

"I can help facilitate that if you would like."

I laughed, but Happy just stared at me with that damned red smile and his yellow eyes. He was serious.

"Quit messing around with that droid and meet me over here," Brannigan said through the radio.

Happy lifted his face to the sky and pointed. "Mecha Scaly is coming back."

I turned but saw only sunshine and fluffy clouds drifting by. "What are you talking about, Happy? There's nothing there."

"I suggest preparing for an aerial attack," Happy said.

"Did you hear me, Guillermo?" Brannigan asked.

"Happy is saying Mecha Scaly is coming back."

From where he stood, Brannigan looked at the sky as he turned in a circle with his arms extended. "I don't see a damn thing. That droid needs its head looked at."

"I will step away now," Happy said, walking backward. "Your power jump is recharged. You may need it."

I shook my head. "It's not coming back. It would have attacked us by now if–"

A sound came from the sky, like a distant chair being dragged over concrete. Where there had been nothing, now I could make out a small shape in the sky. It grew bigger and louder and as it did, I realized it was aiming for me. Mecha Scaly had returned.

"Happy was right," I shouted at Brannigan. "It's coming in hot."

"Oh shit," Brannigan said. "Run!"

I took off in the direction away from town. My laser sword thrummed as I swung my arms. In front of me, bare earth stretched all the way to the horizon. Where was I running? There was nowhere to hide and I couldn't outrun the dragon.

"What do I do?" I shouted.

Mecha Scaly's rusty growl made me pump my legs harder. A rumble followed. A wall of heat pelted against my back. Even in the daylight, I could see the glow of fire lighting the ground ahead of me.

"Power jump," Brannigan said. "Straight up. Do it now."

I hit the button and sailed upward. A stream of fire passed under me and then the dragon sailing on its shiny metal wings. I floated to the ground as Mecha Scaly clomped onto all fours ahead of me, swinging its tail over my head as it turned to see where I'd gone. I rolled and stayed behind it, out of its view.

"Good," Brannigan said. "Stay at its rear and keep it blind to you. Watch the tail. Try to move in and stab its underside."

I was huffing, couldn't get a good breath. Every time I tried to sneak closer, Mecha Scaly would turn and I'd have to move with it. The big tail flicked violently to the side and I squatted into a shuffling run. Stopping between its hind legs, I was close enough to plunge my laser sword into its... well, whatever you call that space on a robo dragon.

But then I saw the door on the back of its leg, the one Happy had used to turn it on. I ripped it open and grabbed the lever. Mecha Scaly roared and lifted its leg, taking me with it. I hung from the lever by one hand.

"Come on, come on!" I pulled and pulled but the switch wouldn't move. I had no leverage.

The dragon bent its neck and moved in to bite me, widening its mouth enough to swallow me whole. I lifted my legs and kicked against its snout. Pain shot up my leg. Mecha Scaly reared back for another bite.

I felt the lever shift... just an inch. A little more and the dragon would be done. If I let go, I'd have to contend with Mecha Scaly face to face. Or it would crush me with a single step. I had no other option.

Again, I swung back to dodge its teeth, but Mecha Scaly stopped short. It wasn't going for a bite. Not when it had easier weapons to use. It opened its mouth and showed me the flickering flames at the back of its throat.

I should have just stabbed it when I had the chance.

The lever in my hand dropped. Mecha Scaly crumpled into a lifeless pile of metal, but I fell along with it. I caught a good look at its giant tail falling toward me before I rolled over and covered my head. The tail smashed into my back, knocking the air from me. I lay there coughing and drooling as Brannigan threw a litany of swear words at me over the radio.

"You had to be a hotshot, didn't you?" he said, when he stood over me. "You couldn't just stab it like I told you, you had to figure out a smarter way to do it. How smart do you feel now?"

"Not... very," I squeaked out.

"Hey, droid," Brannigan said. "Come over here and lift this tail off of Contreras. It's the least you can do for fucking up our training. If I didn't know any better, I'd think you did that on purpose."

"As you wish," Happy said. He squatted and lifted Mecha Scaly's tail enough for me to crawl out.

Brannigan patted me on the back when I got to my feet. "Real dragons aren't going to have off switches. We'll try again tomorrow."

"Great," I said. If he caught my sarcasm he didn't show it.

We started walking toward town, Happy following behind us.

Brannigan looked over his shoulder then got close and whispered, "And I'll make sure this metal bastard isn't a part of it."

When we got back to Cannon 15, ready to doff our power suits, Renfro was suited up and going through the bins and checking equipment. Something was off.

"What's going on?" Brannigan said.

Renfro thumbed toward the long house. "I'll let T tell you."

We left our suits on and walked into the house. Afu and Tamerica were geared up and standing beside Lot as all three gathered around looking up at a floating holographic image of Big Base. At least, I was pretty sure it was Big Base. It was shaped like an octagon and tiny clusters of green soldiers were pictured at various points. Red lines marked entry points. Blue spider tanks were positioned outside every corner. I didn't see any markers for rideable dragons, but how could you map something like that?

Tamerica turned to us as we walked in. "How'd training go?"

"Mecha Scaly lives on," Brannigan said. "Why is Renfro prepping the rig?"

"Because we need it prepped," Tamerica said. "Lot was able to get in touch with Yolanda. The Nusies are up to something. They ordered her and the rest of the propellerheads to prepare a bunch of medical and surgical equipment. She doesn't know what's happening but they're gathering the prisoners and want everything ready by tomorrow morning." Tamerica pointed to the hologram. "She sent us this. It's the most recent image she had of their base, but it's still three months old."

"And it doesn't give us any indication of what's inside," Lot said. He pushed his glasses onto his nose. His long hair fell off his shoulder when he turned to me. "There's only one halfway decent way to get in there."

"What do you mean by 'halfway decent'?" Brannigan asked.

Afu began chewing on his lip, looking from Tamerica to Lot. "It wasn't my idea, by the way."

"You gave me the idea," Tamerica said.

Afu threw up his hands. "I was just remembering a story, wifey!"

"You can save the lover's spat for later," Brannigan said. "What fucked up idea did you guys come up with?"

"Well," Afu said, toeing his boot into the floor. "You remember that time we flew to New Mexico and you got pushed out of Jet-1 and you thought you were going to die, but then the glider kicked in on your suit?"

Brannigan blinked. "What, you guys are going to shove me into the front gate?"

"As much fun as that would be," Tamerica said, showing her teeth in a big smile. "We're going to glide onto the roof."

"It's the only way to do it." Lot nodded.

Brannigan laughed and rubbed his face as if he was trying to wake himself up. "We'd need a plane for that."

"Exactly," Tamerica said.

"I'm done with surprises," Brannigan said. "Just tell me where it is and what we're doing."

"Cedar Point," said Afu. "We thought it was the best place to hide it."

"Hide what?" I asked.

"Jet-1," Renfro walked in. He crossed his arms and stared at the hologram. "We left it fueled. All we have to do is go get it."

"Goddamn," Brannigan said. "It's been sitting there for ten years?" Remind me never to hunt Easter eggs with you sneaky bastards. Chris, that means you're going to have to fly it and that's going to leave us short a smoky."

Renfro nodded. "I know, but I don't see a better way to do this."

"When do we leave?" Brannigan asked.

"Now," said Tamerica.

While they continued to go back and forth, I studied the map floating above my head. I was still thinking about the dragons the soldiers rode. Jet-1 would make a lot of noise over Big Base, even flying at a high altitude the Army would get wise to us dropping in one way or the other, and I was sure Calhoun would use the dragons to guard the sky. Why wouldn't he? Jumping out of a plane would be bad enough. Being snatched out of the air by one of the Nusie scalies was even worse.

"It won't work," I said.

They all turned to me.

"We have to make it work," Tamerica said. "They've got it guarded everywhere else."

"They'll have it guarded in the sky, too," I said.

"What are you thinking, Gilly?" Brannigan asked.

"If this is going to work," I said, "we need the Nusies too busy to notice us. We need a distraction."

"Man, it would be impossible to create a distraction if we're jumping out of a plane," Afu said.

"He's right," said Tamerica. "We'd need someone on the ground and we don't have anyone else."

"Yes." I smiled. "We do."

CHAPTER 18

A haze of mildew emanated throughout Cedar Point.

Tamerica told us they'd hidden Jet-1 by a roller coaster. Renfro parked outside the amusement park grounds, which meant we all had to power jump over a concrete wall. The ash kickers jumped without thinking. Whilst I didn't hesitate as much as I thought I would, I'd been leaning too far forward so on the way up, I gouged out a chunk of rock with my chest plate and missed the top. Renfro had been waiting and caught my hand to pull me the rest of the way over. Brannigan went last and landed into a grumbling walk.

Lot Scynch had come along with us to stay behind in the cannon truck. Once we had Jet-1 in the air, his job was to drive the truck back to the Williams' town, send our planned distraction to Big Base, load everyone up and transport them to Brannigan's castle settlement. It was a big job, but he seemed happy to do it.

Tamerica's dad, Carl, had balked at leaving his home, but finally relented when even Brannigan told him it was better to get as far away from Ohio as possible. If things went awry, the Army would surely find him and Rebecca. If one of us was captured at the base, we could be forced to talk. And I knew enough about Calhoun to know he'd only shown me half the things he would do for information. Everyone has their breaking point.

There inside Cedar Point night was coming on fast and all we had was the turquoise glow of our laser swords to see by. Brannigan was quiet as we neared the park. He didn't even groan. I almost forgot he was there, and that was the first sign of impending doom. The old man usually never shut up.

Everything in the amusement park had a touch of gray to it that I couldn't quite put my finger on. It wasn't just ash, it was a lifelessness that coated everything like a fog. I hadn't seen many other places that had been left to rot like that, while still being able to show a glimpse of the world that used to be. All without being able to enjoy it. The carousel was especially decrepit. The top had fallen over and most of the horses were either bent on their poles or had broken off.

"Hey," Afu said, running up to the damaged ride. "Remember this one, Chief?"

"You motherfuckers took us this way on purpose," Brannigan said.

The others laughed. I didn't. The place had me feeling eerie. If I hadn't known it'd been abandoned since E-Day, I would have been worried a gang of wraiths would rise out of the half-scorched funnel cake stand to kill us.

We moved on. Oscar Mike, as NUSA would say. I kept thinking that my boots were too loud against the ground. It was all I seemed to hear. Army boots had rubber soles. These power suit kicks were all metal. I had no reason to be quiet but I softened my steps anyway. That just made me fall behind, so I ended up being even louder trying to catch up.

The coaster we were headed for lurched into the sky ahead. It was called the Iron Dragon and so much of its track was missing it was a wonder any of it still stood. Just outside the coaster's turnstiles, a large shape stood under the Iron Dragon's shadow, covered by what looked like a large sheet.

"Well," Renfro said. "At least it's still here in one piece." He stopped abruptly. His voice dropped to a whisper. "Stop. Nobody move."

I froze.

Tamerica took a few more steps and turned to look back at Renfro. "What's wrong? You step on your nuts?"

Renfro kept his red eyes on the murky shape just ahead of us. I squinted and tried to make out what he saw that the rest of us couldn't.

"T," Brannigan said. "I'd listen to the guy who can see in the dark."

Tamerica must have realized the joking was over. "What is it, Renfro?"

"All of you be quiet for a second," he said. He held a hand up as if it was some kind of antenna that could help him see better. Despite my hopes, his eyes didn't glow red in the dark. That would have been awesome.

We all stood silent, watching Jet-1, waiting for something to happen. I thought I saw movement on the jet's surface, but when I blinked and looked again it seemed no different. I listened, but all I heard was distant water from the lake and the death knell creaks of old wood and steel beams.

"It's moving," Renfro said.

Brannigan's whisper sounded like he was gasping for air. "What, the jet?"

"Someone beat us to it?" Afu said.

"Shut your damn mouths!" Tamerica curled a fist at us. Somehow I knew if she started swinging Afu would get socked first.

"I mean something is moving under the tarp," Renfro said. "The jet is stone still. Looks like a squid crawled under there and started getting busy with my plane."

"Scaly?" Afu asked.

"Leviathan," Brannigan said. He wasn't asking, he was being cocky, thinking he knew the answer.

Renfro took a cautious step forward. He shook his head. "No. I can't tell much without seeing it out of that tarp, but there are too many... heads? If it's a Leviathan, there are at least three of them under there. And they're moving too in sync, too rhythmic to be more than one scaly. I'm telling you, it looks like a giant octopus."

"Ha," Tamerica whispered to Brannigan. "You even remember the difference between a Wyvern and a Drake?"

"This isn't the time for jokes, Cappie," Brannigan said. "And you don't know what's under that tarp either."

Tamerica stiffened her chin and looked toward Jet-1, where I thought I began to see the swaying shapes Renfro was describing. She guessed. "Behemoth."

"Nah," the other three men said in unison.

"Then all four of you chauvinistic bastards can go pull that tarp off and see for sure," Tamerica said.

"Wait a minute," I said. "I didn't disagree with you."

"You didn't agree either."

Afu showed me a sympathetic pout.

Brannigan groaned and pushed ahead of us, stomping down the path toward Jet-1. "Come on. We need that plane."

I hustled to follow behind him. My body moved before

my mind could talk my sore legs out of it. I blamed Mecha Scaly for the soreness, but it was my damned curiosity that got me going. I'd studied dragons twice as much as I had the smoke eaters. Nothing Renfro had described jumped out at me, and that meant if there *was* something under that tarp, it could be a scaly I'd never heard of before.

That would take some doing.

Reynolds and I used to play this game where we'd have to guess a dragon type in as few characteristics as possible. It was like twenty questions. We'd always end in a draw, and I'd always wonder if she asked for more hints than she really needed, tying the game on purpose. Maybe if she'd been there with me in Cedar Point, she would know the answer.

Tamerica, Afu, and Renfro followed behind me. I looked back and saw Afu and Tamerica holding hands as they clogged along in their big, metal suits. It was both cute and oddly hilarious.

A deep rattle came from underneath the tarp. I skidded to a stop. We were twenty, maybe twenty-five feet from the jet. I could see the rustling shapes Renfro had mentioned. They rose against the tarp briefly then dropped back against the jet. It looked like one of the park's rides, operating silently under a big sheet. But the things moving under there were too imperfect to be mechanical. They confirmed what that rattling, like a thousand broken tambourines, had already told me.

"Hydra," I sputtered.

The others swore under their breath and stopped.

"No way," Tamerica said.

"That's funny, bruh," Afu smiled at me.

"I'm serious," I said. "The rattle and all the heads moving

under the tarp. Only thing that makes sense. Dragon Field Guide Volume Three. Fun Fact section on Mediterranean scalies. Each hydra's throat has a–"

"Man, you read the Fun Facts section?" Afu said.

I blinked at him. "Yeah, didn't you?"

Afu laughed. "It's not a Hydra. That rattling sound make you think that? All you heard was one of the coaster cars moving or something. You have nothing to worry about. Promise. Here, I'll show you."

He broke away from Tamerica's handhold and ran ahead to grab one of the tarp corners.

"Hold up," Tamerica called.

But Afu was already charging back toward us with the tarp corner draped over his shoulder as if he were pulling a spider tank by a rope. He was able to tug off enough of the tarp to uncover the orange brown jet we already knew was under there...

...and three swaying scaly heads at the end of three long, skinny necks. All three visible heads were the size of hover cars and all three were dancing side to side. Its skin was the green white of cheap glow-in-the-dark stickers. All the Hydra heads had only two teeth, but they were huge, too big for their mouths – all of which had underbites.

To someone who hadn't read the Fun Facts section of DFGV3, they might have thought the Hydra was sleeping. Its eyes showed no irises, they looked to be covered in the same scales as the rest of it. But here's one of its tricks: Hydras have no eyelids and their eyes are completely white.

Afu stopped and turned to see how much more tarp he'd have to pull, but it fell the rest of the way, revealing four more dragon heads, for a total of seven, all connected to a slug-like body sticking to the side of Jet-1. As one, the heads rattled in their throats for an instant. The one nearest Afu struck so quickly, I didn't realize it had attacked until it had the big man up in the air, wrapping its neck around his body

"Hydra!" Renfro and Brannigan shouted.

"Shit!" Tamerica ran toward her husband.

The Hydra's teeth grated against Afu's suit, but as soon as it realized it couldn't crack into it, the dragon dropped him from its mouth and squeezed its neck around him like a python. I could see Afu's head poking out of the dragon's coils. He couldn't even scream and his face was turning blue.

The other Hydra heads unlatched from Jet-1 and lowered to the ground to hold itself up. A hydra doesn't have legs. It uses its heads to move over the ground like a speeding storm cloud, and it can do it on as many or as few as it decides. A Hydra was essentially a big tangle of angry mouths and wiggling necks. Now it was slinking toward us.

One head dove and shot across the park pavement. Tamerica jumped over it, then launched higher into the air on her thrusters. She slapped her suit's laser arm and blasted several shots into the top of the dragon head. A gory gash appeared and spurted a puff of gray smoke. A rattle escaped its throat, but the head was dead before it stopped sliding.

The Hydra tried to bolt forward, but the dead appendage slowed it, dragging behind and tripping up the heads the Hydra was using as legs. It fell back onto its body and the remaining six mouths closed in and began chewing through the dead neck. The huge fangs dug into its flesh like a bulldozer shoving through chocolate cake. When the neck was severed, the other heads fought to gobble up what they could.

"Goddamn," Brannigan said. "That's recycling."

Tamerica landed against the neck squeezing Afu. The Hydra heads were busy eating their own detritus, so they didn't notice her placing her laser arm against its flesh. Blood and a splatter of scales flew into Tamerica's face. The neck fell and Afu with it. Just before the other heads snapped at where she'd been standing, Tamerica jumped to the ground and ran over to untangle Afu.

The Hydra was pissed. It rolled up and stumbled forward. I thought it would fall over again, but it saw the opportunity to keep itself upright and snag meal at the same time. It just had to put one of its heads onto Tamerica and Afu.

Brannigan saw the scaly's attempt before it could pull it off. The old man launched into the air and lopped off the attacking head before it could swallow Tamerica and Afu. But the Hydra was just as smart. Another of its pale heads zipped in to catch Brannigan while the other two mouths plowed into the ground. The old man dangled upside down in the Hydra's teeth, while the dragon ground its jaws against Brannigan's suit.

"Come on, kid." Renfro patted his helmet and ran toward the dragon. He placed his laser shots toward the two heads standing on the ground, but the scaly jumped out of the way, tucking its heads – including the one gripping Brannigan – into its body. It rolled off toward a broken-down tilt-a-whirl. Renfro chased after. "Squirrelly bastard!"

I ran over to Tamerica and Afu. White chunks and blood stuck to their suits and helmets. Afu was sitting on the ground and spit out a glob of slime.

"We're fine," Tamerica said. The way she held her husband's head suggested she'd never allow him to move from that spot ever again, but I took her word for it and followed after Renfro.

The Hydra had crawled onto the tilt-a-whirl and balanced on one head. The second swung high in the air, continuing to chew and dodge the slashes of Brannigan's laser sword. The third head bent over Renfro and snarled.

"Get up here, Guillermo," Renfro's voice came through my helmet. "I need you."

My breath caught in my throat. I huffed but couldn't find any inhalation that would calm my nerves. I kept running.

The Hydra swung Brannigan toward the ground. His boot grazed the top of my helmet and then he was back to dangling from the Hydra's full height. It was playing with him. From a hundred feet up, the old man was swearing. Out of everything he was saying, it was the only thing I could understand. He hadn't cast his radio, and his distant shouts went garbled every time the dragon would shake him from side to side.

Renfro tried a few shots, but the Hydra dodged them or switched to balance on the other head. If I had been in Brannigan's place, I would have puked.

"My shots aren't going to work," Renfro said. "Guillermo, you need to get in close and use your sword."

There was no way it could have understood Renfro, but the free head turned and looked down at me as if it knew I'd be the next to make a go at it. The Hydra's scales began to glow with that dim Halloween mask green. The head watching me rose to its tallest. I had to bend my head all the way back to see Brannigan's legs kicking between the dragon's two big teeth. The head hissed, daring me to just try if I thought I was salty enough.

But I just stood there. It was like my problem with sleep paralysis had crept into my waking life.

All the pep talks my Uncle Pedro had given me, the sayings I'd repeat in my head to pump me up and force myself into action, they were all gone. The only thing my mind would give me was an image of my father, standing in front of me, spreading his arms to hug me. I remember the day he'd done it, because it was the only time in my life he ever had. It was the day he'd dropped me off with the platoon in Peoria. The day I signed up. I'd refused to hug him in front of the other soldiers because it seemed weak. I thought it would make me look bad and that they'd give me a hard time about it. If I'd only known they'd do worse for no reason at all. When I shook his hand instead of hugging him, my father had nodded and smiled as if he understood, but as he walked back to his white Wilheimer hover pickup, it looked like he was hunching a bit, as if something invisible was weighing him down.

I didn't want to be there in Cedar Point, standing in front of a dragon. I wanted to be back there in Peoria with my father. If I could just wake up a few years earlier, I'd do things differently.

"Gilly!" Renfro shouted. "I'll distract it. Move in."

"I... I can't." My eyes watered. I was so angry with myself. I wanted to fight, but I couldn't move.

"What do you mean?" Renfro asked. "It's going to kill Brannigan."

I tried to tell him, but my throat tightened. All that came out were croaks and sighs.

The thing about this kind of paralysis, it's sharper than anxiety, more than fear. Those words don't really do it justice. The feeling petrifies and shakes your whole body, and not just the obvious arms and legs. It feels like a parasite digging into your central nervous system and shutting your shit all the way down. And people like me, those who've been smothered by sleep paralysis more than twice, we know it's just a matter of time before it happens while we're awake. And when it does come, there's nothing you can do to stop it.

"Goddamn it!" Renfro jumped at the Hydra. He was aiming for the neck holding Brannigan.

But the head that had been staring at me whipped toward him. It didn't bite, but I don't think it had been trying to. The neck snapped like a whip and the Hydra's head smacked into Renfro. It sent him flying into the Iron Dragon roller coaster. He broke through several support beams before dropping to the ground, out of my sight. The track above creaked once, then imploded in a cloud of dust and metal clanging against itself like a giant wind chime.

The Hydra turned two of its heads toward me. It hopped off the tilt-a-whirl, landing just a few feet away. The pavement shook but I still couldn't move. I was blank. Numb. I knew there was a giant monster coming to eat me, but that only cemented my boots more firmly to the ground.

"Contreras, get down!" Tamerica's voice came through my helmet.

A sliver of light flew over my head – a laser axe. The burning blade dug into the Hydra's body. The dragon roared and fell back, extending all three of its remaining heads toward me. Afu flew over and began chopping into one of its necks with his sword.

Brannigan must have finally realized he hadn't been casting. His shaking voice came through my helmet. "Get the one holding me... for... Chrissakes!"

Afu punched the mouth trying to bite him, then looked up to see which neck to leap onto next.

I felt something grab my arm. I flinched and turned. Tamerica was there at my side. She looked angry but concerned.

"Get out of the way if you can't fight," she said.

She might as well have dropped a nuclear bomb on me. I was devastated. It shook me out of the funk enough for me to stiff-leg it over toward a set of bathrooms with a cartoon hound dog hanging on the wall.

Tamerica stayed just outside the Hydra's strike zone and fired lasers at the closest head. She was trying hard to keep her shots low to avoid hitting Brannigan. She barely grazed the scaly as it swerved out of the way, but Tamerica got the attention she was after. Afu cut into the neck holding Brannigan. The other heads had been going after Tamerica, but sprang back toward Afu. They were too late. The big man severed the neck and Brannigan dropped from the scaly's mouth, landing on the other neck Afu hadn't finished cutting. The weight ripped it the rest of the way off and both old man and dragon head landed onto the pavement.

Two perfectly-aimed lasers sank into the flesh just under the last head's mouth. The Hydra flopped dead to the ground.

Brannigan stomped a boot into one of the head's eyes. "This was supposed to be fucking easy!"

"Where's Renfro?" Afu asked.

I limped over and pointed toward what used to be the Iron Dragon.

They called Renfro's name. Their voices echoed into the debris dust still floating in the air, but he didn't answer.

"We have to go find him." Tamerica ran toward the fallen coaster. "He could be trapped under all that shit."

Brannigan ran to the gate and extended his thermagoggles, scanning the area from left to right. "I don't see his heat signature. There's a bunch of water in there. Basically a small lake. Maybe he fell into it. Did he have a respirator?"

"He couldn't put it on if he was unconscious, Chief." Afu ran after Tamerica. Both of them continued to shout his name, even through the radio.

Someone coughed to my right. He was walking toward us from the path leading from a rise-and-drop ride called the Corkscrew. Renfro was dripping water. "Relax. I'm okay."

I ran over to him. "Renfro. Man, I'm so sorry."

Renfro glared at me for a second then pretended I wasn't there.

Tamerica and Afu ran over to hug Renfro. She squeezed him and grunted out all of her frustration. "I thought you'd... you know."

"Nah," Renfro said. "It'll take a lot more than that."

"You sure you're not hurt," Tamerica stepped back and looked him over.

"That scaly flicked you away like a damn house fly," Afu said.

"You should get out of your suit," Tamerica said, "just so we know there's no internal bleeding or anything."

"I said I'm fine." Renfro walked toward the jet. "If you want to check in on anyone, it should be the rookie over there. Dude turned into a wet noodle. Make sure he's up for this."

Tamerica and Afu looked at me. She sighed.

Brannigan stepped forward and waved them off to

follow Renfro. "I got this. You guys get in the jet. We'll be right behind you."

They moved quickly, as if the old man had saved them from doing something they didn't want to. Brannigan stared at the dead hydra as they walked away. When they were climbing into Jet-1, he spoke.

"What should you have done?"

I swallowed, thinking about it. There were a million things I *should've* done. But like my dad always used to say: shoulda, coulda, and woulda never did *mierda*. "I... guess I should have thrown the Haymo."

"No." Brannigan shook his head. "It had one of us in its mouths pretty much the whole time. That would have been dangerous. But it still would have been better than what you did."

I felt nauseous. I bent over and held myself up with my hands against my thighs. "So, the answer is I should have done *something*."

"See," Brannigan said. "You're smart. So tell me what happened. You've been doing great until now."

I'd been doing great? I felt like I'd been bumbling my way alongside the real smoke eaters the whole time. I'd been severely lucky, probably due to some blessing my family asked for as they died. That's the only reason I still held breath.

"It just..." I stared at the pavement, trying not to think about it again. "It came over me all of a sudden."

"What did? You got diabetes or something?"

"My family," I said. "And I know you'll tell me I should bury it. I've been trying. Sometimes I don't even think about them. But you bury enough long enough it'll eventually spew out. I'm sorry."

Brannigan sucked on his teeth. It was obnoxiously loud. He walked over and patted me on the back. "You going to puke?"

"No."

"You want to?"

"No." I stood up. Breathing felt a little easier.

"You think I bury it?" Brannigan asked.

I turned to look at him. He hadn't shaved in a few days and gray stubble covered everything below his eyes. "You?"

"Yeah. You think I don't see my wife dying every single day? Firefighters and smokies I've seen killed? And there have been a lot. It's like a movie on repeat and life keeps adding more horror scenes to the reel. I'm not judging you. Everybody deals with their shit differently. You can take what I say and use it or you can figure it out yourself. But would you like to know what I do?"

I nodded. Most of the words that came out of Brannigan's mouth were bullshit, but every so often he offered a rough gem.

"I use it," he said. "I take it out on every dragon I come in contact with. Every Nusie for that matter. It's a damn miracle I was in a decent mood the day you showed up at my door."

"How?" I asked. "How do you use it? It always feels like it's using me."

He took a big breath as he thought about it. "Blame them. Put all of that pain on the scalies. Thing is, you wouldn't be wrong to do it. Believe me, I feel justified as hell. Dragons killed your family. Nusies allowed it to happen. If you don't expel that shit inside you, it's going to eat you alive and get one of us killed. Normally, if you were under my command, I'd recommend you get therapy and take some time off, but this isn't a normal situation is it?"

"And I'm not a smoke eater," I mumbled.

"Shut up."

"I mean it. I just showed how I'm not–"

"No, I mean really. Shut up."

I turned and saw Brannigan was staring at the dead Hydra's body. A sharp, wet sucking sound was coming from it, like squids dying on a tile floor.

"How much of that Fun Facts section on the Hydra did you read?" Brannigan asked.

"All of it," I said. "But there wasn't much. Just a paragraph."

Brannigan took a cautious step toward the headless body. "You know, given its name, I thought it would sprout two more heads for every one we cut off. That's what the one from Greek mythology did."

Jet-1's engine turned on. Dark orange lights were piercing through its windows. Renfro turned it toward the long stretch of pavement cutting through the park. It was going to be a tight squeeze. He'd left the hatch open for us, and it looked like it was time to go.

"What the fuck," Brannigan whispered.

The Hydra's body was convulsing, steaming, issuing black sludge from each of its headless stumps.

"We should get on the plane," I said.

"Yeah." Brannigan nodded and took a step back, but he couldn't stop watching the dead dragon.

One of the severed necks exploded. Blood and flesh hit me in the face and somehow found its way into my mouth and nostrils. It tasted like what I would guess a pickled cadaver tasted like.

Another head, from deep within the Hydra's body, pushed out of the same hole where the neck had broken apart. It looked like a monster being birthed. It screeched and shook gunk from its face. A little smaller than the head it had replaced, it was still big enough to be dangerous. It looked down and noticed us. It screeched again.

Brannigan engaged his laser sword. "Guess there's one more for the road."

Five more wet splats came from the Hydra's middle, and five more heads appeared. It was as if the smoke eaters hadn't done anything. The Hydra was back to the way it was when we'd arrived.

"Should," I said, my fingers trembling as I reached for my pocket, "should I use my Haymo grenade now?"

"No," Brannigan said, as the heads moved in to lurch above us. "Run."

"What?"

"Run, goddamn it!" Brannigan turned and bolted for the jet.

I ran after him, but I was clearly aware of the slithering sound behind me, the rasps and snapping teeth. Ahead, Tamerica stood at the edge of Jet-1's hatch, squinting to see what was going on.

"Start the plane!" Brannigan shouted.

The Hydra roared. It no longer sounded like a fledgling scaly, but a full-blown monster intent on murder. Tamerica turned and shouted something toward the front of the plane. When she looked back, I could hear her plainly as she saw what was chasing us. "Oh fuck."

The air *whooshed* behind me. Something heavy struck at the back of my legs. I would have fallen, but I hit my power jump and sailed the rest of the way to the jet's hatch. It was gaining momentum and beginning to roll down the concrete path.

Brannigan was still far behind. The jet was picking up speed. The way it looked, the Hydra would make it to him before he made it to the jet.

"Power jump!" I shouted.

He raised his left arm and hit the button. As he launched into the air, the Hydra's heads moved in to snatch him. It all seemed to happen in slo-mo. Brannigan flew upward. One of the Hydra's many heads had its mouth surrounding him. And then he was out of the way, flying forward toward the jet.

I caught him when he landed against the hatch floor. We quickly fell back while Tamerica closed the door behind us. I could hear the Hydra roaring, as if it was still just beyond that metal door.

I would hear it all the way to Big Base.

CHAPTER 19

We were somewhere over Ohio and that was about the only thing I was sure of after being in the air for the last three hours. Renfro was taking the plane in a shortening spiral, supposedly around the central point of Big Base, but all I saw when I looked out the window was darkness and maybe the odd cloud.

A flash of lightning.

I tapped my forehead against the glass. A question kept running through my mind: What the fuck was I thinking?

"Quit it, you'll get grease on the glass," Brannigan said beside me. He looked out the window. "This motherfucker better hurry up."

The back of Jet 1 was just a big cavity, bare except for the cushionless, metal seats lining the side of the cabin. It was more military grade than first class commercial. Neon orange steel. Our power suits were soft enough in the backside, but it was the seat's damn angle that made you fidget. You couldn't get comfortable.

"Fuel is getting low," Renfro said. "We need to decide if we're doing this, with or without Guillermo's brainchild."

"Why'd you have to say that in the weirdest way possible?" Brannigan asked.

"We're doing it one way or another," Tamerica said.

"I know, I know," Renfro said. He kept one hand on the plane controls and rubbed at his eyes. "I'm just saying, we need to know *when* we should move in. You know, like a now or never time marker."

"How much longer can we keep flying?" Afu asked. The seatbelt across his chest looked so tiny.

"Maybe another hour," Renfro said. "Maybe. We're going to have to ditch it at this point."

Everyone looked away from each other and listened to the air flowing outside the plane.

"I'm sure they'll call us any minute," I said.

"Hell, I didn't even see if Lot made it out of there," said Brannigan. "The Hydra could have snagged him and we're waiting around up here for nothing."

"That's not funny," I said.

The old man bobbed his head slowly. "It wasn't a joke."

"The point remains," Renfro said. "How much longer?"

Tamerica tapped her armored fingers against her suit's knee. "Ten more minutes. Then we jump. Sink or swim."

Renfro and Afu nodded. I did as well, but I felt horrible. Once again the odd man out, the young punk who knew nothing. I thought I'd come up with a good idea. Maybe it could have been. The way it was looking, I would never know for sure.

What was I thinking?

Brannigan cleared his throat. "And if Contreras is right and those dragon-riding bastards are in the sky trying to pick us off?"

"Then we shoot and slice our way down," Tamerica said.

Brannigan frowned and looked at me. I shrugged. What else could we do?

Yolanda, according to what they'd all been telling me, knew every single piece of equipment a smoke eater or propellerhead would use. She'd designed most of it. Besides that, she had extensive medical knowledge, due to having a doctor mother who kept old textbooks in the house, and being a little girl with insomnia who was determined to read them. She was the one who created Ieiunium Curate, which healed thousands of people, and... subsequently caused everyone who'd received the dragon blood to burst into flames if the Phoenix was near.

Well, if what she'd seen down there in Big Base was enough for her to think a mass medical procedure was happening in the morning, I wasn't going to argue. We all knew the Nusies would eventually do something to Captain Jendal and the other captive smoke eaters. Something permanent.

There was no other choice. It would have really sucked to get eaten or shot in the face with a laser attempting to rescue these people, but I was convinced I'd feel worse if we kicked rocks without even trying.

Another flash of lightning outside the window.

For a second, I thought I saw a dragon gliding out in the clouds next to the jet. It had been made entirely out of electricity. Appearing in one instant and gone in the next. It had to be an illusion. If an electro scaly had really been there – I tried to convince myself – I would have seen it even after the lightning subsided. Besides, there was no such thing.

I turned from the window feeling sick. "Are we really going to jump through storm clouds?"

"A real smoke eater wouldn't say that." Brannigan slapped the back of his armored fingers against my suit.

I opened my mouth to agree. But then Tamerica's holoreader rang.

Lot's holographic head appeared. "If I got my numbers right, they should be flying with you now."

"You always get your numbers right." Tamerica turned to her pilot. "Renfro, do you see them."

"Yeah, I see them now," Renfro said.

"What?" I unbuckled my belt and wide-legged it to the cockpit. "They're really here?"

"You're not supposed to unbuckle," Afu said.

"Oh, shove it," Brannigan said. "It's the apocalypse. Who gives a shit?"

I leaned in behind Renfro's seat, searching the dark through the window. I was looking for them, but then I remembered Renfro was the only one who had any chance of seeing anything. "Where?"

Renfro pointed toward the left. "I got 'em, kid. They're just over there. Looks like your plan might work after all."

"Yeah, well," Brannigan said, trying not to look disappointed, "showing up isn't even half the battle. Let's see if they stick to the plan."

A bolt of lightning lit up the sky ahead of us. The flash reflected off a metal dragon with shiny jet wings. It was flying exactly where Renfro had pointed out to me. Riding on top of the dragon was a stocky droid, whose face was painted with a big, red smile.

"Happy now?" Renfro asked.

I clapped my hands against the back of Renfro's chair. I laughed in two big *ha ha*'s that sounded a little too triumphant. "That's exactly right, man."

"How'd you program them so fast?" Tamerica asked Lot. "Did you connect them?"

"Wasn't time for that." He shook his enormous green glowing head. "He just... agreed to do it."

"You *asked* that droid?" Brannigan said.

"Yeah," Lot's eyelids drooped. "Carl said I should request his help nicely."

"All right, they're diving," Renfro said. He squinted, hiding most of his red eyes. "Hey, uh, Tamerica, did... did your daddy give that droid a laser rifle?"

"What? Why do you say that?" Tamerica sat forward, staring out into the dark sky. "Oh shit."

I imagined Happy raising that rifle as Mecha Scaly pulled them toward the ground, disappearing beneath the thunderclouds. I wondered if we would see the laser shots and fire commingling below. It would be the best way to know where to jump.

"Hello, fellow warriors." Happy's depressing voice crackled through our helmets.

"Oh for fuck's sake." Brannigan struggled with his seat belt, stumbling into a clumsy walk after escaping it. He moved to the back of the plane.

Afu watched him the whole way. "You know that's where we're jumping from, right Chief?"

"Yeah."

"And you want to be first?"

"I need the wind blowing into my face at a hundred miles an hour. It's the only way to drown out that droid's voice!"

"Chief got brave since we saw him last," Afu said, toward the cockpit. "He wants to jump."

"He should," Tamerica said. "He had to escape the Phoenix the same way."

"I don't know what you're talking about," Brannigan

said. "I've always been brave."

"Don't let him fool you, Guillermo," Renfro said, "he was more nervous than you are on his first jump."

"Yeah," Afu said, "New Mexico. Thought he was going to have a heart attack right there mid fall."

I looked at Brannigan. "I believe it."

The others cracked laughs.

Brannigan looked away but he was trying to hide a smile. "I'm the one standing here ready to go while the rest of you are comfy in your seats talking a lot of shit."

"All right, all right." Tamerica unbuckled and got up.

Afu followed behind her and I caboosed the line toward the hatch.

Through the radio, Happy said, "I will begin engaging the enemies. See you soon. Huzzah."

"Oh, sweet Jesus hurry up!" Brannigan yelled toward Renfro.

The pilot laughed and pulled a lever. The hatch began to lower. Air rushed in and filled my ears, pushed at my face. Thin lines of tears leaked out without my permission. I looked out to what I was about to jump into. It looked like a pool of pure nothingness. I didn't see any dragons flying around down there.

"Gilly, listen to me," Tamerica pointed two fingers from me to her eyes. "You have a device on the back of your power suit. When you're clear of the jet, stretch out like you're lying face down."

You mean, like I'm about to hit the earth face-first, I thought.

"You don't have to do anything but point with your head," Afu said.

"And you'll be following behind me," said Tamerica. "Stay close, but don't get kicked in the face."

"Then I guess that means I'm first?" Brannigan said.

"You're not too old to miss the mark are you?" Tamerica smirked.

Brannigan stepped up to the edge of the hatch. The wind was blowing so hard, I was sure it would reach in and take him. He put his back to the sky. "I really hope this is the last time I have to do shit like this."

He spread his arms, reminding me of the crucifixion, and fell backward. Tamerica stepped up next and turned to make sure I was right behind her. My stomach felt like it had wandered back to buckle itself into a seat, but both it and me didn't have a choice in the matter.

Tamerica jumped out as if she was cannonballing into a pool.

Happy's voice broke in. There was screaming and the sound of laser fire behind the droid's words. "Hostiles are returning fire. We took them by surprise. Three dragons have come down from the sky. There are soldiers riding them."

I turned to Afu behind me. He made a circle with his lips.

"I told you guys," I said.

"We should hurry after them yeah?"

"Yeah," I said.

Afu grabbed me in a big bear hug. I started screaming before he launched into the clouds. I couldn't see anything. It was like we'd fallen into an endless well. Afu had to shout into my ear. "Stop screaming. This is a covert mission. Remember?"

I slammed my gums shut. Afu pushed me away gently and what little I could see of him disappeared. The thrusters in my suit kicked in. I began to hover. The air didn't rush against my ears as loudly and I didn't feel like I'd been thrown into a washing machine.

Once I broke through the clouds – which surprisingly felt nothing like cotton balls – I could see Big Base below me.

Lasers of different colors zipped all over the ground. Some flew toward the sky, but only one got close enough to make me flinch. Mecha Scaly was buzzing over soldiers and spider tanks. The Nusies tried to lead it with their shots, but the metal dragon was too fast for them – and apparently much smarter.

Happy was firing his laser like a professional killer, switching the rifle to different hands, spinning his torso around to pop off a difficult shot. All with that damned red smile that seemed to brighten against the glow of Mecha Scaly's flames. Brannigan had been right to be wary. Thank god the droid was on our side.

I spotted Tamerica's suit, flashing green and red lights on the back of her shoulders. I pointed my head toward her to follow. As I did, dragons, real ones, were being ridden to crawl along the side of the base's outer wall, or circling the muddy ground around the outer perimeter. The Lung dragon, and I assumed Reynolds, was zipping through the air after Mecha Scaly. The Lung's enormous wings flapped strenuously as it tried to keep up. When it got close enough, the Lung breathed a cone of fire that grazed the droid dragon's tail.

Brannigan landed on the center of the roof, hovering just before to silence his boots. He caught Tamerica by the forearms and helped her do the same then they turned to watch me. I had been so focused on pointing my body flat like Tamerica had told me to, I didn't remember to pull up to land.

Tamerica caught me by the ankle and lowered me to the roof. The thrusters shut off and she helped me to my feet.

"Thanks," I whispered.

Tamerica nodded and turned when Afu fell hard onto the roof. "I swear."

"What?" Afu whispered.

"Nothing." Tamerica shook her head as she pulled out the holoreader and followed the digital map to a particular spot. "You and Brannigan make a cut right here."

The two men bent over and began sawing into the roof with their laser swords.

"What about me?" I asked. "What do I do?"

"You keep look out."

Another boring job. I huffed and watched the battle below. Things were catching fire and a glow of orange rose up, but I didn't want to look over the edge. Instead I looked up, where I saw Jet-1 making a pass.

"Y'all make it?" Renfro's voice came through my helmet.

"We're good," Tamerica said. "Get above cover. You're too low."

"Had to at least see what was happening down–"

Happy's voice cut in. "There is a new development. Doors have opened and dragons are coming out. They all have riders. My initial count is ten of them. Will report more."

Everyone on the roof stopped and looked at each other.

"Did that droid just say ten?" Brannigan asked.

"Ten more," I said.

"*Don't stop.*" Tamerica whispered, swishing her finger toward the nearly finished hole in the roof.

Brannigan and Afu hunkered down and moved a little faster, if sloppier. Chunks of burnt metal curled up like snakes escaping hell.

After a few short gasps, I forced myself to take a full breath and moved toward the edge of the roof. I slowed to a creep when I saw a neon spotlight coating a Nusie lying just outside the base gate. A look of horror on his face: eyes huge and sunken, lips wide and wormy. The blood had misted his face. His torso was bloody. Arterial blood, Reynolds used to point out. Contents under pressure. The soldier had been bitten or blown in half at the belly button.

I couldn't see Happy's rifle doing so much damage. Besides, there were no scorch marks. Even if Mecha Scaly hadn't been going damn near Mach 1 without landing, I didn't see the droid dragon biting someone in half.

I took a step closer to the edge.

The ground shook just under me. A snarl rippled through the air and drew a twinge up my back. A dark shape shot into the air to my right. Then another on the left. And another. Happy had mentioned doors. They must have been right under me. I found myself counting each fleeing dragon and got to nine.

I waited. Took a step. Maybe Happy had counted wrong. It didn't seem possible a walking calculator could foul that up, but–

A dragon rose above the edge in front of me. I squatted and hid. The scaly faced out, so I got a good look at the dragon's rider. Calhoun rode atop a tactical black saddle that had plenty of pockets and straps to hold everything a modern soldier could ask for. Calhoun was not wanting in killing devices. All his saddle was missing was a cup holder. The red Fafnir looked from left to right as Calhoun shifted his own head in the same motion. It looked like he was controlling the scaly with his mind. With a scratchy roar, the Fafnir leapt into the air and was soon spiraling alongside the other dragons.

They were circling just below Jet-1.

"Chris." Tamerica didn't try to whisper this time.

"I'll see you all in a bit."

"No, you've got company. Dragons right under the jet. You need to eject."

"Shit."

A continuous yellow beam shot from the underside of Jet-1's nose, toward a dragon with a very long, spiky tail. The laser made it a *short*, spiky tail. The scaly shrieked and dove into the side of Jet-1. Renfro tried to follow with the laser, but he wasn't fast enough. The other dragons, led by their riders, followed. It looked like a pack of airborne piranha making a kill.

"Get out of there!" Tamerica screamed.

"I'm on my way," Renfro's voice sounded so calm.

We all saw the fire build before it left any throats. It was hard to miss in the dark. Like an expected chain reaction, the scalies all breathed fire as one. Some didn't even stop chewing at the side of the plane while they did.

There was no way Renfro could have made it out.

The plane exploded.

I heard screaming. I thought it was Tamerica, but she stumbled in front of me to watch the bits of flaming jet fall from the sky. She said nothing. Afu beat a fist against his chest and wailed something I didn't understand while the light from the explosion highlighted the streaming tears on his cheeks.

The dragons scattered when the plane blew, but none of them sustained injuries. All ten of them were flying just fine. A couple of the smaller ones attacked any random pieces of airplane they came across as they dropped back down.

"We need to get inside before they see us," Brannigan said.

Tamerica rushed over to the hole they'd been cutting. She stomped on it and caused the metal to drop through. I turned back and watched the sky. I was trying to see if Renfro had gotten out, just in the nick of time. That was a smoke eater's thing.

But there was no sign of him.

Tamerica grabbed my arm and led me to the hole. She didn't have to push me.

I jumped right in.

CHAPTER 20

"Move!" Tamerica whispered as she dropped into the hall behind me.

Afu and Brannigan ran down the hall. The wall to our right was glossy metal. To our left, glass separated us from another hallway, where I expected to see soldiers running toward the fight. There were only blinking lights and another metal wall.

Tamerica had the holoreader out, the map of the base floating in front of her face. "There should be a right turn up ahead. Take it."

There indeed was a right turn up ahead. Two Nusies rushed around it and were just as surprised as us. The soldiers raised their rifles.

Afu made a short, scared wail and grabbed the Nusies by the heads, smashing them together. The soldiers dropped to the ground atop of each other. The big man blinked and looked down at the bodies as if he hadn't realized what he'd done.

Brannigan ran up and looked at the Nusies around Afu's huge arm. "Damn. I thought that kind of thing only happened in movies. They're out of commission."

Afu looked at his hands and then at the two on the ground. "Are they dead? Check their pulses!"

"I'm not getting out of my suit for any Nusie," Brannigan said.

"They're breathing." Tamerica pushed past Afu and stepped over the Nusies. She put the holoreader into her pocket and raised her left arm. "Come on."

We followed after Tamerica.

"What's she going to do?" Brannigan asked under his breath. "Make 'em slip on some foam?"

If any townsperson heard Brannigan cracking jokes at a time like that, they would have thought he'd gone insane. But at least he wasn't saying some of the dark things rushing through my mind. They were horrible things: Renfro could see in the dark, but he couldn't see that fiery death coming.

What the hell was wrong with my mind? I was a good person. Good people didn't think those kinds of things, did they? I was beginning to understand why Brannigan was how he was. He battled his demons in his own way, a way he thought worked. Seeing death consistently, not being able to process it properly, it would make anyone crack a little. But grief couldn't keep up with a smoke eater.

Around the corner and a little farther down, the hall widened into a big room. A black woman sat in a chair, sprawled out on a desk in front of floating holographic screens that showed several tabs stacked on each other, each with a different person's name.

"Yolanda?" Tamerica stepped toward her with a hand out.

The woman didn't move. Her hair was soaked in sweat.

"Yo-yo?" Brannigan tried.

Nothing.

This is too much to take, I thought. Even for someone like Brannigan.

Tamerica put her armored hand on Yolanda's shoulder.

The propellerhead jerked and sat up straight, a smear of saliva beside her mouth. "I'm sorry. I'm sorry. I'm awake."

"Yolanda, it's us." Tamerica grabbed Yolanda's other shoulder and turned her to face us.

"We thought you were dead," Afu said.

"Oh my gosh." Yolanda blinked at each of us. "It's you. I thought… I thought…"

"It's okay." Tamerica kept her hands on the propellerhead's shoulders. "Just relax."

"They don't let me sleep. I know I should have run or hid, but when they all left to see what was attacking, I couldn't help myself. I had to grab some sleep." She looked like she hadn't slept in a month. Her eyes were sunken and her lips were dry. "I should have known it was you guys attacking."

"Well," Brannigan rolled his eyes, "technically it wasn't us. We got Mecha Scaly out there giving the Nusies some hell."

"And a droid riding it," I said.

"What?" Yolanda blinked and stared off as if she was from another planet.

"Don't worry about it. We're going to get you out and somewhere safe." Tamerica looked back at me, worry plastered on her face. "Somehow."

How *were* we going to make it back without Jet-1?

"Where's Naveena?" Brannigan asked.

"She…" Yolanda yawned and dried the side of her mouth with the back of her hand. "Naveena?"

"Yeah," Afu said. "And the other smoke eaters. You said the Nusies were going to do something to them. Medical equipment?"

Yolanda sat there quietly for a moment, then her eyes

got wide and she gasped. She stood quickly, but then wobbled back into the chair. "What time is it?"

I looked at the floating screens at the desk and told her. "Ten fifteen."

"Not too late then." Yolanda relaxed a bit into the chair. She looked at me. "Is that Harribow?"

"Contreras," Tamerica said. "New guy. Now where are Naveena and the others?"

"Downstairs," Yolanda said. "Sub Level Three."

"Sub Level Three?" Brannigan said. "Like a basement?"

"A third basement," Yolanda said. "They built more stories below ground."

Tamerica sighed. "Of course they did. Yolanda, where can we hide you until we get back?"

Yolanda shook her head, about to cry. "There is nowhere to hide in here."

"Not even a broom closet?" Afu said.

Yolanda blinked at the big man. "They have tiny, wheeled droids that do the cleaning. Everyone knows that."

Brannigan grunted. "I'll stay here with her."

"We're going to need you, Chief," Tamerica said. "Yolanda will be okay."

"I can do it," I said. Shoutout to my Catholic upbringing. I felt like I had to pay a penance for locking up at the amusement park.

"No." Brannigan nodded his head at me, as if he was finalizing a decision. "If a group of them come in here, it'll be better for me to greet them. I don't want you getting shot. Or worse."

"What's worse than getting shot?" My voice cracked.

"You freezing up and getting captured and blabbing your mouth," Brannigan said.

"Are you okay coming with us, Contreras?" Tamerica said. "Can you handle yourself?"

Fuck no I couldn't. But I answered, "Uh, yeah. Yeah, sure."

Yolanda dropped her head back to the desk and mumbled against the surface. "I can stay here by myself. I just need a nap."

Tamerica looked from me to Brannigan, then huffed. "Yolanda, how do we get to the third sublevel?"

"Oh," Yolanda said. "That's easy. You take the elevators."

Yolanda's sleepy directions were flawed, but we found the lift she'd described. It was plain, dark-silver metal with a keypad to the right of the doors.

Afu stepped up to the pad, finger ready, but stopped himself short. "Damn. What was that code again?"

"Eight, six, seven, five," I said.

"Thanks." Afu tapped the buttons gently. "How'd you remember that?"

"I don't know," I said. "The sequence just has a musical quality to it."

The elevator came. We all squeezed into it. I was shoved against the back corner as Tamerica and Afu kept trying to move their arms and legs to find a comfortable stance. The only way this could have been more ridiculous is if terrible music had been pumping through a speaker above us.

Tamerica stretched her arm to hit a blue button labeled "S3" and the elevator shifted, going down.

"Brannigan," Tamerica said into her helmet, "we're in the elevator."

The Chief's voice came through but it was choppy and drowned in static.

Tamerica craned her head toward me and Afu. "Did you guys get anything out of that."

I tried to shake my head but, seeing as I'd been squished in, my helmet hit each side of the corner. I never thought of myself as claustrophobic, but I guess it's never too late.

"Radio signal must be blocked," Afu said. "Yolanda didn't say how deep this was."

Groaning, Tamerica slammed her elbow into the elevator wall. "Okay. Okay, okay."

"Okay?" Afu's eyebrows met.

She shushed him. "We don't know what's going to be on the other side of those doors when we get there, so this is what I want: Afu you go right, Contreras you go left. I'll lay down some fire to give you cover."

"And who's going to cover you, babe?" Afu asked.

"It's not the time to be calling me babe," Tamerica said.

She never gave him an answer about her cover. The elevator dinged. The doors slid open.

Sub Level Three was only a few notches of above pitch black. There were lights in the ceiling but they'd been turned down to a candle light luminescence. A hallway lay in front of us and seemed to go on forever. Something didn't feel right, but I put it off on the lack of electrical buzzes or distant battle sounds. It was quiet as a grave and just as deep.

"What the hell is this place?" Afu whispered.

"Stick to the plan," Tamerica said. "Afu go right, Contreras take the left."

"I thought you said I was going left," the big man said.

"I know what I said." Tamerica stepped out of the elevator. She pointed the laser arm to each side as she crossed one boot in front of the other. "Come on."

The sublevel hall was similar to the one a few stories above in one way. We were enclosed at each side by a long wall of glass. Something was on the other side but it was too dark to see what.

"I'm not gonna be able to follow your orders, babe," Afu said, still whispering. "There *is* no left or right."

Tamerica pulled out her holoreader map. When she did, the device's glow illuminated what looked to be a large reptilian eye on the other side of the glass beside me. I stumbled backward.

Afu caught me. "Careful there, man. There's only so much room in here."

"There's no sublevel anywhere on this map, let alone a third one." Tamerica had been too focused on the map to notice what had happened. Afu was... well, just Afu. They hadn't seen the eye. But I had.

I pointed toward the glass. "There's something in there."

"In where?" Tamerica put down her holoreader and looked at the darkened glass around us.

I pointed again to show her.

She held up the holoreader and turned on its flashlight. Her steps sounded like gunshots against the floor as she got closer. Her breath fogged the glass. She squinted to peer through it. With a sigh, she turned to me. "I don't see anything. Just relax, man. We're all jumpy. Let's just keep moving."

I was sure I'd seen it, but I hadn't been able to rely on my own senses for a few days, so I followed Tamerica and her husband deeper into Sub Level Three. Ahead, a red light glowed like a cigarette in the dark. I jolted slightly and stayed back, but as I stared at the red light, I realized it was digital and not biological. Maybe Tamerica had been right. Maybe I was just jumpy.

Tamerica stepped up to the red light and pressed an armored hand against a flat surface. At each side of her, the hallway split into a T-shape. "Told you, *babe*. Left and right. It splits here."

It did. But that made me feel worse. I'd be walking in the dark by myself.

"What's that in front of us?" I asked.

"A door," Tamerica said. "Or a gate. Something. Big space on the other side, I think. Feels like it. Might be where they hold–"

The elevator dinged behind us. When it opened, multiple armored bodies poured out. One of them punched something against the wall and turned the overhead lights bright as day. I flinched and covered my eyes. A group of Nusies stood at the end of the hall. They had rifles and tactical masks.

As bad as it was to see them, there was something worse. I had been right about seeing something behind the glass.

Dragons. There were at least six enclosures at each side of the hall. And when the lights turned brighter, the scalies lost their shit. A Jabberwock slapped flammable, black oil against its cage. A two headed Wyvern scratched at the glass with one of its huge talon-like feet. Flames pelted the glass from the throats of Drakes and Lindwyrms. A Popper slammed its head against the glass. It didn't break, but everyone in that hall could feel the vibration. Everyone tensed, expecting them all to come crashing out.

The Nusies turned to us, but they didn't give us any commands. They just raised their rifles.

"Left, right, go!" Tamerica shouted.

I picked a direction and ran for it. I forgot which way Tamerica had told me to go. Was it left or right? Which one had I taken? It didn't seem to matter. Afu was barreling the other way and Tamerica was doing her best to follow him.

The hallway lit up like Chinese New Year as the Nusies fired. The air filled with a light haze of laser discharge. Tamerica and Afu had gotten out of the way in time, but one of the lasers struck Tamerica in the side of the helmet, catching her hair on fire. She slapped a hand against it until the flames were gone.

"You motherfuckers!" Lasers spit from a barrel in Tamerica's arm. None of her shots struck the soldiers, and I wondered if she had purposely missed them.

I quickly realized she had. Her lasers bounced up and down the hall, striking each side of the glass holding the dragons. Every inch of the glass along the hallway shattered.

The scalies tore from their cages. They'd been watching hungrily. Most of them had already been attacking the glass, so when it was no longer there, their oil and flames and teeth engulfed the Nusies. They didn't have time to turn their rifles.

A Blood Drake with crimson eyes and scales took a soldier into its mouth. The Nusie squirmed and screamed until the Drake smoked him like a brisket in a furnace. He quit moving, and the scaly bit down, causing his roasted arms and legs to drop to the floor, where a trio of baby Wyverns dug into the scraps.

A Jabberwock, dripping black oil and standing on its two, webbed feet, wrapped itself around two Nusies. It spewed oil from its rat-like mouth, grunting, *"Ooh, oooh, unnngh!"*

I didn't see what the Jabberwock did next. The hall began to fill with fire and smoke and flashes of electricity, lasers and blood, flapping wings and twisting tails, all accompanied by human and dragon screams that conjoined into one hellish outcry. I'd stayed to watch all of this, peeking around the corner, because my legs were stuck to the ground, and hell, it's not something you see every day.

But I should have known the scalies weren't going to stay in that hallway.

Green, glowing eyes shone behind the smoke. A skeletal dragon head broke through, followed by a long, leathery neck. It was a Jersey Devil. It stepped out on two big claws, standing upright, with its winged, almost human-like arms tucked against its side. It saw me and began to spew out even more dark smoke from its nostrils. There was immense pressure behind the smoke, and it quickly covered the Jersey from sight. The thick smoke was its main defense... and its primary attack. Jerseys liked their prey blind.

If I got even a whiff of the Jersey's smoke, I'd asphyxiate and drop to the ground while it ate me in my death throes. I pried my boots from the spot and bolted down the hall. My helmet's thermagoggles helped me see a little, but I still bumped into blurry neon objects in the way. I was going too fast to tell if it had been a Nusie or a psyroll I'd dodged. Everything was blobs of orange and purple. But I needed speed more than sight. Hell, I would have used my power jump if I thought it could propel me forward.

The Jersey growled and it sounded so close I thought I could feel its breath on my neck. I yelped and tried to run faster. A door on the left opened at my passing. I twisted and charged through.

When this new room's overhead lights snapped on, tiny clouds of black smoke floated at the door behind me as it sliced shut. I backed away. Heavy clawsteps beat against the floor just on the other side of the sliding door. I saw no way to lock it, and I sure as shit didn't want to get too close to the motion sensor.

The door would open when the Jersey got close enough. I didn't want to be standing there when it did. I turned and faced some kind of science lab. A large case stood in the middle of the room. Most of it was metal, but the front was glass so I could see what was inside. Orange and purple lights illuminated what was on display: a power suit.

I stepped closer.

This armor was different from the kind I was wearing. This suit was bigger, bulkier. The metal was matte black and the glowing tips at the boots and elbows were red. Additional red lights had been fixed to the tops of the shoulders. The right arm had a huge attachment around the wrist and forearm.

"Gnarly," I whispered.

Behind me, the lab door slid open. I flinched, backing into a desk and smashing my helmet through floating holographic qwerty keys. Yolanda's holographic head appeared and began to speak.

A hungry screech came from the open door.

I got low and dove behind a solid work table.

"Colonel Calhoun," Yolanda's recorded head was saying, "I think you'll be pleased with our new power suit design."

Shut up! I thought.

The Jersey stepped slowly into the room. Its claws scratched against the floor.

"We included all of your requests," Yolanda's head continued, "including the recent ones from this morning, all of the modifications that were possible and functional, that is. With all of the–"

The Jersey leapt onto the work table I'd hidden behind.

I turned my head to look up from where I was squatting. Rows of shark-like teeth opened in front of my eyes. Sulfuric breath pelted my face when it shrieked.

I slapped my right arm to engage my laser sword and swung up. The Jersey caught my arm with one of its human-like hands, stopping the blade just inches from piercing the side of its head. Its wing, under its arm, spread out in front of me and I was reminded of my abuela's red and orange chunk jello molds. The Jersey snapped its teeth toward my head. I veered away and hung loose from its hand, dead weight. The Jersey held tight. I dangled there for a second, until the Jersey grabbed my other arm.

As it pulled me toward its skeletal jaws, I shoved my boots against its chest. It fastened its grip, but I'd slipped to where its claw brushed against my power jump button. My suit's thrusters threw me from the Jersey's teeth, and I landed against the display case in the center of the room.

The dragon roared and flitted its arms and wings violently. I still saw the jiggle of a jello mold. Dark smoke poured from its nostrils. The Jersey rasped and rocked back and forth, but soon I couldn't see it through all the smoke.

I had to get out of there, back into the hall. But the smoke was already blocking the only way out.

I was trapped. My mind was focused on preservation, and the only place I could escape was the display case. I thought I'd be safe in there. I got to my feet as the smoke filled the room and rolled toward me. I grabbed the door at the back of the case. but the opening was too small for me to enter... with my power suit on.

Any other time I would have second-guessed giving up my armor, but the smoke was coming fast and I didn't have any other choice. I doffed my power suit and crawled into the case, slamming the door behind me as the smoke engulfed the space I'd left behind.

The upgraded power suit glistened in front of me. Sensing my presence, the suit popped open at the back.

"Whoa," I whispered. The suit was just begging to be put on. But I still hesitated. It had been made for Calhoun. What if it did things I couldn't handle? What if Yolanda had booby-trapped it for him and I'd be stupid if I used it?

The Jersey's muffled screeches surrounded me. A burning smell filled the case, but I didn't see any smoke making its way inside. I couldn't see much around the power suit, and I definitely couldn't see anything through the smoke on the other side of the glass. I didn't know where it was lurking, but the Jersey would find me eventually. And maybe, just maybe, I could hold my breath long enough to fight my way out of there with the thermagoggles protecting my eyes. Slim possibility, but I knew I'd have even less of a chance if I stayed in only my t-shirt. I needed armor.

"Fuck it," I said, and stepped into the black suit.

A hum vibrated through my body, as if the suit was connecting to my spine. I tensed, thinking it would make sense for it to be horrible, but all I felt was the hum, and the suit's insides inflating to match my size.

A feminine robotic voice said, "Ready."

"It talks," I said.

The Jersey roared. It must have heard me. Or the suit.

I didn't have much room, but I needed to get a feel for the armor's movement. See what I had to work with. Brannigan always said to check your gear every time. The black suit was bigger, and I didn't have the muscle strength Calhoun did. It didn't matter how cool I looked if I was slow and dead.

The display case was taller than it was wide, so I could only move my arms and legs up and down. I felt ridiculous, like I was practicing moves in an old holorobic class on the Feed. Still, moving felt lighter than in my other suit. The motions were more fluid, natural. That was good. I'd need to move as fast as possible.

And what weapon did this suit have? Foam and lasers or a sword? It didn't look like either, with that big tube around my right arm. It had been built for a Nusie not a smoke eater. Maybe it was just a big club for beating people. That would check out. Wasn't like Calhoun needed a suit for slaying scalies. He rode them. And he'd always preferred a standard laser rifle.

But the arm had a button.

I wasn't scared or dumb enough to depress it and see what would happen. Not encased as I was.

The top of the display case was ripped off. I had the good sense to engage my thermagoggles and take a gulp of air as it happened. I'd had my arms in front of me, so I'd managed to dodge most of the shattered glass. I tasted blood on my lip. I prayed and prayed that no smoke had gotten into my mouth. I wasn't dying or coughing. Not yet. I could still move.

The Jersey was a snapping blob of red above me. I fell over the broken pieces of the display case, onto the floor, then onto my feet and running. It was too easy to move and I was too used to the old clunky suit. I stumbled forward like a fledgling baby Behemoth on its new legs.

Where was the door? Every wall looked like the sliding exit, and every time I thought I'd found it, I would collide into a new wall. I felt like I was going to die. It popped into my mind as a fact, but my body raged against it. I had to find a way out. If I could just calm down and think. Time wasn't slipping, it was gone. An empty tank. Not even fumes. I was about to lose my breath and I'd be forced to inhale. That would be the end.

I hit another wall, then turned back. My helmet connected with the Jersey's skull. An accident. I must have surprised the dragon when I reversed course so quickly, and we charged into each other like fighting mountain goats. But it didn't matter if it was an accident or not. The blow caused me to evacuate every puff of air I'd been holding in.

And my body did what came naturally. It inhaled.

Every muscle was tense. I froze, expecting to choke and burn and fall. But I remained standing. My head hurt from the game of chicken with the scaly. I could see the Jersey in front of me all thermal and fuzzy. It was shaking off the impact, groaning like a drunk.

I exhaled. Took another breath. I tasted bitter char, but my lungs took to it like fresh air. I was... I was... eating smoke.

"Holy shit," I said. My breath came out clean. I really was a smoke eater.

The Jersey roared, stretched its neck all the way back, and spit a ball of fire into the air. The smoke ignited and the entire room burst into flames. My fear dropped away and I was more angry that I'd gotten confirmation of something I could only previously dream of, and this *púchica* scaly was going to burn me to death before I could realize it.

Tiny, cool jets blasted me in the face from little holes in my new suit's chestplate. The suit's voice spoke: "Reducing heat."

Flames swam around me but I could breathe. In fact, I was huffing, dumped with adrenaline. I retracted my thermagoggles. The heat stung my eyes a bit, but I could see the Jersey blowing added fuel toward me.

"Cooling mist nearing empty," the suit said. "Bail out."

"Fuck that," I said.

I aimed my big right arm at the scaly and slapped the button. Hot orange discs spit out of slots in the arm's clunky appendage, right past my hand. They tore through the Jersey's neck. Its head hit the ground before I could register what had happened.

The flames died. Everything in the lab had melted: all the glass tubes and vials, the computer desk. The lights had been killed.

Even though I couldn't see, I held the big arm in front of me in amazement. I'd never heard of a dragon going down that fast with everything the smoke eaters had. It was a good thing I'd found it before Calhoun could put it to use. He would have sliced and diced us in one sweep of his arm.

I felt like I was going to puke.

The Jersey's head lay in front of me. To my left, only inches away, was the door leading out. I could almost graze it with my fingers.

An alarm went off in the hall. Flashing red and yellow lights extended from a port above the door as something *popped* above me. Droplets of water leaked from hidden sprinklers in the ceiling. The downpour started slow, weaker than the power suit's cooling mist, but then it really came flooding out, soaking me. I closed my eyes and raised my head. Why not enjoy the free shower?

The fire was already out.

CHAPTER 21

Tamerica and Afu were running down the opposite hallway toward the place we'd split up. Intermingling, gory pieces of humans and dragons littered the hallway leading back to the elevator. The walls held blood splatter and burn marks. I avoided looking at all of it, but I couldn't avoid the smell.

The ash kickers slowed to a chug when they saw me in the new suit.

Tamerica frowned so hard it squished her face. "What the flying fuck are you wearing?"

"Bro's suit is hulked out," Afu said.

I had a huge smile on my face. "Guys, I'm a smoke eater."

They both patted me on the shoulder and walked around me, toward the big door with the red eye.

"We know you are," Afu said.

I spun around. "I'm not joking. I was just locked in a room filled with scaly smoke and I could breathe it just fine. And I survived the fire, too. But I think the suit helped a lot with that. Still, I killed a Jersey right in the middle of a flaming room."

Tamerica pulled out a key card. "Snagged this off a Nusie just before a Popper swallowed her."

"That's great to hear, bro," Afu patted me on the shoulder.

That was it? That was all I got? "You don't believe me.

"We believe you," Tamerica said. She stepped up to the red digital eye. "Like Afu said, you've always been one of us. Didn't matter if you could breathe smoke before. Why should it matter now? Old news, man. Now, if you don't mind, you have some fellow smokies to release from behind this door."

Looking closer, I realized it was a card lock device. It was older technology, but safer from hacks through the Feed.

Tamerica shoved the card into the red-eyed slot. The door began to rise, clanking on its joints. It sounded like someone was taking a hammer to it. A gap grew under the door, and pale light flooded in from the room on the other side.

Tamerica pulled me out of the doorway and shoved me against the wall. I didn't appreciate that, even if she was trying to protect me. I was a smoke eater, too. Officially, damn it! I had a better suit but I could follow her orders. I was an adult. Maybe I'd been too nice before. Too submissive. I'd been trying too hard to get them to like me. I needed to take charge.

Slowly, Tamerica peeked around the corner. The big door finished raising, slamming to a halt. It jolted me into action and I ran around Tamerica, dodging her grasping hands. I had a hard time keeping my gun arm straight as I ran for the light behind the door.

"Contreras. Guillermo. Gilly!" Tamerica's whisper felt like a razor-blade. "Get back here!"

I swung around the corner and crossed into the new room.

At least fifty men and women stood in front of me. Smoke eaters, I assumed. They wore clothes that were a cross between hospital gowns and pajamas. Lime green. These smoke eaters had gathered together like an army in ancient Rome, facing me, squatting low. A device with blinking lights had been strapped to each of their arms. Clear tubes connected from the device to individual IV stands they were now holding like spears. They'd pulled them from their wheeled base and had somehow found the time to whittle the ends of the metal into a fine point meant to stab Nusie necks.

Two or five of the spears launched at me. A woman's voice broke out from the front of the pajama legion as a spear bounced off my chest, leaving a faint scratch.

Oh, thank Christ, I thought.

Another almost impaled my eye. I turned in time for the IV spear to strike my helmet.

I guess I hadn't thanked Christ hard enough.

"I said stop throwing," the woman shouted. She stepped out from the others, dragging her IV stand with her. She stood in front of me and held her hands out as she faced the other smoke eaters. "Can't you tell a power suit when you see one?"

She turned to me and my mouth dropped open as recognition hit.

"Please, tell me you're a smoke eater and not a Nusie," she whispered.

I didn't whisper. "You're... you're..."

"My what?" she said.

"No." What the hell was my mouth and brain doing. Was I having a stroke? "You are Captain–"

"Naveena Jendal," she said. "Who the hell are you?"

"A fucking dumbass," Tamerica's voice came up behind me.

Naveena ran around me, crying as she passed. Tamerica

gasped as she stopped short to welcome Naveena's embrace. They hugged like that, sobbing and mumbling things to each other.

Afu hugged Naveena next.

And there was Brannigan, coming down the hall outside, pushing Yolanda in a wheeled chair. The propellerhead was asleep. "I was getting bored upstairs so I–"

"You." Naveena wheeled her IV forward, walking toward Brannigan on stiff legs.

"Well, shit," Brannigan sighed. His face had turned red. "All right, get it over with. Tamerica already gave me a good knuckle sandwich. I'd hate to make you jealous. And fuck I guess I deserve it. Go ahead and hit me."

Naveena stopped in front of Brannigan, close enough for an uppercut. She didn't strike. She just looked up into his eyes, like she was searching for something.

Brannigan groaned. It was short, but sounded painful. "Naveena..."

She fell forward, catching herself around Brannigan's neck. When she pressed her lips into his, they both closed their eyes as if they were in the deepest of sleeps. The kiss lasted too long to excuse as an accident, and when they began moving their mouths together, it was probably better than any kiss I'd seen in any movie.

I thought of Reynolds.

Why the hell did I think of Reynolds?

I wish I'd kissed her that night in Waukesha. No, I wish she would have kissed me. Not that I was lazy; I've always been scared shitless I'd do something wrong or misread a signal. Everyone in the platoon would have told you I was horrible at reading signals. Hand signals, morse code, or knowing if someone liked me. I was shit at it. If Reynolds kissed me, it would have answered a lot of questions that liked to bounce around my head at night while the platoon slept. The kiss wouldn't have had to be a big deal. Just a peck. Platonic. It would have shown that maybe she cared about something else besides the Army and I would have felt a whole lot less alone. I would have had a friend. A friendly kiss. A one-timer.

But I'd be bullshitting myself if I really thought I'd have left it at that.

I wouldn't want to seem desperate or clingy or – again – misread everything. I would have gotten more upset than usual when she didn't stick up for me when the other guys in the platoon started in on their bullshit. I'd wonder why she didn't kiss me again, what I did wrong. I'd be even more stressed and ostracized. More questions would stuff my brain at night. More ideations. Then I would have regretted the whole damn thing and would wish instead to give back the simple, friendly kiss. Maybe Reynolds had had the right idea to begin with. Maybe I was just confused because of Brannigan and Naveena's kiss on display right in front of me. It was one to envy.

"All right, you guys," Tamerica said. "Goddamn."

"Hey, T. I want to kiss like that again," Afu said. "When this is all over."

Tamerica blinked in confusion as she looked up to her husband.

"Who's this guy in the extra large power suit?" Naveena pointed to me as she clung to Brannigan's neck.

He didn't seem to mind holding her. "This is Guillermo Contreras. He's with us."

"I'm officially a smoke eater," I said.

"Yeah, that's what I meant," Brannigan said.

"No," I said, "I mean–"

"Hey," Tamerica shouted and clapped her armored gloves together. "There are other smokies here besides you two PDA-ing motherfuckers. Let's get these folks upstairs. There's only one small elevator and we have to wade through blood and guts to get to it."

Naveena turned to Brannigan. "She's a lot tougher now."

"She's always been tough," Brannigan said.

"Wait." Naveena looked around as the other smoke eaters made introductions. "Where's Harribow and Renfro?"

The devices on the captives' arms, Naveena explained to us, acted as both a tracker and a regulator. The only nutrition they'd been receiving was through the IV connected to the device. If they attempted to detach it, or if they tried to run, the IV would shut off for a few days. And even if they managed to escape, the Army could easily find them. None of them had been able to detach the device from their arm.

One of the more malnourished smoke eaters, a man named Craig, had tried to escape when they'd started moving the smoke eaters down to Sub Level 3. He didn't get far, and he'd been starving for the last two days. I wish I'd had a snack to give him. His eyes were sunken and he looked like he'd pass out at any minute. Where his skin showed, I could see his skeleton moving. He leaned on my shoulder as I walked him to the elevator and waded over the gore. The hall had taken on the smell of dead fish.

"They want our blood," Naveena said after we sent up another group of smokies. "They want to be able to breathe smoke and do what we do without going up in flames. No one's forgotten the Phoenix."

"And they think a direct transfusion will do that?" Brannigan said.

"They're willing to try. They think it's more stable than dragon blood. More accepted by the body."

"Yeah, who knows?" Afu said. "There might be another Phoenix."

"Don't bring that evil down on us." Tamerica took off her helmet and leaned against the wall. "We have enough shit to deal with besides another bird."

Though she looked as bad as the other captives and could have used a rest, Naveena demanded to fight with us. She put on my previous power suit, the one I'd left in the room with the Jersey. When Brannigan and the others saw the dead dragon and the charred walls of the science lab, they all told me they believed me and that I was a real smoke eater, but I think they just did it to shut me up and get back to business.

"Never had a doubt," Brannigan told me as he tapped his boot against the Jersey's headless body.

"I did," I said.

"So that suit," said Brannigan. "Are you sure you want to wear it?"

"Hell yes," I said. "This gun is awesome."

I'd said it a little too loudly. We'd been wheeling Yolanda around in her chair, allowing her to sleep, but my voice woke her up.

"Huh?" She jolted to sit up straight. "Breakfast. Moonshine."

"What the hell is she talking about?" Afu said.

"Yo-yo." Naveena got onto her knees in front of the propellerhead. "You're okay."

"And you're okay." Yolanda smiled at Naveena. "Thank

goodness. I knew the others would bust you out of here."

"Couldn't have done it without you," Tamerica said. Her voice was strained and shaky. The nerves must have finally caught up to her. She'd been trying to get in touch with Lot with no result. She was worried about the smoke eaters we'd sent upstairs, even though Brannigan said the coast had been clear when he'd been up there. She paced, impatient. She was ready to get out of Big Base. I was, too. "We should really go. There are still dragon-riding Nusies above ground and I don't know how we're all going to get out of here."

Yolanda opened her mouth to speak, then she looked at me and pointed, bouncing in her chair. "You found the suit. You found it."

"Yeah," I said. "I hope you don't mind."

Yolanda grabbed Naveena's arm, the one with the device strapped to it. "And I could use this smoker for the short-range signal."

Brannigan looked at us. "I don't know, guys. When she hasn't been asleep, she's been spouting weird streams of sci-babble."

Yolanda tensed her eyes. It was the first time I'd seen her look anything close to angry. "I'm in my right mind and I know exactly what I'm talking about. What Naveena is wearing, the Nusies called them smokers. They thought it was funny. You want to get us all out of here safely? You'll listen to me."

Naveena ejected her laser sword and slashed it through the air a few times. *Phrum, phrum.* "We're listening. Go on Yolanda."

"The Nusies riding the dragons control the scalies with the headsets they wear. Well Calhoun wanted the same thing but in his suit. The suit Guillermo is wearing. Oh, remind me to tell you something else about the suit. It's important."

"Okay," I said. She was talking so fast I almost hadn't caught that she'd been speaking to me.

"I can use the parts in Naveena's smoker," Yolanda said. "I can wire them to Guillermo's suit, using the scaly signal, and he should be able to shut down any Nusie headset he gets close to."

"That's great," said Afu.

"Hold on," Brannigan said. "She said he has to get close to them. How close are we talking, Yolanda?"

"Given the time I have to do it?" Yolanda's eyes fidgeted as she stared at the ceiling. "It would have to be within twenty feet."

"Oh hell," Tamerica said. "No way. I'll wear the suit. I'll do it."

"Fuck that," Brannigan and Naveena said as one.

"I'll wear it," the Chief said. "I'm old enough, it won't matter."

"Like I'm going to let you die again?" Naveena shook her head. "I'll wear it."

"You can barely stand up," Brannigan said.

They all continued arguing as Afu and I watched. I was tired of everyone else making decisions for me. Thinking of me as only the kid, or rookie, or private.

"I'm wearing the goddamn suit." My voice boomed.

They all turned to me.

"I found it," I said. "I killed the Jersey with it, and I've been doing a pretty good job of not dying. I like the suit. You haven't seen what this gun can do. I'll be fine."

"The discs are very formidable." Yolanda nodded in her

chair, but looked like she would fall asleep again. "Highly volatile, though."

"Besides," I said, "these Nusies have a vendetta against me. It won't be hard to get close to them. They'll want my ass."

"You don't have to get close to be killed by fire or lasers," Tamerica said.

"No," I said. "But if I was scared of dying I wouldn't be here. I mean, I am scared. But I'm doing this anyway. I want to do it. And I won't let you stop me."

Tamerica looked to Brannigan as if the old man would talk some sense into me.

He grumbled and nodded his head. "This one is all on Contreras."

CHAPTER 22

Afu ripped open a fridge locker. MREs and nonperishable food stores poured onto the ground for the captive smokies to dig through. For those who couldn't move or eat on their own, Tamerica and Brannigan helped them sip water cups and chew on protein bars.

I was glad to be out of the Sub Level, but I was nervous to be so close to where most of the Army was located. The Nusies had only sent one squadron to engage us downstairs. There should have been more soldiers. Something didn't feel right. But we had little choice. If Calhoun had something waiting for us, we'd still have to engage the Nusies if we wanted to nullify their dragon control. If we wanted to go home.

I felt like a coal mine canary. Or a Judas goat. I didn't hate every single Army grunt. Just because my platoon sucked didn't mean there weren't diamonds amongst the bullshit.

Reynolds was still a good person. A medic's job is to help people. You can't be completely corrupt if that's your cause. She was just confused and hadn't known anything outside the Army for too long. It wasn't her fault, and there had to be other soldiers like that. Orphans adopted by the wrong ideology. I was a poster child for one-eighty turnarounds. I'd been a card-carrying Nusie a lot longer than I'd been wearing a power suit. It wasn't a simple change of teams. It wasn't only because they'd tried to kill me. I had woken up, and I wasn't special. There were probably a hundred or more brainwashed young adults in Big Base that would have seen reality like me. But where was the point you knew for sure you couldn't change their minds? When did you have to use force? When did you know they couldn't be reasoned with?

In a cold room inside Big Base, Yolanda worked on my suit. I stayed with her.

We'd used a flathead screwdriver to pry off Naveena's smoker. She screamed when we finally got it loose, and I could see why. A long syringe was sticking out from the device's underside – a long, nasty looking thing. Blood seeped from a hole in Naveena's arm where the needle had been lodged. Brannigan rushed over to press his armored fingers against the wound, but Naveena stopped him.

"Back off, Brannigan. I'm fine. Goddamn. It was a kiss, not a marriage proposal."

Brannigan blinked and backed away. He looked confused, almost drunk. Tamerica's punch hadn't made him that loopy. Achilles had his heel. I guess Brannigan had his heart.

Yolanda broke into Naveena's smoker and pulled out only the necessary wires. She connected these to a panel in the back of the suit.

Sparks flew from inside my suit as she worked a small laser cutter to patch the wires. I didn't know much about electronics, but it looked unsafe. "So what do I have to do?"

"Just get close enough." Yolanda took a big breath as she put the cutter down. "The dragons will... twitch. That's how you'll know."

"Twitch?"

"Well," she closed the panel to my suit, "their body will react to your presence. In some way. When you're close enough. They won't be able to help it. It could look like a stroke... who knows?"

"Who knows?" My mouth went suddenly dry. But we'd given out all the tinfoil-covered water cups.

"That's how neurology works. Afterward, they'll go back to being regular scalies of their own minds... I think."

"So, we'll still have to deal with the dragons like normal. The Nusies just won't be able to control them. And I'll know when this happens if I look for a... sign?"

"Basically."

Dios mio.

"Oh," I said. "You asked me to remind you about the suit?"

"The suit?"

"Yeah, you said to remind you. That you had to tell me something about it."

"Huh." Yolanda leaned against the power suit and looked into the air as if she was searching for a thought. "Can't remember what it was."

I could have cried.

"Give me a second," she said. "Maybe it'll come to me."

I waited.

"Nope. Sorry, Guillermo. But, hey. I'm sure if it was important I would remember."

If it wasn't important, I thought, *why did you ask me to remind you?*

I just hoped the suit wouldn't explode with me in it.

"All right," Tamerica said, jogging over. "We're going out the same way we came in. We'll have a good vantage. It's better than the front door."

"I don't think this place has a front door." Brannigan followed behind Tamerica. "They'll be watching the roof. I'm sure of it. But it's still our best option. We'll have to defend ourselves. I hope everyone here is okay with that."

Afu sighed and looked away, rubbing the armor around his laser arm.

"And what about all the other smokies?" I asked.

"They'll be fine here in the holding area," Naveena said. She was jumping up and down in her suit as if she was about to rush out onto a stage to give a motivational speech. She hadn't said anything about Renfro after we'd told her. She hadn't said much at all until now. "They need to get their strength up."

I wondered why she wasn't included with them.

"Are you sure you don't want my helmet?" I said.

Naveena shook her head. "You need it more than I do."

She'd refused to wear one of the Nusie helmets we'd taken off one of the unconscious soldiers.

"We're going to stay around Contreras and give him cover," Tamerica said. She turned to me. "Please just go toward one dragon at a time if you can."

"Don't worry," I said.

"Seriously," said Afu. "The riders will stay in groups. We'll have to isolate them."

"They won't stay clumped together once they realize what his suit can do to them."

"But they'll try to take him out one at a time from a distance."

"So," I said, "you're saying this is just going to get easier."

We left Yolanda with the other smoke eaters and headed down the hall, to the hole in the ceiling we'd originally entered through.

"We'll have to power jump out," Tamerica said. She stopped just under the hole, leaning her head back to look through it. She extended her thermagoggles for half a minute, but retracted them with a shake of her head. "Be ready to shoot or slash. I don't see anything, but I'm not going to lower my guard."

"Um," I said, swallowing at my dry mouth. "Who's going first?"

Tamerica lowered her stare to me. "You wanted to wear the cool suit, right?"

Well, shit.

"Step up, smokie." Brannigan extended his hand like some showy butler.

"Sink or swim," I said.

Before I could hesitate, I got under the hole and engaged the power jump. The button was easy to find. It was in the same spot in the left glove. But this new suit's thrusters had kick. I was launched sixty or so feet into the air. It could have been more. Looked like more. But I was never a good guesser of heights. I wasn't much of a fan of heights either.

Night surrounded me. The roof lay far below. Naveena – looking the size of an action figure – launched out of the hole next, but her jump was weak. She didn't reach anywhere close to my altitude, but landed gently onto the roof. She looked up at me and waved her arms.

At first I thought I'd simply overshot. But I wasn't slowly lowering like in the other suit. I wasn't moving at all.

I was flying.

"What the hell are you doing up there?" Brannigan's voice came through my helmet after he'd made it onto the roof.

"I don't know," I said. "I'm stuck."

I could hear the suit's thrusters burning at my back, keeping me in the air. From where I floated, I could see destruction all around the building. Bodies, burning tanks. Thankfully, no dragons or Nusies.

A nearby water tower had been punctured and steadily poured precious liquid life onto the ground. Smacking my dry lips, I unconsciously leaned toward the depleting water. My suit moved me forward. I yelped and leaned back to hover again with my feet toward the ground. This slowed me to a stop.

"Huh," I said.

If I leaned forward, with my belly parallel with the ground, the thrusters would jet me ahead like a superhero. Leaning back to "stand" was like the brakes.

I took a shaky breath and tried the maneuver again. Big Base became a blur and then was gone from sight as I reached the edge of the compound. Turning was easier than I thought. I just had to lean in the direction I wanted to go.

For a brief second I found myself enjoying soaring like a scaly, but then I felt guilty. About Renfro, about Naveena and everyone and everything else. Not to mention the terrorizing knowledge of dragon riders flying somewhere close, and the fear of falling out of the sky if I moved the wrong way. I turned back toward Big Base's roof, where the others were watching me.

"Bro," Afu's voice crackled through my helmet. "You can fly."

"Clear some space," I said. "I just want to be on solid ground again."

From above, a huge hunk of metal careened through my flight path. I almost crashed into it, and would have been torn to shreds, even in my power suit. The mass seemed to roar as it plummeted toward the roof. The bottom half of Happy the droid followed. The head and torso came next. The red smile flashed past my eyes. That's when I knew what had happened. The metal dragon had been chewed on, balled up, and thrown to Earth missing its shiny wings and most of its head.

On the roof, Brannigan tackled Naveena to get her out of Mecha Scaly's path. The dead dragon bot broke through the roof and sent a final flash of blue flames into the sky as the roof began to cave in.

Naveena screamed for them all to run, and though she didn't have a radio I still heard her. My guts twisted as I watched the roof rupture like a black hole. Tamerica and Afu had power jumped to the edge. Afu, being closer, made it there before his wife and had to catch her by the arm when her boots had no floor to land on. The big man pulled Tamerica up and they straddled the edge, watching the rest of the roof drop.

Naveena had managed to run fast enough to grab onto a set of antennae outside the hole's reach. Brannigan was limping.

Let's do it! My uncle's voice came to me.

I fell forward and shot out of the sky like a damn comet and felt like I was going to release my guts out of all three orifices. But I could see and move well enough. The suit had extended two glass panels in front of my face when I hit a certain speed. My own personal windshield.

The hole swallowed every inch of the roof. Like Tamerica, Brannigan suddenly found the ground to be missing. But Naveena's hand hadn't been close enough to grab him. Malnourished as she was, she wouldn't have had the strength to pull him up anyway. She was barely holding herself from the antennae.

Brannigan landed in my outstretched arms. My back popped as I yanked myself upward enough to shoot back to the sky without stopping.

The Chief was whooping like he was on a roller coaster.

"Stay still," I said.

"I'm not moving a fucking inch. Don't drop me. How 'bout that?"

I scoped out a clear enough area on the ground outside Big Base and pointed my nose toward it. All I could hear was the thrusters. Afraid I'd plow into the dirt, I leaned back. We slowed to hover, but we were still ten feet above the ground. I wasn't going to press the power jump button to find out what would happen. It might have killed the flight but it also might have launched me back into the sky.

So I dropped Brannigan.

He landed with a grunt and began cursing me for an asshole, a bastard, and other things he said so fast I couldn't catch.

"Sorry, Chief," I said. "But I don't know how to land this thing."

Brannigan staggered to his feet. "I could jump up there and hit the button on your chest."

"Then I'd fall out," I said. "Backwards. Without armor."

"I know," he said. "It would be fair."

Three orange bursts came from the top of the building. Tamerica, Naveena, and Afu jogged over.

"The dragons from Sublevel Three are starting to crawl out into the open," Naveena said. She looked up at me. "Nice catch by the way, Gilly. That thing hard to control?"

Captain Naveena Jendal got a personal hero pass to call me Gilly. Naveena Jendal could call me whatever she wanted.

"He can't come down," Brannigan said.

"Have you tried hitting the jump button again?" Tamerica asked.

"Wouldn't it be more of a fly button?" Afu asked.

"You still want that romantic kiss?" Tamerica said.

Afu clenched his lips.

"I haven't hit the button again," I said. "Not yet."

I was about to. But a roar cut through the air above me. Reynolds, gripping the reins of her yellow Lung dragon, was soaring toward me like an incoming nuke. Murder tensed in her face. The woman I saw in memories looked nothing like this pissed off Valkyrie coming for my head. I flinched at first. Then I remembered she had more to worry about from me and what was in my suit.

When the dragon flipped out and regained its mental liberty, it would dump her toward the ground and eat her either before or after she landed. If Yolanda had been successful.

"Stay back!" I shouted.

Reynolds opened her mouth. The Lung opened its jaws in sync. When Reynolds screamed, the dragon responded by shooting its golden fire.

"Shit!" I raised my arms and flew straight up.

The Lung's fire remained in the air like burning streamers lighting up the night. An additional twenty feet separated me from the ground, and I was too busy watching it fall away. I didn't look up. A laser struck me in the chest, sending me spiraling horizontally. Dark smoke blew into my face as the suit wailed a small siren noise. The suit's voice was telling me that I had only fifty percent armor sustainability. I was good enough at math to understand one more hit would finish me.

"Forty percent," the voice said.

Less than one more laser hit then.

I dropped my arms and came to a stop. The Nusie who'd fired was barreling at me on the back of his Spike-Crown Wyvern. The scaly's horns looked like several racks of antelope antlers, but twice as sharp. The dragon's cat-like eyes glowed orange, while its bird-like mouth, full of teeth, snapped repeatedly. The Nusie was riding closer to the dragon's horns than I would have, but he seemed too preoccupied with aiming his rifle at me. I readied to fly out of the way, but I held still. Told myself to wait a little longer. I had to see if my suit would work.

"I surrender!" I shouted. I couldn't throw up my arms because then my suit would take me higher.

The Nusie laughed and lowered his rifle. But the dragon didn't slow down. It sped up. The soldier made a chomping motion with his teeth. The Wyvern lunged, biting. But just before it could sink its teeth into my suit, it flailed and careened backwards, shrieking as if its head was going to explode.

Feedback screeched from the speaker in the Nusie's ear. As he fought to control the scaly, he reached up and jerked off the device he'd been wearing and tossed it to the night. The Spike-Crown thrashed its head back. Two of its horns pierced through the soldier's head. The dragon flapped its wings to hover there, and when it lowered its head back, the soldier's body was lifted out of the saddle, left to dangle on the scaly's crown.

The scaly saw me and roared, flapping its wings twice to pick up speed. I already had my weapon up.

The first two discs sliced into the mess of horns on its head. The lasers severed the ones where the Nusie's body was impaled. The dead man fell toward the ground and soon, after the other laser discs sliced into the Wyvern, I sent scaly pieces tumbling down after him.

Reynolds and the Lung came in hot.

"Wait!" I shouted. "Sarah, please."

She pulled at the reins and circled back to slow down. The Lung hovered there, thirty or so feet away, the tendrils below its nostrils flapping in the air. The dragon was far enough that Reynolds still had control of it.

"You just can't stop killing good soldiers," Reynolds said, "can you?"

"Don't come near me," I said. "I didn't kill that guy. But it's not safe to be around me. I don't want you to get hurt."

"You're gonna hurt me, Gilly?" The Lung's roar sounded like a thousand trumpets.

Heavy whooshing came from above. "Why are you wearing my suit, you shit stain?"

The big red Fafnir sailed down and circled us. Calhoun had his pistol drawn and aimed at me. Three more dragon riders fell from above to join us. I felt like a duck surrounded by a horde of alligators. But I was hoping they'd get closer. All of them except Reynolds. And I couldn't explain to her why. Not with the others there.

"Lieutenant Reynolds," Calhoun said. "Why haven't you eliminated this enemy?"

"I believe I heard him surrender, sir."

"Surrender? Thanks to this asshole and his friends, there isn't a base to put the prisoners we had to recapture."

What? We'd saved all of the captive smokies.

Calhoun noticed the look on my face. "Oh, yes. Those smoke eaters didn't get far after the roof caved in. And that backstabbing propellerhead, too. We've got 'em cordoned off over there."

He pointed but I didn't look.

"Sir," Reynolds said. "I think he did something to Bowers's dragon. He's been telling me to stay back."

"He's a liar. Can't trust a liar. He has my suit, but this ungrateful bastard is surrounded now, isn't he? I think some waterboarding would be a nice start for him. But not the end. Oh no, Contreras. There are plenty of techniques I've been dreaming of trying out. And I bet I could learn so much about what you've been doing since you left us in Waukesha." Calhoun brought the Fafnir in to hover beside Reynolds. "Did I ever introduce you to my dragon, Contreras?" Calhoun patted the Fafnir's neck. Its dark red eyes were motionless as it stared at me. "This is Sitri, demon of lust and death."

Calhoun smiled and the dragon bared its teeth. I thought I saw a few pieces of shiny metal stuck between them, but the dragon closed its mouth before I could know for sure.

"See Tree?" I said. "I haven't seen any trees for a long time. You and those fucking things you're riding made it impossible."

"Show some respect!" Calhoun shouted. His dragon growled. "I'm taking that suit back. We can do that with you still alive in it, or we can all fry you here and have that propellerhead fix any damage. Dig out all your burned guts and bones. Your choice."

They were all flying side by side now. Reynolds was right in the middle.

"Guillermo," Brannigan's voice came through my helmet. "What's stopping you. Move in. This is the perfect opportunity."

I couldn't. Reynolds had been the only ray of light for me in a dark place, even though she didn't get to shine it often. A life debt twice. That's what I owed her. I owed her more. What I was about to do was stupid as hell, but I counted it as payment

"Come and get me, you assmunchers." I dropped into a fall, my head pointed down, soaring for the dirt.

Lasers flew around me. They raced ahead of my path, chewing up the dirt. When I saw an opening, I took it, zipping straight ahead.

"Where are you guys?" I cast through my radio.

"We never left our spot," said Tamerica. "Had to take out a few of the dragons from the sublevel. We see you. To your left. What can we do?"

"Help me fucking land," I said. I spotted them to my left and turned for them.

The lasers chewed up the ground behind me.

"Oh, great," Brannigan grumbled. "Kid, just get above us, as close as you can."

I leaned into a hover and hit the button. My whole body dropped like an anvil. Brannigan and Naveena caught me so I didn't fall onto my face, while Tamerica, having the only laser suit, ran across the dirt firing rounds back at the incoming dragons and Nusies. Her lasers struck one of the scalies in the wing. It dropped into a tumble and the Nusie flew off. I jumped over to the dragon and blasted a few of my own shots into its body.

I heard someone swear and groan to my right. The soldier was back on his feet, and although blood was pouring from his head, he had his rifle pointed at me.

Brannigan flew in, used his laser sword to slice off the rifle's barrel and punched the Nusie in the face. The man dropped and writhed on the ground. Heavy thuds sounded nearby. I turned and saw that Calhoun, Reynolds and the others were riding toward us on the ground, as if the dragons were slow-moving horses.

"Fuck the torture," Calhoun raised another gun, a snub-nosed rifle, to join his pistol.

A scream filled the air. Naveena soared into a power jump, flying right for Calhoun. He turned his guns and fired. The shots hit Naveena in the chest and she dropped from her jump. Landing in a heap, on both of her knees, she bent all the way back to slide across the dirt. It would have looked cool if it had been intentional. She remained lying in the dirt when she stopped.

"You son of a bitch!" Brannigan raced toward the colonel with his laser sword raised.

The red Fafnir breathed hot orange flames at the old man. Brannigan dropped onto his face. I had to leap out of the way to avoid getting fried.

When the flames died, Calhoun was speaking. "You goddamn smoke eaters are like a virus. You won't go away, fire doesn't kill you, you grow and grow. But we don't have to kill you, do we? We can use you, your blood. We're going to fix the world you left to burn."

One of the soldiers to Calhoun's right made a confused gasp as he turned around in his saddle. Afu had climbed up the back of the Nusie's scaly, a green Drake with a fat tail, and had his laser axe lifted over his head. He brought the blade down. The soldier screamed as he was cut and burned. The soldier dropped onto the ground, swearing and screaming, but still alive

Sitri, Calhoun's dragon, reared back, snatched Afu by the leg and threw him fifty feet away. The big man tried to get up, but his armored leg looked like it had been squished by a car crusher. The green dragon began to slither over to Afu. The soldier he'd cut with his axe laughed and winced from the dirt, apparently still able to control his scaly.

I looked at all the smokies around me. Tamerica was the only one left standing and she was bent over, huffing breath. She'd been going for a long time and looked to be running out of steam.

"Contreras," Calhoun called. I heard a click and turned to see he had both guns trained on me again. "I changed my mind. I'd rather just have the suit."

CHAPTER 23

A digital howl came out of nowhere. The Nusies looked around. I looked around. It wouldn't have surprised me if a gang of wraiths showed up to make everything worse. Suddenly, Kenji appeared, leaping through the air in front of Calhoun. The robo dog snatched the colonel's snub-nosed rifle in its mouth and the other gun in its metal paws. Calhoun wailed, nearly falling off his saddle in confusion.

Kenji landed and ran off barking something harsh in Korean.

Brannigan looked up from the ground. "Was that my dog?"

"Look at that!" Tamerica pointed toward the road behind us.

Charging over the horizon, Cannon 15 and an assortment of different hover cars, trikes, and wheeled clunkers came barreling toward us with their headlights blaring in the dark. The cannon on the back of the truck rose and blasted a single, huge green wad of laser at Calhoun and Sitri.

The colonel yelled and pulled at his reins. Sitri leapt in time to dodge the blast and soared off roaring into the distance. The green Drake near Afu wasn't so lucky. The cannon blast blew the scaly apart. Its guts covered Afu so plentifully I thought he might drown in them.

"Are you okay, baby?" Tamerica asked through the radio.

Afu spit something out. "Always so gross. Ah! Shit! I can't walk."

Far off, he lay pounding the ground and rocking from side to side on his back.

Cannon Truck 15 stopped in front of us. Lot poked his head out of the driver's side window. "How's that for a propellerhead?"

"Holy shit," Tamerica said. "You're supposed to be in–"

"I know," said Lot. "But we ran into Bethany and her people coming this way, and we were closer to here than there, so we all decided, why not come kick a piece of Nusie ass."

"Where's my daughter?" Brannigan said.

"Up here, old man." Bethany stood at the cannon controls, wearing a smoke eater power suit. She didn't wear a helmet. Her dark curls moved with a passing gust of wind. She wore a cocky smirk that looked too much like Brannigan's.

"What the hell!" Brannigan began chugging toward the truck. "Is that the broken suit I kept in the back of the shed?"

"Got to go," Bethany said. "We saw them moving a bunch of people over that way. Lot, engage!"

The propellerhead laughed as he pushed his glasses higher onto his nose. He shifted into drive and sped the truck after Reynolds and her dragon.

"Brannigan, get Afu," said Tamerica. "I'll get Naveena."

"But–" Brannigan started to say.

"Do it," Tamerica said. "You're stronger than I am."

"All right, all right." Brannigan took off toward Afu.

I looked over to Tamerica because she was the closest to me. "What do I do?"

Both she and Brannigan said it together. "Go after Calhoun."

Reynolds and her Lung dragon were flapping above the oncoming calvary of carburetors. The Lung breathed its golden fire and caused the cars to split around the flames. One of the braver vehicles kept straight on, right through the fire. Like a clown car, droids began crawling out of every door. One fell out of the smoking trunk when the car hit a bump in the ground. It rolled across the ground, then got up and ran after the car. The other droids took turns leaping at the yellow dragon. Most of them fell and got run over by their own car, but one caught the tip of the Lung's claws. The lone droid held on, dangling like an ugly earring as Reynolds steered the Lung to soar away.

"Don't hurt that woman on the Lung," I said into my radio. "She's a friend."

Brannigan spoke through my helmet. "Are you serious?"

"Your *friend* has been trying to kill us just like all the other Nusies," Tamerica said.

I refrained from arguing about it. I couldn't defend Reynolds, and I had a colonel to find. Raising my arms, I rose into the air to search for him. There was no moonlight, but it seemed my eyes were adjusting to the dark. To my left, I thought I saw a red scaly tail disappear into the middle of a cloud. I couldn't be sure, but I had nothing else to go on. I flew into it. Puffy mist flowed past my face and I was soon out of it on the other side.

I made the mistake of looking down. Cannon 15 and the other vehicles looked like toys as they charged toward a cluster of spider tanks. The Nusies were guarding a group of people held inside a holo-cage. It had to be Yolanda and the other smoke eaters. The prisoners were packed close to each other in the center, avoiding the zap of the digital bars.

Bethany and everyone on our side with a weapon began shooting the same time the Nusies opened fire. If weapons weren't fixed to their vehicles like Cannon 15, each car's passengers held laser rifles out the window and squeezed off as many rounds as they could before return fire caused them to dip back into the car. The blind shots were surprisingly accurate, blowing chunks of metal off the spider tanks. Lasers from both sides lit the scene. Soldiers on foot stood behind and to the side of each spider tank. All of them advanced toward the fiery vehicle that had held all the droids. One of the spider tanks sped up and used its long legs to trample the car. But just as the tank was beginning to climb off, the droid car exploded, obliterating the front half of the spider tank.

The other spider tank rolled around and ejected two antennae from its sides.

"Oh no," I said.

Wraiths – maybe five of them – erupted from the tank. Cannon 15 slowed and sped off to one side, but several of the other cars kept on. One of the wraiths entered through one of their windshields and the car zoomed off into one of the columns keeping the holo cage energized. The digital bars disappeared and the prisoners ran as fast as they could, away from the wraiths.

I almost forgot about Calhoun. Turning in midair, I searched the clouds around me. The movement made me feel queasy, especially when I bobbed like a fishing lure. Turning back the way I came, I looked down at my suit and said, "Please don't run out of juice."

Hot red fire blasted out of the cloud in front of me. It

toasted the front of my suit and my face felt like it had been torn off, but since I'd been looking down, my helmet caught most of the fire. I fell backwards into a dive toward the ground.

"Armor failing," the suit said.

I looked back. Calhoun and Sitri were in a freefall just behind me. With no other choice, I raised my weapon arm and fired.

I was answered with several empty clicks.

"Diverting power from weapon to maintain stability," the suit said. "Get to safety."

"What do you mean?" I shouted. I again tried to fire a laser disc, but all I got was more blank button pushes.

"Shit." I looked back toward the ground and tensed. I could fight dragons a lot better than I could fight gravity. I could have flown up and given the scaly a big hug to send its brain back to normal, but I ran the enormous risk of having the suit fall to pieces or getting chomped by the Fafnir.

I didn't have a weapon, but neither did Calhoun. When I was thirty feet from the ground, he screamed at the top of his lungs. A *whoosh* brought heat against my back. Sitri was breathing its fire after me. My suit felt looser, shaking against the wind.

Come on, come on.

When it looked safe enough, I hit my jump button and let myself fall.

Calhoun and Sitri flew over me, scorching a big line of flames into the ground as they went. Sitri cut to the right and they began to turn back.

A growl came from over my shoulder. I turned to my side. The Lung dragon hovered just above me.

Reynolds pulled on her reins and said, "Down." The Lung lowered onto its feet.

"Sarah," I said, backing away.

"No, you don't get to call me that anymore," she said.

I lifted my hands, straight up. Maybe I could fly away one last time.

"Power Hover disabled," the suit said. "Please seek immediate repair."

"Looks like you're all out of tricks." Reynolds smiled and kicked a heel into the side of her Lung. The dragon stepped forward, and I stumbled backward. Laughing, Reynolds pulled on her dragon to stop.

"Oh, I might have at least one surprise up my suit," I said.

"Why are you scared to come close, Gilly?" she said. "Lucky won't bite."

"You named your dragon Lucky?"

She looked offended. "Yeah, why not?"

I shook my head. "Just give this up. The Nusies are done. You want to know why I couldn't ever say that was my platoon? Because they're bad people, Sarah. How long have they been torturing smoke eaters? You're a medic, it goes against everything you're about. You don't have to stay with them anymore. You could come with me."

She directed a hand to the wasteland around us. "Go with you where? The Army was the only thing going on. The only thing we had. You just gave it up. Now you're trying to take it away from me. This world really belongs to the scalies now. What is wrong with you?"

"I'm trying to help you."

The Lung roared, shutting me up.

"You never answered my question," she said. "Why'd

you tell me to stay away? Did your smoke eater friends strap a bomb inside your suit?"

I couldn't tell her. She'd tell Calhoun. And I had no other way to either escape or fight back. "You'll just have to trust me."

The corner of Reynolds' lips curled up. Then she frowned and moved the dragon forward. The Lung's eyes turned red as it slithered its head from side to side. Its tendrils lifted. "You're in no fucking position to ask for trust."

The air shifted and dust flew into the air around me. Sitri dropped behind me with its big, red wings spread. The Fafnir hissed, filling the air with the smell of sulfur.

"Corporal," Calhoun said, out of breath. His beret had flown off somewhere above us. "Shoot this traitor between the eyes."

Something quick and fragile passed over Reynold's face. Was it hesitation or regret? It was gone in a blink. She raised her rifle.

"At least you can die like a soldier," Calhoun said.

I looked at Reynolds, silently asking her not to pull the trigger. When I saw the dark hole of her rifle's barrel, I squeezed my eyes shut and thought of my family. I missed them. I would have given anything to see them again, but I wasn't ready to go. I didn't move, afraid it would make Reynolds shoot.

The sound of clanking footsteps distracted me. When I opened my eyes, a droid was walking up the Lung dragon's back. Reynolds heard the sound a second after I did. It was a second too late. She turned in her saddle as the droid tackled her, pulling her to the ground. Fighting to pry her rifle out of the droid's hands, Reynolds grunted and pulled, but the droid wouldn't let go.

"Useless," Calhoun shouted. Sitri's steps shook the ground as the dragon stomped toward me. "I have to do everything myself."

Reynolds let go of the rifle and drew a pistol holstered at her side. She blew a hole through the droid's head, dropping it. Smoke rose from its metal skull as Reynolds retrieved her rifle.

Sitri roared and spread its jaws wide around me. I was inside its mouth, feeling the teeth close in. I screamed, but the scream kept going till I was out of breath. The dragon had stopped short of biting me in half. It just stood there.

"Kill him, bite him," Calhoun was shouting. "Do it, you stupid fucking scaly!"

A gap between the Fafnir's teeth was big enough for me to slip through. I made it out before Sitri began convulsing, shrieking, and thrashing around. Calhoun yelled as he tried to get control of the red dragon, but the scaly was bucking the colonel around like a ragdoll.

Reynolds was on the ground, running toward me with her pistol aimed at my head. But her Lung beat her there. It bent its head to nudge me, but it barely bumped its snout against my chest when it too began to twitch and rasp.

"Lucky!" Reynolds ran to her dragon.

"Sarah, stop," I shouted. "Get away from it. You're not in control anymore."

She didn't listen. She tried to climb into the saddle, but the Lung snatched her by the leg and threw her toward Sitri. The red Fafnir came out of its fit and bent its head to watch Reynolds crawl across the ground.

"Hold on, Sarah," I said. "I'm coming."

The Lung growled the sound of wind chimes. In response the Fafnir bent low, looking like a viper about to strike.

Calhoun kicked at Sitri's sides with his boots. Both dragons roared and circled each other. I dodged the Lung's foot as it came down and nearly crushed me. The dragon was blocking my way to Reynolds. She was caught between them as they did their territorial scaly dance. I moved to run after her, but the Lung's tail whipped into my path and knocked me back. I soared a few feet and landed. Everything hurt. I struggled just to lift my arm.

Both dueling dragons inhaled.

"No!" I shouted.

Reynolds got to her feet and tried to grab the reins dangling from the Lung's neck. Light glowed at the back of both dragon throats. The fire rushed from their jaws. The Lung's golden blaze covered Calhoun from sight while Sitiri's dark red fire mixed against it and scorched Reynolds as she tried to run away.

The Nusies screamed. For a second.

"Reynolds," I shouted.

She didn't answer. When the fire cleared away and the dirt began to fly, as the dragons began clawing and biting each other, there was no sign of Reynolds anywhere. Sitri had a pile of ashes on its saddle. What looked like charred human legs crumbled onto the ground as the Fafnir lunged for Lucky's neck.

The Lung dragon was quicker, though. It curled around and snatched the Fafnir's neck in its teeth and twisted with a wet pop. A huge chunk of Sitri's throat remained bleeding in the Lung's mouth. As the Fafnir dropped dead, the Lung spit out the meat in its jaws and turned to me.

I was still lying on the ground. I didn't think my suit was good for anything more than weighing me down at that point. But after the Lung took two inquisitive looks at me, blood coating its tendrils, it looked to the sky. With a single leap, Lucky flapped its wings to get higher. It glided away into the night. I never saw it again.

"Contreras," Tamerica's voice came through my helmet.

I lay there stunned, numb. I couldn't speak. I realized how cold the air was when my breath made steam.

"Contreras," Tamerica said again. "Are you okay?"

"Yeah," I croaked.

"Where's Calhoun?"

"They're… they're all gone." Sarah, too. "They're dead."

"We can't stop yet," Tamerica said. "Bethany and the others are having problems with some wraiths and a spider tank. We all need to head that way. Yolanda and the smokies are caught in the middle of them."

"My suit is fried," I said.

"I don't have a wraith remote," Brannigan chimed in. "Does anyone else?"

"No," I said. I looked down at the smoking metal I was still in. My old suit had a remote, though.

"I'm on it," Naveena said.

She leapt through the air and landed in front of a wraith flying after a silver coupe. Naveena pointed a remote at the ghost and sucked it up before running toward the next nearest wraith. I was in awe. I remembered why she'd always been my favorite and it was a pleasure to watch her work. How she could survive the torture the Nusies put her through, a dragon attack, the loss of her friends, and still keep going… it was beyond my understanding.

I lay my head back and closed my eyes.

CHAPTER 24

I woke up in the back of a speeding vehicle. The first things I recognized were the sounds and sensations of the hover wheels sensing the rough terrain below. Daylight flashed on the other side of my eyelids.

"He's waking up," a man said.

I sat up and blinked awake. Lot sat in the seat in front of me. I'd been laid out in the third row. The power suit was gone, and they'd haphazardly bandaged me in spots I hadn't known to be injured before I passed out. Yolanda was behind the wheel. Ahead of us were a few other cars. I assumed it to be morning and, based on the position of the sun, that meant we were headed west.

"Heading back to Brannigan's?" I asked.

"No, we're heading south," Lot said. "One of the smokies they were holding has a town with enough space down in Arkansas."

Yuck, I thought.

"Oh my gosh! You're alive." Yolanda bounced in her seat. "I remembered what I'd meant to tell you about the suit, but you'd already left."

I looked to Lot and asked, "Am I going to be okay?"

He snaked his head left and right, as if he wasn't sure.

I could feel my pulse quicken. But then he smiled and his uncertainty morphed into a nod. "You had us scared there for a minute, but as far as I can tell, yeah, a little more sleep and some food, I think you'll be just fine."

"You guys have gallows humor worse than the smoke eaters." Back to Yolanda I said, "It's okay. Honestly, I wish we had another suit just like that. But more durable. It fell apart after only a few hits."

"Oh, I had another prototype that was better in balancing energy and protection." She had to slow the van as the vehicles ahead were coming to a fork in the road. She didn't continue speaking.

"What happened to it?" I asked. "This other prototype."

"It's on Cannon 15," Lot said. "Just relax, man. They told us to take care of you. We've got snacks and water in the back. Even a little morphine Yolanda snagged from Big Base."

I blinked at him. "What happened with the Nusies?"

"The signal worked," Yolanda said. "You saved the day." She looked more alert and oriented, but she sounded loopy. Me? Save the day?

"I don't know about that," I said.

The last image of Reynolds flashed before my eyes. She was engulfed in red and golden flames. Screaming. I hadn't saved a damn thing.

I brought myself back to the present and looked around and confirmed I was in a hovering minivan. It was just the three of us.

"Where are the others?"

"We lost a few," Lot said. "Hey, if you want to go back to sleep you can have a bump of morphine."

"No, I'm good." I watched the cold wastes fly by the

window. "Where are the other smoke eaters? Brannigan and Tamerica?"

The propellerheads looked at each other.

"What the hell?" I said.

Cannon 15 pulled up beside us. Afu was behind the wheel and waved at me before the road forked and took him, the other smoke eaters, and Cannon 15 away, down the other path.

"Hold on," I said. "Where are they going?"

"They didn't want you to worry," Yolanda said.

"Brannigan didn't want him to get hurt," Lot corrected. "Said he'd earned a vacation. They left you this. Said you should keep it as a souvenir."

Lot handed me my helmet. The one I'd been using since Brannigan gave it to me. I squeezed it in my hands. With angry, jerky movements, I strapped it onto my head.

"Like hell." I crawled over the seat and plopped down beside Lot.

He leaned back and combed his hair behind both ears. "What's your problem, man?"

"I'm not going to fucking Arkansas." I leaned toward Yolanda. "Please turn around and go after that truck."

"But we're in the middle of the caravan." Yolanda's eyes widened. "Oh my goodness! That's where the word 'van' comes from."

"Yolanda, go after Cannon 15!" I yelled.

She flinched and jerked the steering wheel. We pulled out of the line of cars and made a u-turn off the road. The hovering minivan left behind a cloud of ashes and bounced as it crept back onto the pavement. In less than two seconds, we were zooming toward the fork at ninety miles per hour.

"Sorry I yelled at you," I told Yolanda.

"No worries," she said. "We're about to be even."

I opened my mouth to ask what she meant just as she took the turn to follow Cannon 15. She didn't slow down. The force of the turn threw me into the side of the van and held me there. My vision was too blurry to tell, but I was sure the van had hovered completely on its side before Yolanda straightened it.

My shoulder ached as I sat up. "What the hell?"

"You said you wanted me to go after the truck," Yolanda said with a small grin.

I couldn't help smiling back. At least she hadn't refused. Her foot was to the floor, driving the engine to maximum octave. Cannon 15 was just ahead.

"They're not going to like this," Lot said. "You're supposed to be grieving your family and your friend."

I turned to Lot and opened the van's sliding side door. "My family and friends are in that truck."

Yolanda put the van's bumper just behind Cannon 15's rear wheel. "What do you want me to do now, Mister Bossy?"

"If you would please," I said, "get on their right and stay beside them."

"Holy cow, man." Lot's long hair tussled around violently in the wind. "You really going to do it? You don't even have a suit on."

Yolanda sped up the van.

Sneakers planted firm, I grabbed the sides of the open door and watched the truck's black and purple metal pass by, until I was in line with the rear window. Brannigan's gray head leaned against the glass. His eyes were open. When he saw me, he sat up and...

Was that a smirk on his face?

He rolled down the window and yelled over the rushing air. "Can I help you?"

"Open the door," I shouted back.

Brannigan put a hand behind his ear and squinted his eyes. "I didn't catch that. Sorry. I'm *old* and hard of hearing."

"Come aboard?" He laughed. "Are you a smoke eater and a pirate now?"

"You can't leave me behind," I shouted. "I'm one of you. We're... we're family!"

The door swung open. Brannigan stood there leaning on it. "Well, then jump over here, Guillermo."

"Call me Gilly," I said.

The van hovered closer to the truck. I looked into the cab ready to take me off to another adventure, and all the people inside who I'd looked up to most of my life. I didn't hesitate. I jumped. Brannigan caught me and closed the door once we were both inside.

"Goddamn, guys," Tamerica said from the captain's seat. "We could have just stopped and let him get in."

Brannigan mussed up my hair and patted me on the shoulder. "What took you so long?"

I took the chair beside him and buckled up. Then I glared at him. "You were going to send me to Arkansas to grieve?"

"Why do you assume it was me who made that decision?" Brannigan said.

When I didn't say anything, he shrugged.

"I gave you a choice," Brannigan said. "You could have gone

and relaxed, took some time. But you chose to come with us. You want to be here. That's what makes you a real smoke eater."

Naveena, sitting in the seat across from me, leaned forward, touched my knee, and said, "Don't listen to anything that man just said. Brannigan is full of shit."

Afu laughed and hit the horn to say goodbye to Yolanda and Lot, whose blue, red-cross-covered minivan slowed to fall away and turn back to catch up with the others heading for the Natural State.

"Of course Brannigan's full of shit," Tamerica said. I could hear her through my helmet speaker now that the radio had synced with theirs. "He was always full of shit, he's always going to be full of shit, and there isn't any geritol or stool softener powerful enough to clear that bastard out of all his cockstrong shenanigans."

"I love how you say shenanigans," Afu said.

"That's not the word I was focused on," Naveena said.

Everyone laughed.

"What's the plan?" I asked.

"Well we've got to get you a suit," Brannigan said.

"Yeah," I said. "I'll take the one Yolanda gave you. The prototype."

Brannigan squinted. "She told you about that, huh? Okay. When we stop, I'll arm wrestle you for it. Loser gets my old one."

I mirrored his look. "Where are we stopping?"

"Fort Bragg," Afu said.

"What?" I wasn't sure if I'd heard him right. "North Carolina?"

"I mean, eventually." The big man put a stick of gum in his mouth. He reached back to offer me a piece, which I took. "I found a whole box of these at the base. Every flavor you could think of. Why the hell would they need all that gum?"

"Why the hell do we?" Brannigan asked.

"That's not all we found, though, Gilly," Tamerica said. "Your Big Base was only the big base for the midwest. There are still a shit ton of Nusies out there. All over the country. We only took out a rung in the middle of the ladder. We're going to start from the top and work our way down."

"And that means North Carolina," Naveena said. "Fort Bragg."

"I got the coordinates," Tamerica said. "I'm thinking there'll be a whole lot of dragon riders. Experienced killers. We need to scope it out to know what we're dealing with."

"Just the five of us?" I asked.

"At first," Brannigan said. "Then my daughter, Yolanda, Lot, and an army of smoke eaters are going to ride in and help us kick some Nusie ass. You would have been there either way."

"So I wasn't going to be left behind." I nodded to him.

He nodded back. "We don't leave family behind, Gilly."

As the truck rolled on, I looked out to the wastes and remembered that spring was even closer. I wondered if it would look any less gray this year, if we were any closer to a time where things weren't left to ash. It was worth a shot. We could try.

I guess that's what the smoke eater motto is really all about. Sink or swim. Sometimes you don't know what's going to happen but like my Uncle Pedro, you say, "Let's do it!" and jump in anyway, because it's the right thing to do. Because it isn't just about you.

Maybe someday I'll sink. Maybe we all will when the dragons have their fill. But until then, I'm going to try like all hell to swim.

CHAPTER 1

That's one thing they never told Lena Horror about space – how damn dark it is. Her gang sped down the glowing glass streets of Oubliette, but it was only a tease of light, false and too dim for comfort.

Their cyclone motorcycles didn't exactly have wheels, even though Grindy had always called them that. They were round like wheels, they spun like wheels, but the bikes hovered on swirling circles of blazing light. Pretty as Christmas in Hell and three times as hot.

No wind blew on Oubliette, but Lena wasn't about to let that stop her. If she just went fast enough the illusion of wind could be created. She adored feeling her hair *thwap* against the back of her shoulders and tickle her ears, the flapping brown strands a lot louder than the low hum of two-wheeled death between her legs. But most of all, she liked how the cyclones lit up the city, piercing the shadows and letting everyone know, when they saw blue light bouncing off the buildings, the Daughters of Forgotten Light were coming.

Always traveling in a V formation, they rode five strong now. Only a month before it had been six. Even missing a rider, their bikes took up the street's width and anyone in their path had better move or get run down. Riding like that, each Daughter was at another's side. If another gang shot at them from behind, they had more chance of seeing it coming, or at least one of the sheilas in the back could scream an alert before the rest of the Daughters got blasted.

There was a truce on, wasn't there? Truce or no, Lena wasn't about to drop her guard. Lena told herself a leader shouldn't question her own decisions, just like those under her shouldn't challenge them. Did they think paranoia had her all fucked up? This was still Oubliette, and trust had long gone extinct.

"The shipment just came through the Hole," Hurley Girly shouted from Lena's right. Her blond pigtails bounced as she whipped her head up, looking to where the box hurtled toward them like a meteor.

Shit. Lena could have spit if she didn't think one of her gang would have caught it in the face.

Beyond Oubliette's towering buildings, outside the city's green, fabricated atmosphere – the Veil – the quarterly shipment jetted from the space gate. The Veil made Oubliette a sprawling roach motel. Whatever came in never went out, and that included all the stale air, and all the sorry sheilas confined to the city.

Lena had watched every shipment entry over the last ten years. That made her – she always had to take a minute to remember – twenty-seven. The other Daughters were only a few years younger, except for Hurley Girly, who'd turned twenty the last quarter.

The shipment was the same metal box it always was, coming from Earth with the same fanfare. Emptiness and starlight filled the circle made by an oversized, ivory gate – the Hole – and then *snap*, a new shipment came through with a couple thrusters to guide it. A million miles cut out of the trip, so the shipment could reach its eternity quicker. At least, that's how hyper drive was explained to them before they left Earth.

Faster, damn it!

Lena leaned into her cyclone, but she had her bike at full

speed and all tapped out of patience. She just had to ride. The street curved round into a ramp that rose between the upper floors of two adjacent buildings then dipped into a steep drop. The downward slope helped, but the shipment neared and, fuck it all, they were late. It was the only disadvantage of claiming territory across the Sludge River and far away from the main thoroughfares, where trouble always waited.

Above the Daughters, the shipment broke through the Veil and green static sizzled around the descending metal, waves rippling outward toward the horizon like digital gelatin until the expanse settled again.

Two klicks still separated them from the receiving stage.

"They're not taking this from us," Lena shouted. "We've got first pick this time."

Someone was waiting for them at the bottom of the ramp, a dark shape against a dark canvas, save the minuscule lights scattered throughout the dwellers' buildings. Their unexpected guest had been leaning against her cyclone when the Daughters rounded the curve, but now she jumped onto her bike.

For a millisecond, a quiver in time, Lena considered slowing the gang behind her. But that would mean more seconds lost and the first choice of the delivery going to another gang. Worse, it would show weakness. Lena ground her teeth and let the false wind push her hair back. The bitch at the bottom of the ramp would have to make way or get flat.

The mystery woman lit up her cyclone – orange wheels. Amazon colors.

Those cheeky….

It wasn't enough that just a few quarters ago – before the truce – the Amazons had been hunting down dwellers under the Daughters' protection, butchering them in alleys and leaving behind the parts they didn't have a taste for. Now, they'd left one of their own behind to fuck with Lena and her gang.

This Amazon was the scrawny one, the one with the busted teeth Ava gave her for making cracks about her Down syndrome. Even in the low glow of the glass street, Lena could tell it was her. The Amazon didn't try to run. By the looks of it, she controlled her speed to stay at Lena's right side.

Lena gripped her cyclone's handles and smiled, wide and crazy. The rushing air dried the inside of her mouth. *Try it. I want you to. Raise your arm and give me a reason. Please.*

The rang gun on Lena's forearm pulsed to the same beat as her blood, begging to be discharged. When had she shot it last? Long ago enough to have flashing delusions she'd never fired it at all, like how aging hookers-turned-nuns could convince themselves they'd always been virgins.

Lena raised her left hand above her head, shaping it as straight as a shark fin, keeping her eyes bobbing from the street ahead, to the Amazon at her right, then back. The Daughters' wheels sparked and hummed in a slightly different octave. She didn't have to look. Her sheilas changed formation, gathering in a line behind her.

The Amazon's hair stood straight in a long mohawk. The streaks of purple and red staining the strands looked like a chemical fire in the glow of her cyclone's wheels. The colorful sludge the Amazons put in their hair was just one of the specialty items commissioned from Grindy – one of the reasons the Amazons didn't try to kill everyone and take over Oubliette. Lena thought the mohawk would make an excellent trophy when she cut it off at the scalp, brought it back to the ganghouse, and glued it to a wall.

But that damned truce. It ruined Lena's fantasies as quickly as they came. She knew it was for the best in the end. A means to create some form of order in the chaotic city. Still.

Do it, you twat.

The Amazon made no motion to raise her weaponed arm; only

scrunched her face in a disdainful frown. A burn scar ran from her left cheek, down her neck, and then farther into the dark of her jacket. She was trying hard to keep her mouth squeezed shut, hiding the fucked-up grill.

Ahead, maybe a klick or less, the lights for the shipment receiving stage blasted on. The shipment, that big box of metal, hovered above the stage as if it had met the resistance of an invisible pillow. Slowly, it came down.

As much as Lena couldn't stand the mohawked Amazon's ugly mug, it became worse when she tilted her head and smirked. It was the eyes, twitching with secrets. *I know something you don't.* Lena's own grin faltered and she had to squeeze the cyclone handles to refrain from shooting her rang into the smug bitch's throat.

The Amazon zipped left, swerving into Lena's path, causing every Daughter to slow.

Angry shouts from her gang; Lena cut into the other side of the road. The Daughters followed in exact movement. Babies following mommy ducky. Lena regained her speed and cruised alongside the Amazon, whose frown had returned.

Lena laughed into the fake wind. So that was it. *Have one of your cannibal ass-plungers stay behind and slow us down, huh?*

"Put a rang in her ass, Lena!" Ava's voice could carry over any machine and always sounded clear and enunciated. Her tact was a different matter.

They neared the receiving stage. If the cyclones were more like motorcycles on Earth, the roar of the engines could have announced their impending arrival, but with the low hum of their bikes the Daughters had to rely on speed.

Lena raised her unarmed fist to the Amazon and extended a very direct middle finger. The cannibal widened her eyes and huffed from swelled cheeks. To make the insult dance at the edge of injury, Lena tapped the same finger against her bared, fully-intact teeth.

The Amazon snarled, giving Lena a fantastic view of what few teeth Ava had left inside the cannibal's mouth. The orange of her cyclone wheels only reflected against a tooth or three. The rest of her mouth was as dark and barren as the rest of Oubliette. The Amazon swerved again, this time not speeding ahead first. She zoomed straight for Lena.

A ramp came up on their right. Lena took it. Had to. The stage disappeared behind a black building and whatever ground they had gained now dwindled farther behind them. The Amazon came along, staying close to Lena's left. The Daughters berated the Amazon with an unfiltered assault of four-letter words and shouts of, "Truce-breaker!" and "That counts! Let it fly!"

"You trying to get killed?" Lena asked the Amazon.

That counted. She attacked you with her cyclone. That's an offense. What other reason do you need?

The Amazon laughed in her own gruff, self-satisfied way. She'd done her job. And even if the Daughters of Forgotten Light were to stop and reverse course, they'd lost time. The Amazon would surely follow them, too, a mosquito in the ear. Not that Oubliette had any insects. It had enough pests already. Well, this bug ached for a squishing, and Lena wanted to give it another stretch of road, give the Amazon another chance to make an offense, something Lena couldn't argue away as a misdemeanor. What was another lost minute?

Draw your rang, Lena. Do it. Blast that glorious ball of light and send her off her bike.

Grindy's voice kept coming up to put a lid on the boiling pot of Lena's wrath. "The truce is the best thing to happen to this place since they started dropping every motherless child through the Veil," Lena could hear her say. "I'd do my damnedest to keep to it."

Damn it!

Lena raised her left fist. And the cavalcade slowed. They

turned round, leaving the Amazon to hover off into the dark, and headed back toward Oubliette's center, the receiving stage.

"You should have done it," Hurley Girly said.

"We're late." Lena ground her teeth, wanting to scream.

She was about to signal them to return to the V formation, an ironic two-fingered peace sign, when a sparking noise rose from behind. Lena looked over her shoulder. The Amazon was back.

Yes!

No. They had no time for this distraction. They'd been short on supplies for weeks, not to mention the lack of a sixth Daughter. Lena would just have to ignore the Amazon and get to the drop. There'd be plenty of time for retribution later.

They came to the ramp that arched over the Sludge River, where Oubliette's fecal waste flowed, when the Amazon returned to Lena's side. With a sneer, she gave Lena a return on her universal "fuck you."

But the dumb bitch must have thought more about the "doing" than the way to do it. She'd used her *right* hand. The rang gun, strapped to the forearm, was pointed at Lena's head. Lena reacted. The pot had boiled over. Her body gave her no time to deduce what really happened, and it didn't matter. With her left hand, Lena snapped the handle back, killing the front wheel, and leaned forward with every ounce.

Aided by a lower gravity, Lena and the cyclone, together in one kamikaze package, soared into the air in a somersault. She laughed rabidly as it happened, not just for the thrill of going airborne, but for the release, the removal of the truce's crushing formality.

The cyclone dropped on top of the Amazon. There may have been a blip of a scream but the rest of the noise was snapping and searing, bones breaking, flesh burning, and the cannibal's cyclone crumpling under the weight and heat of Lena's blue wheels. Lena almost flew off her bike as the cyclone buzzed and tottered over the wreckage, careening toward the edge of the bridge before she remembered to jolt the dead side of the wheels back to life.

Free of the debris, Lena spun in a circle. To the rest of the Daughters, it must have looked like a celebratory doughnut, but they didn't have much time to gander. The line of cyclones split, dodging the mess Lena had left in the street.

"Holy fuck!" Dipity, who, even though third in command, always insisted on riding caboose, hadn't seen what happened after Lena's short aerial journey. She swerved her cyclone to the right with dark-skinned, muscled arms. After avoiding the pile of metal and meat, she looked back to it every other second, as if trying to decipher what had happened.

The Daughters circled around Lena in an impromptu huddle.

Lena stared at the dead Amazon over Ava and Hurley Girly's shoulders and giggled. Then frowned. "Shit."

"Truce is broken," Dipity said.

Ava nodded. "She raised the rang."

"What was with the fucking flip?" Hurley Girly thumbed back to the wreck, putting her amusement on full display with a big grin.

Sterling, their fifth, hand-signed something so quick Lena couldn't catch it.

"Swallow your words, ladies," Lena said. "This didn't happen."

Ava began to object. "But–"

"Grindy's right about this truce," said Lena. "And that pile back there can muck it all up."

They stared at Lena. The cyclones buzzed beneath them. Sweat beaded on Dipity's forehead.

"You wanna go back to before?" Lena asked. "One of us dying every week? Having to keep our supplies under lock and key? Getting dragged off and eaten by one of those shitheads," Lena nodded toward the Amazon, "if a straggler got cornered? No fucking thank you, ma'am. We got to keep things nice and orderly."

"But now we can have war, right?" Ava's peanut-brown hair hung over an eye.

"Maybe," Lena said. "But that's more chance to die. And I still plan on flying out of this dump."

The other Daughters traded glances. Sterling looked to the Veil above, probably fighting the urge to roll her eyes. Lena remembered when they used to laugh as she'd tell them of her escape plans. She'd let it slide since they went along with the many failed attempts to turn a shipment box into an escape ship. Now that Lena was leader of the gang, her pipe dream didn't seem to be so funny to them anymore.

"I've got it," Hurley Girly said. "I know why Lena got sent here. She was a serial killer."

Shaking her head, Dipity said, "Like she'd admit to that, even if it was true."

"This isn't the time for your stupid bet," Lena said. Then, after a silent moment had passed, "But no, goddamn it. That's not why."

Hurley Girly kicked the ground, mumbling a few swears. She'd have to put another manna loaf into the pot for guessing wrong.

Dipity cleared her throat. "So what do we do, Head Horror?"

Lena looked over the side of the overpass, down to the Sludge. It coursed through the glass river banks like rotten molasses. "Toss her over, whatever is left. It'll look like she crashed."

Ava shot her left hand into the air. "Not it."

"We all do this," Lena said.

They each grabbed a chunk of the Amazon. Ava and Lena shared the weight of what they guessed was a torso, while the others grabbed a severed arm or foot. The head must have flown over the side when Lena came down on her. It didn't even feel like pieces of a human being. They were just warm, squishy objects that smelled mildly like pork steaks sizzling on a grill. It had been a long time since Lena had eaten meat, and she was disgusted to find her mouth watering. She could almost sympathize with the cannibal mentality. Her stomach heaved, and she almost vomited the little bit of manna she'd swallowed before they left the ganghouse. She and Ava tossed the torso over, but the river lay too far down to hear a splash.

All five of them pushed the wrecked cyclone to the edge of the road, against the glass overpass where they'd ditched the Amazon's remains. From there, they sped toward the crowd gathering round the quarterly shipment, freshly sent from Earth, a place none of them were meant to see again.

Faster! Lena pressed.

They were late.